BAI GANYO

BAI GANYO

Incredible Tales of a
Modern Bulgarian

Aleko Konstantinov

Edited by
Victor A. Friedman

Translated by
Victor A. Friedman, Christina E. Kramer,
Grace E. Fielder, and Catherine Rudin

THE UNIVERSITY OF WISCONSIN PRESS

The University of Wisconsin Press
1930 Monroe Street, 3rd Floor
Madison, Wisconsin 53711–2059
uwpress.wisc.edu

3 Henrietta Street
London WCE 8LU, England
eurospanbookstore.com

Originally published as *Baj Ganju: Nevěrojatni razskazi za edin sûvrěmenen bûlgarin*
(Sofia: Pencho V. Spasov, 1895)

5   4   3   2   1

Printed in the United States of America

Library of Congress Cataloging-in-Publication Data
Konstantinov, Aleko, 1863–1897.
[Bai Gan'o. English]
Bai Ganyo: incredible tales of a modern Bulgarian / Aleko Konstantinov;
edited by Victor A. Friedman.
p.   cm.
ISBN 978-0-299-23694-6 (pbk.: alk. paper) — ISBN 978-0-299-23693-9 (e-book)
I. Friedman, Victor A. II. Title.
PG1037.K58B38713   2010
891.8′132—dc22
2009041983

Contents

Preface

ABOUT THIS TRANSLATION

I first became acquainted with *Bai Ganyo* in 1970, when I began studying Bulgarian at the University of Chicago with Howard I. Aronson, and for most of us who study Bulgarian in North American universities, *Bai Ganyo* is a high point of our first year of study and the gateway into a deeper understanding of the Balkans. A number of years ago Christina Kramer, of the University of Toronto, suggested gathering together a group of North American specialists in Balkan linguistics to translate *Bai Ganyo*. Its subtle and masterful use of the Bulgarian language makes translation a daunting task for anyone. Kramer's idea was that each of us would take responsibility for a section of the book, and then we would convene to read each other our translations aloud and work as a group to come up with the best version possible. We would thereby make available to a wider audience a beloved book worthy of translation, and we would also have a good time sitting around and reading each other the funny stories. In this respect, the idea reflected the setting of most of *Bai Ganyo*, in which each vignette is narrated as a first-person experience by one of a company of friends at a party.

Owing to the endless commitments of academic life at a research university, the idea remained unfulfilled until 2002, when Daniela Hristova, then of the University of Chicago, told me that the Bulgarian foundation Aleko was planning to sponsor the publication of an English translation of *Bai Ganyo*, and she was planning to bring this project to fruition. Thanks to Hristova's inspiration and energy and the interest of Aleko, we set about turning the idea into a reality. Kramer, Grace Fielder, of the University of Arizona, Catherine Rudin, of Wayne State University, and I divided *Bai Ganyo* into four parts, and we each translated our respective sections.

Hristova, as well as Wayles Browne, of Cornell University, read the entire first draft of the manuscript for consistency and offered additional input. Marta Simidchieva, a translator and literary scholar in Toronto, was consulted by Kramer during the initial translations of her sections. Thanks to funding from the University of Chicago's Center for East European and Russian/Eurasian Studies supported by funds from Title VI of the National Defense Education Act, we were able to hold two two-day conferences in 2003, and the entire group went over the whole translation in a series of marathon sixteen-hour days. Aronson attended the sessions and contributed his thoughts as well. Bill Darden, of the University of Chicago, also sat in on some of the sessions. The result was an almost complete translation, but there were still gaps and many rough spots: the punctuation was chaotic, there was a need for footnotes and a glossary, the stylistic differences of the four translators needed reconciling, and many minor errors had managed to slip by everyone's gaze. As in any translation of a complex work, we were constantly faced with choosing between faithfulness to Aleko's words and capturing the intent and spirit of their meanings.

I took on the task of editing the translation. When I finished, all the other members of the team read it and sent suggestions. Ronelle Alexander, of the University of California at Berkeley, and James Augerot, of the University of Washington, read an early version of the manuscript and commented helpfully on it. Alexander also read the final version and offered a number of important suggestions. Dale Pesmen and David Kramer also read the entire translation, Pesmen for style and punctuation, Kramer for style and flow. T. David Brent, of the University of Chicago Press, also read the entire manuscript and provided valuable input. I am indebted to all of those mentioned above for many helpful suggestions and corrections.

I also wish to thank the Research Center for Linguistic Typology of the Center for Advanced Research of La Trobe University, where in 2004, as a visiting fellow engaged primarily in writing a book on the Balkan languages, I was also able to complete most of the editing of this volume, including all of the footnotes.

The footnotes benefited in specific details from those in Tihomir Tihov's four-volume edition of Konstantinov's works (Aleko Konstantinov, *Sŭbrani sŭchineniya*, 6th ed. [Sofia: Bŭlgarski pisatel, 1980]), which served as the basis of our translation of *Bai Ganyo*. Tihov's edition also gives a complete concordance of manuscript variants, and their choices are the ones I have followed in this translation.

ORIGINAL PLACES AND DATES OF PUBLICATION
OF THE CHAPTERS IN *BAI GANYO*

The first edition of *Bai Ganyo* ended with what is chapter 12 in the present book. It was not until T. F. Chipev's edition of Aleko's collected works (1929) that all the available chapters featuring Bai Ganyo were grouped together. Since then, it has been traditional to include them all in editions of *Bai Ganyo*. The order in which they are presented here is not chronological, but it is the one used in most editions. In all Bulgarian editions of *Bai Ganyo*, only the nine chapters of Bai Ganyo's adventures in Europe are numbered, and the novel is not divided into parts. I have added numbers to the remaining chapters for ease of reference and divided the novel into two parts (chapters 1–9 and 10–18).

CHAPTER	ORIGINAL PUBLICATION
Bai Ganyo Starts Out for Europe	*Misûl* 4, no. 1 (April 1894): 13
1. Bai Ganyo Sets Off	*Misûl* 4, no. 1 (April 1894): 13–17
2. Bai Ganyo at the Opera	*Misûl* 4, no. 1 (April 1894): 17–19
3. Bai Ganyo at the Baths	*Misûl* 4, no. 1 (April 1894): 19–22
4. Bai Ganyo in Dresden	*Misûl* 4, no. 1 (April 1894): 22–27
5. Bai Ganyo at the Prague Exhibition	*Misûl* 4, no. 1 (April 1894): 28–30; *Misûl* 4, no. 2 (May 1894): 128–29
6. Bai Ganyo at Jirecheks	*Misûl* 4, no. 2 (May 1894): 129–36
7. Bai Ganyo Goes Visiting	*Misûl* 4, no. 2 (May 1894): 136–52
8. Bai Ganyo in Switzerland	*Misûl* 4, nos. 3–4 (June–July 1894): 238–43
9. Bai Ganyo in Russia	*Misûl* 4, nos. 3–4 (June–July 1894): 243–52
10. Bai Ganyo Returns from Europe	*Misûl* 4, no. 5 (September 1894): 419–32
11. Bai Ganyo Does Elections	*Misûl* 5, no. 1 (March 1895): 36–54
12. Bai Ganyo the Journalist	Dated 17 March 1895; first published when *Bai Ganyo* appeared as a book
13. Bai Ganyo at the Palace	*Zname*, 6 April 1895
14. Bai Ganyo in the Delegation	*Zname*, 15 July 1895

A Note on Transliteration

Owing to the fact that we are attempting to appeal to a general audience, we have used an English-based system of transliterating Cyrillic. We use *û* to represent Bulgarian "schwa" (approximately the *u* of English "but"). The letter *y* represents the consonantal sound of the *y* in "yellow," never the vowel sound in "by." In word-final position, however, we have used *i* rather than *y* to indicate the off-glide of a diphthong. Also, the name of the St. Petersburg boulevard is given as "Nevsky Prospekt," as this is the form current in American translations of Russian. Words in languages using the Latin alphabet have been spelled in their original orthography with two exceptions: when the original was purposefully misspelled to reflect Bai Ganyo's pronunciation, we have kept the misspelling, and we have used *ch* rather than *č* in spelling the name of the Czech historian J. K. Jirechek.

VICTOR A. FRIEDMAN

BAI GANYO

Introduction

THE CONTEXT OF BAI GANYO

Bai Ganyo was born in Chicago in 1893, when a young Bulgarian journalist named Aleko Konstantinov (b. 1863) encountered some of his fellow countrymen at the Bulgarian pavilion of the Columbian Exposition. One result of Aleko's journey and those encounters was Ganyo Balkanski, the title character of a series of feuilletons first published between 1894 and 1895.[1] These were subsequently collected and published with an additional chapter as a picaresque novel in 1895 with the title *Bai Ganyo: Incredible Tales of a Modern Bulgarian*.[2] The title *bai* is an old-fashioned term of respect used to address older men and derived from Bulgarian words meaning "older brother."[3] Its nuances lie somewhere between those of English "br'er" or "uncle" and "Mr." Bai Ganyo's surname, Balkanski, is the adjectival form of "Balkan," a word and concept that in Aleko's day had already acquired many negative nuances in opposition to a positively valued (Western) Europe.[4] The novel was described in an American periodical from 1913 as "the first classic of a national literature." And that is precisely what *Bai Ganyo* has become. Not only is it part of every Bulgarian's education, but Aleko himself is the only Bulgarian author to be honored in his own country by being routinely referred to by his first name. Even the words *baiganyovets* (a person who acts like Bai Ganyo), *baiganyovski* (like or in the manner of Bai Ganyo), and *baiganyovshtina* (a quality or act typical of Bai Ganyo) are part of today's Bulgarian lexicon. Although these words have negative meanings, associated with crudeness and vulgarity, Aleko's novel *Bai Ganyo* is itself more subtle and complex.

Firmly rooted in the history of late nineteenth-century Bulgaria, *Bai Ganyo* is also a work of such timeless brilliance that it transcends the milieu in which it was produced. When *Bai Ganyo* was written, the modern Bulgarian state was less than twenty years old, having only recently emerged piecemeal from the Ottoman Empire with the help of czarist Russia, whose designs on the fledgling country left Bulgaria's citizens with a deeply ambivalent attitude. Bulgarians experienced a clash between the old values of a largely agrarian former Turkish territory and those of a new, modernizing European country, indexed by, among other things, Bai Ganyo's attire: a Bulgarian brimless, peaked fur cap (*kalpak*), boots, and a peasant's sash and collarless shirt underneath an urban West European vest and frock coat. In addition to a conflict between old values and new, there was the problem of what we could call an absence of values in the gap between the two. This is the locus of the novel's critique of the political and economic corruption that followed national liberation, a critique that resonates poignantly with what happened in Bulgaria and elsewhere in southeastern Europe—and beyond—during the so-called transition after the fall of communism. It is no coincidence that *Bai Ganyo* has been frequently republished in Bulgaria and was often referenced during the 1990s. In 2003, following the Bulgarian currency reformation of 1999, Aleko's picture and a representation of the manuscript of *Bai Ganyo* appeared on Bulgaria's highest denomination, the 100-lev note.

Part 1 of *Bai Ganyo* is set in the Europe of Aleko's day: in the Austro-Hungarian, German, and Russian empires as well as Switzerland. It chronicles the misadventures of its eponymous protagonist, a traveling merchant of attar of roses (rose oil), an expensive commodity that is still an important ingredient in many perfumes and luxury soaps. Eighty percent of the world's supply of rose oil comes from Bulgaria, and it is a source of national pride. Bai Ganyo himself, however, represents that which was perceived as Balkan in collision with what was perceived as Europe. Here it is worth emphasizing that in Aleko's world, Europe included the Russian Empire, where he studied as an adolescent. This Europe is a world of Victorian politeness, formal education, well-heeled munificence, spotless cleanliness, and virtuous hard work. Bai Ganyo's world, by contrast, is one in which *kef* (sensual pleasure) is the greatest delight and a *kelepir* (something for nothing, a windfall, a free lunch) is the highest achievement. The fact that these two words entered Bulgarian from Turkish (although the latter entered Turkish from Greek) only serves to emphasize the difference between Bai Ganyo and the Europe he encounters. In Bai Ganyo's world, lice are a fact of life, and if your father didn't do something new, why should you? Bai Ganyo is also deeply suspicious and mistrustful of the outer trappings of European "civilization"—he worries constantly about being "fleeced." By contrast, Aleko and the narrators of his novel, as well as many other Bulgarians of their generation, were educated in and completely embraced values and attitudes that they identified as "European."

The first part of *Bai Ganyo* exemplifies an opposition between Europe and Balkan that persisted well into the twentieth century and, to varying degrees, has persisted even into the twenty-first. Although the Balkan part of the Ottoman Empire was called "Turkey in Europe" for centuries, it was Europe beyond the borders of Turkey (or former Turkey) that was Europe for the nation-states that emerged during the nineteenth century.[5] Even in Greece, the generation that grew up immediately after World War II could still say *"Tha pame stin Evropi"*—"We'll go to Europe"—when speaking of a summer vacation in France.[6] Similarly, during the tense years of the Yugoslav Wars of Succession, "Evropa" was used in the Republic of Macedonia as a collective term for the EU, the UN, and all the Western NGOs operating on that territory.[7] By then Greece was exercising its membership in Europe (i.e., the EU), but for the rest of Southeastern Europe, inclusion in the EU remained a sought-after goal. After the accession of Eastern Europe's northern tier to the EU, suggestions that the EU create a kind of second-class membership for countries then still seeking accession reproduced (western) Europe's older attitudes toward the Balkans.[8] Even now that Bulgaria is in the EU, critiques of events still echo Aleko's sigh at the end of the first edition of *Bai Ganyo* more than a century ago: *"Evropeytsi sme niy, ama vse ne sme dotam!"* ("We are Europeans, but still not quite!").

This first part of the novel is marked by a tone of gentle mockery and even of self-mockery, as when Aleko describes the "Bulgarization" of a modern train or when he uses the expression "by our standards" to refer to the relative whiteness of Bai Ganyo's shirt. The Bai Ganyo of part 1 is a crude bully and a hypocritical miser, but as Aleko himself writes, "The evil does not reside in him but in the influence of his environment. Bai Ganyo is energetic, level-headed, observant—especially observant. Put him under the guidance of a good leader and you will see what great deeds he can do. Until now Bai Ganyo has shown only his animal energy, but hidden within him is a tremendous supply of potential spiritual strength that only awaits a moral impulse to be transformed into a living force." In this sense, Bai Ganyo represents a positive Bulgarian self-image and can be compared to the rose oil he sells: natural, powerful, and valued by the West.[9] Unlike rose oil, however,

Bai Ganyo himself has yet to be refined. The satire of part 1 is intended to be both amusing and instructive. Aleko is inviting his fellow countrymen to see how much of themselves they can see in Bai Ganyo, and in so doing he is also advocating an embrace of what he saw as nineteenth-century European values in opposition to those he identified with an Ottoman period that in his day had already been branded as that of the "Turkish yoke" or "Turkish enslavement."

In part 2, however, Bai Ganyo has returned from Europe to Bulgaria (note that here Bulgaria is treated as outside Europe), and the foibles and foolishness of his travels abroad have been transformed into a greed and corruption in his native country that gives very little hope of moral redemption. Aleko's wit is as sharp as ever, and his observations remain acute, but his satire has become mordant, bitter, and deeply disillusioned. Whereas part 1 draws on the experiences of Aleko and his friends as travelers, part 2 is informed by political events in the Bulgaria of his day, which even included his own standing for election in his native Svishtov.[10] The debacle of those fraudulent elections constitutes the subject of one of the chapters in the second part. Two years later, in 1897, Aleko was killed by an assassin's bullet that was, perhaps, meant for the politician next to whom he was riding in an open cab.[11] The saying in Bulgaria is "Aleko created Bai Ganyo, and Bai Ganyo killed Aleko."

In Bulgaria today, *Bai Ganyo* is viewed with a mixture of pride, affection, and embarrassment. Aleko's literary brilliance is a source of pride, his deep love of Bulgaria is a source of affection, and the idea that Bai Ganyo could be construed as representative of a national type is a source of embarrassment. It should be remembered, however, that while the character of Bai Ganyo was based on Balkan realities, the author of *Bai Ganyo* and his friends were also products of that same region. Aleko and his circle were not on the margins of a nineteenth-century Balkan society but rather played a central role in the modernization of southeastern Europe. Although Aleko's life was tragically cut short, his friends went on to become some of Bulgaria's leading citizens. The tales of Bai Ganyo's rapacious greed and corruption are echoed in many societies and in many forms: from Svishtov to Florida, from rose oil to crude oil (see Bai Ganyo's letter to Konstantin Velichkov). Although Bai Ganyo was created in a specific place at a specific time under specific social conditions and reflects those aspects of his creation, *Bai Ganyo* also satirizes characteristics of the parvenu, nouveau riche, petit bourgeois, narrow-minded philistine regardless of where they occur.

Bai Ganyo is a character of the proportions of Gogol's Chichikov and Hašek's Švejk. Although Aleko's novel is shorter and thus does not have the same sweep and depth, it is so sharp and clear in its focus, so deft in its portrayals and characterizations, and so perceptive in its capture of the clash between the "old-fashioned" Balkans and "modern" Europe, between reactionary corruption and liberal values, that it continues to be a touchstone of reference in its own country. Aleko is a Bulgarian Aristophanes, critiquing through satire the failings of his place and time. Some of these failings translate quite well to a different time and place, while others highlight the uniqueness of Aleko's setting. But whatever the mixture of parochial and universal, *Bai Ganyo* is a very funny and entertaining book, and it deserves to be known by an Anglophone audience.

THE LANGUAGE OF *BAI GANYO*

We have tried to capture Aleko's use of language by finding adequate equivalents for Bai Ganyo's earthy speech, as well as for Aleko's own wit and sarcasm.

For all of part 1 and much of part 2, the narrators are a group of young Bulgarians who have had formal educations. They have studied abroad and represent Bulgaria's upwardly mobile youth, who identified their values as "European." Their voices are the voices of Aleko and his friends, who formed a group called Jolly Bulgaria that met for evenings of storytelling and other entertainments just like the ones that frame most of the narratives in *Bai Ganyo*. The sixteen or so men that made up the circle belonged to different political parties but were united in both their enjoyment of life and their love of their homeland. Many of them went on to prominent positions in the Bulgarian government and academic establishment. The voices of these narrators veer from the somewhat formal to the relaxed but still educated-sounding speech of young people in nineteenth-century Europe. By contrast, Ganyo's voice is earthy, of low register, small town, colloquial, old fashioned. Some of the satires in part 2 are written entirely in Ganyo's voice (the mock letters to the editor, for example).

A salient characteristic of Ganyo's speech is his use of words that entered Bulgarian from Turkish. In the Ottoman Balkans, Turkish was the politically dominant language, knowledge of which was a mark of urban sophistication. At the same time, it was also the first language of millions of rural Muslims (as well as the Christian Gagauz of the Black Sea region), and thousands of words entered all the Balkan languages from Turkish. The situation can be compared to the entry of French vocabulary into English after the Norman conquest of 1066. After the independence of the various modern Balkan nation-states, however, most of these Turkisms were rendered obsolete either through changes in historical circumstances or through conscious substitution using vocabulary of native or other non-Turkish origin (usually French, German, Greek, Latin, English, or Russian, depending on various semantic, cultural, and political factors). Some Turkisms became completely assimilated in the same way that many words of French origin such as "table" and "chair" became completely assimilated in English. Another group of Turkisms, however, survives in the various Balkan languages as a specific register that can be colloquial, homey, and intimate or crude, vulgar, and uneducated, depending on the context. Moreover, owing to their historical provenance, these Turkisms sometimes carry specific nuances that are extremely difficult to capture in translation. They are an important part of what is Balkan about the Balkans, and this characterization as "Balkan" has both positive and negative valences just as the register itself does. Turkisms also provide another link between the Balkans of the 1890s and those of the 1990s. Thus, for example, during both periods of transition, the press, and especially the yellow press, made frequent use of Turkisms to produce the effect of rendering the news "hot," shocking, vital; in effect, newsworthy. Already in Aleko's day these words of Turkish origin had been pushed down into the colloquial register. In fact, Aleko's use of Turkisms in *Bai Ganyo* was part of a campaign to turn them into a kind of slang, to create a sense that such words should be limited to very informal speech. Interestingly enough, while Aleko's use of Turkisms has much the same valence today as it did a century ago, the Bulgarian spoken by the young students and intellectuals who narrate most of the novel and who made up Aleko's social milieu sometimes sounds quaint and odd to today's readers. (It should also be noted that some of Aleko's Turkisms are now archaic, and modern Bulgarian editions of *Bai Ganyo* usually have glossaries to explain them.)

   Another linguistic feature of the book is the fact that at times Aleko used French, German, Russian, Czech, Romanian, and Turkish without translation. In Aleko's day, these were all languages with which he could expect his educated readers to be more or less familiar. Leaving most of these phrases and passages in their original languages, however, would interrupt the flow for the ordinary Anglophone reader without imparting any special nuance. Therefore, we have usually translated these passages into English indicating in some other way that they were originally in another language. Where we felt it was necessary or appropriate, we have used footnotes to indicate the original language, and we left a few basic French and German expressions as they appeared in the original.

SOME OF THE MEMBERS OF ALEKO'S GROUP, JOLLY BULGARIA

The following list is based on that given in Aleksandûr Ninchev's *Aleko Konstantinov* (Sofia: Bûlgarska akademiia na naukite, 1964), 29. The identifications for Kolyo, Tsvyatko, Stuvencho, Arpakash, and Gedros are Ninchev's conjectures based on who was known to have belonged to Jolly Bulgaria. The identification of Filyo is my own, but it is based on data in Ninchev (27, 29) that leave little doubt. The others have been positively identified in various memoirs. The identities behind the other nicknames remain unknown.

NICKNAME IN *BAI GANYO*	REAL PERSON TO WHOM THE NICKNAME REFERS
Arpakash	Petûr Abrashev, minister of justice, 1911–13
Dravichka	Sava Ivanchev, vice president of Parliament
Filyo	Filaret Ivanovich Gologanov, a very close friend of Aleko's
Gedros	Another nickname for Arpakash
Gervanich	Georgi Ivanich Kalinkov, mayor of Sofia, 1918–20
Ivanitsa's son	Aleko himself
Kalina Malina	Aleksandûr Malinov, prime minister, 1908–11, 1918, 1931
Kolyo	Nikola Chervernivanov, professor of chemistry at the University of Sofia, 1892–94; later, mayor of Ruse
Marcus Aurelius	Marko Slavchev, law consul at the Ministry of Finance
Stuvencho	Stoyan Beshkov, a classmate of Aleko's in Russia
Tsvyatko	Tsvetan Radoslavov, author of the text of the Bulgarian national anthem and a university instructor of music

FURTHER READING

The following English-language works can be recommended for the modern scholarly perspectives they offer on treatments of the Balkans and on *Bai Ganyo*.

Bakić-Hayden, Milica. "Nesting Orientalisms: The Case of Former Yugoslavia." *Slavic Review* 54 (1995): 917–31.

Bakić-Hayden, Milica, and Robert Hayden. "Orientalist Variations on the Theme 'Balkans': Symbolic Geography in Recent Yugoslav Cultural Politics." *Slavic Review* 51 (1992): 1–15.

Daskalov, Roumen. "Modern Bulgarian Society and Culture through the Mirror of *Bai Ganio.*" *Slavic Review* 60 (2001): 529–49.

Neuberger, Mary. "To Chicago and Back: Aleko Konstantinov, Rose Oil, and the Smell of Modernity." *Slavic Review* 65 (2006): 427–45.

Stavrianos, Leften S. *The Balkans since 1453.* New York: New York University Press, 2000.

Todorova, Maria. "The Balkans: From Discovery to Invention." *Slavic Review* 53 (1994): 453–82.

———. *Imagining the Balkans.* New York: Oxford University Press, 1997 (especially 38–61).

NOTES

1. Another result was a book titled *Do Chikago i nazad* (*To Chicago and Back*) (Sofia: T. F. Chipev, 1929), in which Aleko produced a very perceptive account of his travels.

2. The original Bulgarian uses *sŭvremenen*, which means "contemporary." The word can also mean "modern," however, and this better captures Aleko's irony.

3. The Bulgarian Academy of Science's etymological dictionary (*Bŭlgarski etimologichen rechnik* [Sofia: Bŭlgarska akademiya na naukite, 1971], vol. 1) cites *bai* as a shortened form of *bae* or *bayo*, which it derives from *bate* or *batko*, "older brother." Although *bai* resembles Turkish *bey* (sir, gentleman), Turkish influence is excluded by the authoritative *Dictionary of Turkisms in Bulgarian*, ed. Alf Grannes, Kjetil Rå Hauge, and Hayriye Süleymanoğlu (Oslo: Instituttet for sammenlignende kulturforskning, 2002), which does not include this word among its 7,427 headwords and 3,917 variants.

4. A number of studies published during the 1990s have pointed out that the Balkans as such were constructed by West European discourse as a negative "Other," in much the same fashion as it constructed the Orientalist discourse identified by Edward Said, against which it could define itself positively. Thus, for example, the use of the term *balkanization* to mean "break up into tiny entities" does not date from the nineteenth century, when the Balkan nation-states were separating from the Ottoman Empire, but rather from the end of World War I, when the Austro-Hungarian, German, and Russian Empires were resisting the national self-determination that led to the creation of Czechoslovakia, Poland, and the Baltic republics. The works listed at the end of this introduction do an excellent job of elucidating the relevant arguments.

5. It is worth noting that despite the fact that Eastern Thrace has remained "Turkey in Europe" to this day, the nineteenth-century opposition between Turkey and Europe is again being played out in Turkey's relation to the EU.

6. Joseph Pentheroudakis, personal communication.

7. This was my observation at the time, when I was working as a UN policy and political analyst in Macedonia.

8. See, for example, *The Economist*, 30 May 2005, 23.

9. I am indebted to Grace Fielder for an earlier version of this formulation.

10. A town on the Danube in northern Bulgaria.

11. Gavrail Panchev, in his *Ubiystvoto na Aleko Konstantinov* (The Murder of Aleko Konstantinov) (Sofia: Literaturen forum, 1997), has argued that Aleko himself was the intended or at least one of the intended objects of the shooting. The assassins denied this at the trial, but the question remains moot.

PART ONE

Bai Ganyo
Starts Out for Europe

They helped Bai Ganyo[1] slough off his heavy, felt Turkish cloak, he donned a nice Belgian frock coat, and everyone said that Bai Ganyo had become a real European.[2]

"C'mon, why don't we each tell a story about Bai Ganyo."

"Yeah, let's!" everyone exclaimed.

"I'll tell one."

"Hang on, I know more."

"No, me, you don't know anything!"

An uproar ensued. Finally we agreed that Stati would begin. And so he began.

---

1. Pronounced like English "buy," *bai* is an old-fashioned title of intimate respect used for an older man. The effect in Bulgarian can be compared to the use of titles with first names.

2. The allusion is to Bulgaria's then-recent liberation from Ottoman rule, on the one hand, and to the Belgian constitution, on the other. Belgium's constitution was synonymous with the European model of liberalism and democracy and served as the exemplar for the Bulgarian one.

I

Bai Ganyo Sets Off

Our train pulled into the huge vault of the station on the Pest side of Budapest. Bai Ganyo and I went into the station restaurant. Since I knew we had a whole hour to kill, I made myself comfortable at a table and ordered some snacks and beer. The crowd swarmed around me, and it was a good-looking crowd at that. You know, I'm not crazy about Hungarians, but I've got nothing against Hungarian girls. Distracted by the noise, I didn't notice Bai Ganyo slipping out of the restaurant taking his *disagi*, his woven cloth saddlebags, with him. Where did Bai Ganyo go? His glass was empty. I looked all over, peered into every corner of the restaurant, but he was nowhere to be found. I went outside onto the platform, I looked in all directions; not a sign of Bai Ganyo, nothing at all. What a strange business! I thought that maybe he'd gone into the train car to make sure someone didn't swipe his small traveling rug, his *kilim*.

I went back to the restaurant. There was still more than half an hour till the train's departure. I sat there drinking my beer and staring around. The stationmaster would strike a bell every five minutes and announce the directions of the trains in a listless, lazy voice, "Hö-gösh-fö-kö-tö-he-gi, Kish-kö-rösh, Se-ge-din, Uy-ve-dek."[3] A few English tourists gaped at him, and he, apparently used to the attention he attracted with his peculiar language, grinned from ear to ear and with an even louder and huskier voice kept on going, "Uy-ve-dek, Kish-kö-rösh, Hö-gösh-fö-kö-tö-he-gi," emphasizing each individual syllable.

---

3. The towns in Hungarian are Horgos, Feketehegy (Visegrad), Kiskörös, Szeged (Segedin in Serbian), Újvidék (Novi Sad, now in Serbia).

We still had about ten minutes before the train was supposed to leave. I paid my bill, and I paid for Bai Ganyo's beer as well, and then I went out onto the platform to look for him. At that moment a train came slowly into the station, and just picture it, in one of the cars, hanging halfway out the window, Bai Ganyo came into view. He caught sight of me and began to wave to me with his lamb's-wool cap, his *kalpak*, from far away, saying something I couldn't hear over the locomotive whistle, but I understood what had happened. When the train stopped, he jumped down and came running up to me and told me—with a healthy dose of energetic swearing, which, with your permission, I won't repeat—the following story:

"Don't even ask, pal; I'm worn out from running."

"What running, Bai Ganyo?"

"What do you mean, what running? Weren't you just hanging out at the restaurant staring all around?"

"So?" I responded.

"So! At that moment, y'know, that guy by the door rang the bell and I heard the engine whistle and I went out—I couldn't catch your eye—and I see our train pulling out. Hey, my *kilim*! I make a mad dash for it, running as fast as my legs could carry me—but never mind. Finally, at one point I see that the train has stopped and so, upsy-daisy, I jump on and go inside. I startled some guy and he shouted something at me in Hungarian—*heke meke*[4]—and me, you know, I don't put up with any nonsense. I opened my eyes wide and stared right back at him and showed him my *kilim*. No big deal, the guy was sensible and went away. He even laughed a little. How could anyone know that we would be coming back? These Magyars!"

Sinner that I am, I had a good laugh at Bai Ganyo's adventure. Poor guy. The train was maneuvering to come in on another track, and Bai Ganyo, poor fellow, ran three whole kilometers to catch up to it—after all, his *kilim* was inside.

"But in your haste you forgot to pay for your beer, Bai Ganyo."

"Big deal. As if they don't fleece us enough," answered Bai Ganyo in a tone that did not brook contradiction.

"I paid for it."

"You had plenty of money, apparently, so you paid for it. Come on, get in, get in quickly so we don't go running around after the engine again," Bai Ganyo admonished.

---

4. The syllables are nonsense, intended to imitate the sound of Hungarian.

We entered the car. Bai Ganyo bent over his *disagi* with his back to me, pulled out half a wheel of hard cheese, cut himself a dainty little slice, cut himself a huge hunk of bread as well, and began to chomp away with a prodigious appetite, filling first one cheek and then the other with his mouthfuls, and stretching his neck from time to time in order to swallow the dry bread. Bai Ganyo ate his fill, belched once or twice, shook the crumbs into his palm, swallowed them, too, and muttered under his breath, "Eh, if only there were someone to treat me to a nice little glass of wine." He sat down across from me, smiled good-naturedly, and, after gazing at me kindly for an entire minute, said,

"Has Your Grace traveled, have you seen something of the world?"

"I've traveled quite a bit, Bai Ganyo."

"Really now, well, as for me, I've been all over the place. Tsk! Tsk! Tsk! Never mind Edirne, Constantinople, but even Romania! Would you believe it? Giurgevo, Turnu Magureli, Ploești, Pitești, Brăila, Bucharest, Galați— hang on, I don't want to exaggerate; I can't remember if I've been to Galați or not—I've been to all of them."

The trip to Vienna passed monotonously. I offered one of my books to Bai Ganyo to make the time pass more quickly, but he politely refused my offer, because, he said, he'd read enough in his time and considered it more practical to take a nap. Why stay awake for nothing; after all, he had paid good money for a place on the train, so he might as well get some sleep. And he fell asleep. He fell asleep and began to snore so loudly that, once you'd heard him, there was no need to hear a Barbary lion.

We arrived in Vienna and went to the traditional Hotel London. The hotel porters took my bag down from the cab, and they wanted to take Bai Ganyo's *disagi*, but whether out of thoughtfulness, or who knows what, he wouldn't give them up:

"How can you give these to them, pal? This is rose oil—it's no joke, it's a real strong fragrance; he'll reach in, palm a bottle—just try to chase him down later![5] I know what these guys are like. You don't see it because they're so *slick*"—Bai Ganyo meant to say "polite," but that word is still new in our lexicon, so it gets forgotten—"You don't see how they hover around you.

---

5. Rose oil, or attar of roses, is an essential oil made from rose petals that is an important ingredient in many of the world's perfumes. Eighty percent of the world's supply comes from Bulgaria, and this is a source of national pride. Costing $3,400 to $3,800 per kilogram, genuine attar of roses is still one of the most expensive perfume ingredients in the world.

Why are they hovering? You think they want to do you a favor? *Ein, zwei, gut morgin*, but all the time they're trying to swipe something from you. And if not that, then a tip. Why do you think I'm so careful to slip quietly out of the hotel. Beggars! This one gets a kreutzer, that one gets a kreutzer—there's no end to it."

Since the rose oil that Bai Ganyo was carrying really was a rather valuable commodity, I suggested that he leave it with the cashier at the hotel desk for safekeeping.

"With the cashier?" he exclaimed, in a tone that pitied my naïveté. "You students are really strange. I mean, how do you know what kind of people those are at the desk? He takes your rose oil, sticks it somewhere. Well, and then? What are you going to do? Forget it! Do you see this sash?" And Bai Ganyo raised his vest. "I'll stuff all the *muskali* in here.[6] True, it's a little heavy, but it's safe."

And Bai Ganyo turned his back to me ("The world is full of all kinds of people; who knows what this kid is really like?") and began to stuff *muskali* into his sash. I asked him if he wanted to have dinner.

"Where would we eat?"

"Downstairs, in the restaurant."

"No, thank you, I'm not hungry. You go and have a bite, Your Grace. I'll wait for you here."

I'm sure that as soon as I left the room, Bai Ganyo opened his *disagi*. If a fellow has his own snacks, why should he spend money on a hot meal? He's not going to starve to death, after all!

I took Bai Ganyo to the office of a Bulgarian merchant and left him there, then hopped on a tram and went to Schönbrunn. I went up the arch, looked out over Vienna and its suburbs, strolled along the promenades and the zoological gardens, spent a whole hour staring at the monkeys, and in the evening I returned to the hotel. Bai Ganyo was in the room. He tried to hide what he was doing from me, but he couldn't, and I noticed that he was sewing a new pocket onto the inside of his old-fashioned quilted jacket. Being a man of experience, he wore a quilted jacket under his Western clothes even in the summertime: "In the wintertime keep bread on you, in the summertime keep clothes on you," say the old folks, and that's what Bai Ganyo did.

---

6. A *muskal* (plural *muskali*) is a glass phial containing either one and a half or three drams.

"I just sat down to do a bit of mending," he said in embarrassment.

"You're sewing on some sort of pocket; you must have gotten something for your rose oil," I insisted jokingly.

"Who, me? You're wrong! Why would I need a pocket there? There are ple-e-e-nty of pockets, just let there be money for them. There's no pocket, there's nothing there; my clothes had gotten a little worn out, so I was just patching them up. So where were you? Did you go sightseeing? You did the right thing."

"Didn't you go out, Bai Ganyo, to see something of Vienna?"

"What's to see in Vienna? A city is a city: people, houses, fancy stuff. And wherever you go, everybody goes *gut morgin* and everybody wants money. Why should we give our money to the Germans? We've got people at home to take it from us."

2

Bai Ganyo at the Opera

I persuaded Bai Ganyo to go with me to the opera house to get tickets for the evening. They were presenting the ballet *Puppenfee* and something else that I can't recall. We passed by the Greek coffeehouse, turned at the Bulgarian hangout, the café Mendel, and then headed off toward St. Stephen's Cathedral. In St. Stephen's Square I invited Bai Ganyo to stop in at a pastry shop. It never occurred to me that this small detour would bring out the Don Juan in him. But then, what wonders civilization can produce! I must tell you that at the time, I was studying in Vienna. I had been away for the holidays and had just returned. In fact, it was on my way back to Vienna that I became acquainted with Bai Ganyo. I often went to this pastry shop and had gotten to know the cashier quite well. She was a cute, cheerful girl, lively but proper, and she didn't allow people to take liberties. So just picture this, gentlemen: Bai Ganyo and I enter the shop, we approach the pastry counter, the young lady greets me cheerfully and welcomes me back, I respond with some playful pleasantries and turn to pick out a sweet, and at that moment an indignant shriek deafens the entire establishment.

"What happened? Bai Ganyo, did you do something to her?" I cried out upset and angry.

"Who? Me? Of course I didn't. What would I do to her?" mumbled Bai Ganyo in confusion, and his voice shook.

The young woman, flushed with anger, told me in a loud voice that Bai Ganyo had done something extremely insulting: he had made a grab for her and, grinning with delight, had given her a pinch. She wanted to call the police. What a scandal!

"Just get the hell out of here, Bai Ganyo. If the police catch you, you're a goner. Quick, get out. I'll catch up with you later," I shouted at him, pretending to be angry but barely able to contain my laughter at the tragi-comic figure he cut.

"What's she so high and mighty about?" Bai Ganyo seemed to pluck up his courage as he walked out the door. "What is she, respectable or some-thing? I know these women around here. Just open your wallet, and it's all '*Gut morgin.*' After all, your Bai Ganyo wasn't born yesterday."

As luck would have it, I was to finish off the day with yet another adven-ture in which once again the hero was our Bai Ganyo. As I said, the opera was putting on the ballet *Puppenfee*. We took our seats in the stalls. The theater was full. Bai Ganyo's rustic attire of drab homespun cloth stuck out like a sore thumb against the dark background of formal suits. The curtain rose. Dead silence. Everyone gazed at the dreamlike stage setting. I sensed Bai Ganyo fidgeting, huffing and puffing in the seat to my right, but I just couldn't take my eyes off the stage. The figures of the ballet changed con-stantly at the wave of a magic wand: groups of dancers appeared and dis-appeared; the stage would go completely dark, then be flooded with light, now one color, now another, then a rainbow of colors—a fairyland! One bal-lerina stepped out of the corps de ballet, took a few quick steps forward, leapt up gracefully, and then stood as though suspended in air, touching the ground with only the tip of one toe. Just then, behind my back, hysteri-cal laughter split the air. I turned to my left and saw that everyone in the rows behind me was giggling and pointing to something on my right. I was seized by a terrible foreboding. I turned toward Bai Ganyo . . . Oh my God! What do I see? Bai Ganyo has stripped to his shirtsleeves and un-buttoned his vest, which was constricting the wide sash wound tight around his waist, where he had stuffed—for safekeeping—all the *muskali*. One of the ushers had him by the sleeve with two fingers, gesturing unambigu-ously with his head for him to leave. Bai Ganyo stared back at him and answered with gestures of his own: "What? Who are you trying to scare?" It was his blustering bravado that had made a young girl sitting behind us burst into hysterical laughter, and her laughter infected the entire theater. What a picture! And then, just imagine, gentlemen, there I am dying of shame, and I look toward the box seats, as if someone were drawing my gaze there, and my eyes meet the fixed stares of an entire German family at whose home I had always been welcome. And in their eyes I read sincere pity for my desperate plight. At that moment, Bai Ganyo was tugging energetically at my sleeve:

"C'mon, c'mon, let's get out of here. To hell with these *Chifuti*.[7] I'll show them. Just you wait!"

---

7. The Bulgarian word *Chifut* (plural *Chifuti*) literally means "Jew" (from Turkish). The term is an ethnic slur and is also used to mean "stingy," "mean," "malicious." In his travelogue *Do Chikago i nazad* (*To Chicago and Back*), Aleko evinces considerable hostility toward Ashkenazi Jews as distinct from Sephardi Jews, who were the majority in Bulgaria and whom he describes in favorable terms.

3

Bai Ganyo at the Baths

Bai Ganyo at the Baths

"Let me tell you about my meeting with Bai Ganyo," put in Stoycho.

"Go ahead!" we all exclaimed, because we knew that Stoycho was good at telling funny stories.

It also happened in Vienna. I was sitting in the café one morning, at Mendel's. I had ordered a cup of tea and had just started looking through some Bulgarian newspapers. I was deeply engrossed in an extremely interesting article in which the author was discussing ways the constitution could be tinkered with—well, actually dismantled—and yet somehow remain intact.[8] So I was reading along, really caught up in it, when someone shouted, "Gooood morning!" right in my ear, and a sweaty palm grabbed my right hand. I looked up. There before me stood a broad-shouldered, dark-eyed, dark-haired, swarthy man with prominent cheekbones, a turned-up mustache, and a five o'clock shadow. He was dressed (you'll never guess how) in an unbuttoned frock coat with a broad red sash peeking out from under his vest, a white (by our standards) collarless shirt, a black *kalpak*, which was perched on his head, and a pair of boots, and he had a walking stick tucked under his arm. He was a young man; I'd say he couldn't have been more than thirty at most.

"Excuse me, sir," I said to him, suppressing my surprise. "I don't have the pleasure of your acquaintance."

"Is that so? You don't know me, you say? Aren't you Bulgarian?"

---

8. The reference is to reactionary changes to the relatively liberal Bulgarian constitution that the Stambolov regime proposed making toward the end of 1892. (On Stambolov, see 94n52.)

"Yes, I'm Bulgarian."

"Well?"

"Well what?"

"Well, get up so we can get going. What are you doing wasting your time just hanging out here? They call me Ganyo. Now, get up."

There was no need to tell me that he was a Ganyo.[9]

"Excuse me, Mr. Ganyo, but I'm busy right now."

"What do you mean you're busy? You're just sitting here in the café."

I didn't consider it necessary to provide an explanation. He, however, showed no intention of leaving me in peace and all of a sudden burst out, "Get up and take me to the baths! Where are the public baths around here?"

So that's it! The gentleman wants to be taken to the baths. I felt like telling him to go to hell, but I restrained myself. Not only did I restrain myself, but I was even a bit amused. It was evident that Bai Ganyo was indeed in need of a bath. He smelled acrid even from far away. What could I do? A fellow countryman must be helped, after all. Besides, I figured that I could make use of the occasion to have a shower myself. It was quite hot out. We headed off toward a summer public bath that had a large pool. As we walked along I felt compelled to draw Bai Ganyo's attention to the interesting sights we passed, but I noticed that he barely listened to me. Every once in a while he'd say, in a bored tone, "Is that so" or "I know," just to show me that he was no country bumpkin. Or he'd interrupt me with some question or other that had no bearing on what I was telling him. For example, I was explaining to him something about the monument to Maria Theresa, the one in the square between the museums, when he suddenly tugged at my sleeve:

"See that woman over there, the one in the blue dress? What do you think? How do you people know which ones are *that* kind of girl and which ones aren't? I've headed down the wrong alley many a time, y'know what I mean?" Bai Ganyo punctuated his question with a devilish wink.

We arrived at the baths. My heart was in my throat, as if I sensed what was going to happen. We got our tickets at the cashier's window. Bai Ganyo demanded his change by pushing his hand through the opening under the window and rubbing his fingers together. The young woman behind the glass smiled and gave him the change. Bai Ganyo fixed his lustful eyes on

---

9. Aleko is playing here with the Bulgarian proper name *Ganyo* (which is pronounced "Ganyu" in most of Bulgaria) and the Bulgarian dialecticism *ganyu* (Greek merchant, peddler). As an ethnic nickname, the term carries the connotation of someone who is always looking for a *kelepir* (see 57n28).

her, scooped up the money, and, with a peculiar cough, revealed his feelings. She burst out laughing. Bai Ganyo, enchanted, twirled the left side of his mustache and bobbed his head.

"*Che fromoza esh domneta.*[10] Stoycho, ask her if she knows Romanian."

"*Shtii rumuneshti?*" Bai Ganyo posed the question himself.

Just then another customer came in, so we moved on into the general hall. It was a big round hall. All around the sides were dressing stalls, each one concealed behind a curtain. In the middle was the pool, separated from the walkway by a low wooden balustrade. There were several small ladders for climbing down into the pool. Bai Ganyo and I occupied two neighboring stalls. I undressed quickly and entered the cold pool. Several Germans stood there quietly, dutifully stretching their muscles, huffing and puffing. Bai Ganyo busied himself for quite a while behind the curtain of his stall. You could hear his grunting and the tinkling sound of some sort of glass objects. Finally he drew the curtain aside, and there he stood in his birthday suit. His chest was hairy, and his legs were dappled with coloring from his embroidered, woolen, country-style socks. In his hand he held a knotted cloth: these were his precious *muskali*, bound up in a not-so-clean kerchief, which he had been loath to leave in the dressing stall. "How do you know that the walls are sturdy? Somebody might rip out a plank from the back, and then just try to catch him." He looked along the walls down the corridor, hoping to find a nail that he could hang his bundle on. He figured that if it was a wall, it ought to have nails in it, and he turned to me:

"What idiots these Germans are! It doesn't occur to them to pound in a nail. And they say we're stupid."

Having decisively convinced himself of the Germans' incompetence, Bai Ganyo, with some misgivings, left his bundle of *muskali* on the floor in front of his dressing stall so that he could keep an eye on it while he bathed.

"Listen here, young man," he said, turning to me. "While you bathe, keep an eye on these *muskali*. And pay attention to me, too—don't miss the show." And with these words, Bai Ganyo put one foot on the railing. "You just watch."

He hoisted himself up, put the other foot on the railing, stood up straight, crossed himself, and shouted, "Watch . . . Lord help me . . . Here I go!" And he leapt into the air, tucked his legs up, and splash! Right into the pool. Sheaves of water rose up and then showered down on the heads of the

10. "How beautiful you are!" (in substandard Romanian).

Germans, who were struck dumb in amazement. Waves spread out in circles from the center of the pool toward the edges, splashed up out of the pool and back again, and after a few seconds, when the water had settled back down, everyone in the bath could see Bai Ganyo's exhausting antics under the water. He shot up above the water, then stretched his legs down and touched the bottom, rose up again with his eyes closed and his ears plugged up. Then he shook the water off—pfff!—and sprayed water through his drooping mustache—pfff!—wiped the water from his hair and face, opened his eyes, looked directly at me, and burst out laughing:

"Ha, ha, ha! Eh? What do you say to that?"

I didn't get a chance to respond, because he did a belly flop and began slapping the surface of the water with his hands, swimming "sailor style." Splash! with one hand, then two kicks behind him, splash! with the other hand and two more kicks. The water in the entire pool was seething, as if we were under a waterfall. Waves splashed against the sides of the pool, and cascades of droplets sprayed as far as the opposite wall.

"That's called 'sailor style,'" Bai Ganyo exclaimed triumphantly through the waves. "In a second we'll show 'em the one called the 'steamboat.'"

He flipped over onto his back and began to kick the surface of the foamy water so mercilessly that the spray reached all the way to the ceiling. He churned his arms quickly, in imitation of a paddle wheel, and then Bai Ganyo gave a whistle: "Tupalupa tupalupa toot toot."

The Germans stood stock-still. In all likelihood they assumed my companion to be some newcomer from the east who had not yet been committed to an insane asylum, and I observed in their faces not so much indignation as pity. But Bai Ganyo, of course, read in their faces endless wonder at his talents. He clambered up the ladder, stood with his legs slightly apart, and with a lofty glance at the Germans, he grandiosely thumped his hairy chest, shouting triumphantly, "Bulgar! Bulga-a-a-ar!" And then he struck his chest with even greater vigor.

The proud tone in which he expressed this self-recommendation spoke volumes. It said, "Here before you stands a prime Bulgarian specimen; look upon him! This is what he is; this is the stuff he's made of. You've only *heard* of that genius of the Balkans, the hero of the battle of Slivnitsa.[11] And now

---

11. The battle of Slivnitsa marked the decisive defeat of the Serbian army by the Bulgarians in the Serbo-Bulgarian war of 1885. The Austrians favored Bulgaria against Serbia, and here Aleko is mocking the Austrian press's flattery of the Bulgarian army.

he stands before you, the whole package, from head to toe, in all his natural splendor. Do you see what wonders he can accomplish? But that's not all! Oho! He can do so much more! So, the Bulgarians are uncouth, are they? You miserable *Chifuti!*"

"Hey there, ask them if they have any soap!" Bai Ganyo called to me after his little display of patriotic euphoria had cooled somewhat. "Look at my legs; what a state they're in!"

Indeed, his legs wouldn't exactly serve as the most suitable model for Apollo Belvedere. The colored designs from his embroidered woolen socks were still imprinted on his skin, which in any case was filthy and shaggy. But still, you can't surprise Bulgarians with dirt: not even the most active imagination can come up with anything more sullied than reality itself.

With these words, Stoycho finished his tale.

4

Bai Ganyo in Dresden

"I, too, had an encounter with Bai Ganyo," piped up Kolyo, "in Dresden. Do you want me to tell you about it?"

"Do you need to ask? Tell it!" cried out the entire group.

I don't know if you've heard, but a few years ago Dresden society was shaken by a tragic accident. One victim was a Bulgarian girl, a student, the other a young American. Let me remind you of this sad event in a few words. The Bulgarian girl was studying in Dresden. As you know, there are entire neighborhoods in this city consisting of Englishmen, Americans, Russians, and other foreigners, whose children attend the local schools. A young girl, an American student, became friends with our Bulgarian girl. English and American students have this quirk: they take under their wing one of the most vulnerable of their fellow students. Our Bulgarian girl must have seemed like that type: shyer, gentler, more demure. They became friends, and the American girl started to invite her over to her house on holidays. The Bulgarian girl met the entire family, including, among them, the brother, a young man of twenty who was studying painting. Who knows whether it was because of the inherent proclivity of young artists to be attracted to any live model who differs from the usual type of model around them, or whether it was because of the American penchant for originality, but, anyway, after a few meetings with our modest and demure Bulgarian girl, the young man apparently took a shine to her. He'd take every opportunity to meet with her, to share his artistic impressions, to make himself pleasant. In a word, they fell in love. And it was this love that cut short their days.

On a holiday, during summer vacation, the entire family and the Bulgarian girl set out on a hike through the nearby mountains, the "Saxon Switzerland."

At a particularly rugged and picturesque spot, the young artist and the Bulgarian girl, absorbed in conversation, became separated from the group. A towering cliff caught the young man's attention, and he started to climb, his companion following after him. But they hadn't managed to get even halfway up the dangerous cliff when the American lost his footing, and in his fall he dragged the Bulgarian girl down with him into the abyss. Apparently, their lives were fated to end at that point.

The dead couple was taken to Dresden, to the clinic. The entire city was shocked by this tragic event. Everybody poured in from all over to see them laid out alongside one another on a large marble slab. A telegram was sent at once to the Bulgarian girl's brother, summoning him to Dresden; she didn't have any other close relatives. The bodies were embalmed in order to preserve them until his arrival. Masses of wreaths adorned their bier. Two days later, a telegram arrived from Vienna saying that the brother of the deceased had set out for Dresden. The bodies were transferred to the home of the American family. While they waited impatiently for the brother's arrival, hordes of *Herren* and *Damen*, flocks of ladies and gentlemen, had gathered at this house. The family belonged to Dresden's high society. I had gone there with several Bulgarian students. Since we were Bulgarians, we had been invited because the dear departed was a Bulgarian. Other young Bulgarians had gone to the station to meet the brother of the deceased. We waited. Such a sad occasion. The rooms were all filled with visitors. People spoke quietly, in whispers. The silence was disturbed only from time to time by the bitter sobbing and despairing sighs of the late boy's mother, who was overwhelmed with grief.

During an interval of dead silence, an awful ruckus burst out in the hallway. You could hear the rude stamping of boots as if someone were leading in a shod horse, and voices rang out. "Where is she? Hey, is she here?" "Shhhh! Quiet!" And making his way into the room of the dear departed was none other than Bai Ganyo—with a *kalpak* on his head.

"Good afternoon!" he cried out with a look on his face and a tone of voice that suggested not so much mourning as indignation. It was as if the surrounding people were responsible for the death of his sister.

Bai Ganyo approached the bier and accidentally brushed the shroud off the boy's face. "Who is this? What's this guy doing here?" he asked, scrutinizing almost savagely the entire gathering, and he waited with an intense stare for an answer.

One student, a Bulgarian, dying of shame, went up to Bai Ganyo, took him lightly by the sleeve, and pulled the shroud off the face of the deceased girl. Bai Ganyo took off his cap, crossed himself, and kissed her on the forehead.

"Ah-h-h, poor thing! What a terrible fate. Marika, Marika!" Bai Ganyo shook his head. Say what you will, but that shaking of his head looked more like a threat directed at the visitors than an expression of grief.

He looked suspiciously at the corpse lying next to his sister, and, after tilting his head inquisitively while gesturing with the fingers of his left hand in the Balkan manner, he turned to the student. "And just what is going on here? Why have they put that guy here? What's a man doing in this *pension?*"

"Shh! Please, please, Mr. Ganyo, speak more quietly."

"What do you mean, more quietly? I'm spending money here! Where is the directress?"

"This isn't a *pension*; it's a private home," responded the astonished student.

"What do you mean, 'a private home'?"

"Shh! For God's sake, speak more softly," begged the miserable student, deafened by the roar of blood rushing to his head and on the verge of tears.

Even if you ignored the blustering behavior and manners of Bai Ganyo, which had already begun to seem like sacrilege, like a mockery of the tender feelings of all present, his very outward appearance failed to elicit a favorable reaction from the Americans and the English, particularly those of the gentler sex.

Bai Ganyo was dressed in drab homespun clothes and wearing dirty dust-encrusted boots; a large black cloth was tied around his neck as a sign of mourning. A rather grimy shirt, unbuttoned to the waist, could be seen under this. A walking stick was in his hand, and a package wrapped in yellow paper was under his arm. His mustache was neatly twisted up at the ends, yet his chin was unshaven and stubbly.

"Is this gentleman the brother of mademoiselle Marie?" a member of the household asked me.

I answered him in the affirmative, adding a quickly constructed lie in justification of Bai Ganyo's behavior and appearance. I told him that the telegram with the sorrowful news had found Bai Ganyo on his estate, where he was overseeing the work in his fields, and that without returning to his villa (Bai Ganyo and a villa!), he had set off for the train, supplying himself with money from friends at the station, and that he had arrived in Dresden without stopping anywhere along the way. And his present behavior, odd as it might seem, should be forgiven him in view of the profound impact that the irrevocable loss of his sister had had on him and the substantial losses that he had suffered owing to his precipitous departure from his agricultural affairs.

"Oh, the poor man!" my interlocutor uttered sympathetically and then left to share his feelings about Bai Ganyo with the other members of the household and friends.

I felt relieved, gentlemen, but my relief did not last long. The American, a relative, had already managed to pass on the information obtained from me to a large number of those present; their high-minded indignation, provoked by Bai Ganyo's manners, had been assuaged, and everyone now regarded Bai Ganyo not only benevolently but even sympathetically. The unexpected arrival of a terrible telegram, the unplanned departure on a long trip, huge losses—such surprises could overwhelm anyone. And because of such surprises they condescended to make excuses for Bai Ganyo. But gentlemen, please tell me, I beg you, how could we, the Bulgarian students, come up with an excuse for what Bai Ganyo did next? The student who was hovering next to him in order to stem any sudden bursts of emotion was quietly relating to him how the accident had taken place in the cliffs of Saxon Switzerland. In the course of this story, Bai Ganyo betrayed through various movements of his head and hands the emotions that were disturbing him: he'd cluck his tongue and sigh, "What a damned shame!" He would look at his sister and shake his head. "Oh, you poor thing!" Then he'd glare at the dead boy, shake his head menacingly, his eyes flashing lightning, as if he wanted to say, "At least this idiot got what he deserved!" The foreigners interpreted these facial gestures in their own way and could hardly have guessed their true significance, for otherwise, they wouldn't have looked quite so sympathetically upon Bai Ganyo, whom they regarded as deranged with grief. At one point, Bai Ganyo, deeply affected by the story, clucked his tongue so loudly that everyone stared at him. At that very moment he placed the thumb of his right hand on his right nostril, screwed his eyes and mouth slightly to the right, tilted his head down, and blew as hard as he could out his left nostril. Then he put his left thumb to the other nostril, and he gave it all he had again. We were completely done for.

It would have been possible to excuse even that, you might say, owing to the haste of his departure; in his haste and confusion the unfortunate man must have forgotten to take even a handkerchief, you might say. But no! No, because immediately after this procedure Bai Ganyo unwrapped the yellow paper package and pulled out—what do you think?—a whole dozen handkerchiefs and began passing them out to those present, mainly to the Bulgarians, for the blessing, all the while repeating each time he handed one out, "Here, take it and say, 'God rest her soul,'" or he gestured with his hand for someone to draw near and exclaimed, "Hey, you, young man, c'mere, you take one, too; come on and say, 'God rest Marika's soul!'"

"I don't want to tell you any more, gentlemen," exclaimed Kolyo in despair. "You yourselves must try to imagine the expression on the faces of the English and Americans standing around Bai Ganyo. I'll only tell you that after the funeral service was over, which was Orthodox and took place in the Russian church, after we buried her, Bai Ganyo was invited to stay until his departure from Dresden in the house of the Americans. He spent only one night there. How he behaved in that house I have no idea. But upon leaving he said to the Bulgarian student who saw him off at the station, "Y'know, pal, I almost made a mess of things there. I don't know the ways of these Americans. There was lots of free food, so I ate and ate till I almost burst; and as for that night—don't ask! But never mind that, something even worse happened. In the morning, this woman comes, y'know what I mean, and she knocks on the door. I go, 'Come in.' She comes in, brings me coffee with milk and all kinds of pastries. She puts down the tray, y'know, on the table, and starts sniffing the air. What the hell's going on? I dunno whether she got wind of the rose oil or something else. I wasn't born yesterday, y'know, so I get up right away, grab a *muskal*, and stick it under her nose. She smiles a bit. I look her over—not bad at all. She was dressed so simply, I said to myself that she must be a servant. I give her the eye—she gives a smile. So there I go—hands around her waist. But then she turns around, damn her, and slaps my face. Oh dear, now I've gone and done it. She turns out to be the boy's aunt. Never mind, thank God; one slap, and that was the end of it. Nice people!"

5

Bai Ganyo at the Prague Exhibition

"Hey, wait a minute, let me tell you about how we went with Bai Ganyo to the Prague Exhibition," said Tsvyatko with a grin.[12]

"Bravo, Tsvyatko," we all exclaimed. "Just what we've been waiting for!" And Tsvyatko began.

If you recall, we set off from Sofia with a train made up entirely of our own train cars, even our own locomotive. There were only first- and second-class cars, no third class. They were brand-spanking new, just imported from Europe, impeccably clean and comfortable. Each of the cars had both first- and second-class compartments. There were lots of people, I'd guess around 160; I don't remember exactly. There were old people and young people; men, women, and children; even babies (oh, those babies!).

Who could equal us? We were filled with such pride traveling to the exhibition in our very own Bulgarian train. Let the Europeans see that Bulgaria isn't some sleepy backwater, we told ourselves. Most of all, we were bursting with pride at our new, modern, and immaculately clean train cars. But do you think that our patriotic delight in the supremacy of our train cars or the thought that we would amaze Europe with our progress was destined to last long? As we left the station following a convivial send-off, and then as we crossed the Slivnitsa and Dragoman positions, the battlefields of our glorious victories during the Serbo-Bulgarian war, our enthusiasm grew in direct

12. The 1891 Prague Exhibition celebrated the centennial of the first Prague exhibition. A group of Bulgarians, including Aleko, traveled there in a special train, which was intended to show Bulgaria's material and cultural progress and also to affirm pan-Slavic common interests. This was especially important because at that time Bulgaria was an autonomous part of Turkey and the Czech lands were part of Austria.

34

proportion to the emptying of the abundant wine bottles and food baskets that our practical travelers had packed. "Of course we've packed a few snacks. Why should we fork over our money to the Serbs?" cried out Bai Ganyo, warmed by both patriotism and domestic Pleven wine. But as we approached Tsaribrod, the last station before the Serbian–Bulgarian border, it began to grow dark outside, and as the passengers attempted to illuminate the cars, it became clear that the railroad management had forgotten to put the lamps in working order. As it grew quite dark, the children became frightened and began to bawl. Alas, then did our patriotic enthusiasm begin little by little to slip away, along with the last miles of Bulgarian territory. Some smiled sadly, others smirked with malicious amusement (we Bulgarians weren't the only ones on board), still others grumbled, and even Bai Ganyo whispered in my ear, "A pig can't tell the difference between mud and well water." Some passengers even went so far as to spout unambiguous profanities in the direction of a certain foreigner, an employee in the management of our railways. Emboldened by this, Bai Ganyo shouted, "I just know that it's not our fault. It's those foreigners again, damn them! They've done this on purpose to make fools of us! That's because they're jealous! They're all like that!"

With these words, he glared so ominously at one of the foreigners traveling with us that the man got up and left for another compartment in a fit of coughing. When we stopped at the station in Tsaribrod, it was pitch dark in the rail cars. We couldn't even see one another. At first, we were upset. Then we got angry. And finally, we got silly. Many jokes and sarcastic jibes were made at the expense of our railroad directors. People started shouting, "Hey there, you guys, give us some candles; the children are frightened." "Hey, Mister, go buy us a bunch of candles and keep the change." "How about giving each of us a wax candle, at least?" Bai Ganyo alone wouldn't concede that Bulgarians could possibly be responsible for this mess.

"See that one over there?" he said, pointing at one of our foreign fellow travelers after someone brought in a few candles. "He should be tarred and feathered and set on fire. This is intolerable. Never mind the darkness; who cares about that, but we've lost face in front of the Serbs. See that one over there, that Serbian clerk? The guy's laughing. Of course he's laughing." And Bai Ganyo's patriotism, once aroused, wouldn't permit him to put up with a Serb laughing at him. He scowled at the fellow.

"You there! What's so funny, huh?" And he wanted to jump out of the car and have it out with the Serb. What a hero!

"Shh! Bai Ganyo, take it easy," begged the passengers. "Don't cause a scandal. Keep in mind that you're entering Serbia."

"Yeah? So what if I am entering Serbia? What're they going to do, scare me? What about Slivnitsa? Have they forgotten how they cried, 'Retreat, brothers!' at the battle of Slivnitsa?" Then an obscenity burst forth from Bai Ganyo's mouth like a bomb.

"What fault is it of that Serb over there that our cars are dark?" the others said, trying to calm him down.

"Who? Him? I know his type," answered Bai Ganyo, shaking his head.

They distributed one candle to each compartment and even, I think, managed to set up a few lanterns and get them lit. The train started up again. The passengers dripped hot wax onto the window-sills and stuck on the candles. This was the first Bulgarization of the new train cars. The second Bulgarization also took place that first night: all of the lavatories (if you'll pardon the expression) were turned into cesspools.

Somehow or other we managed to cross Serbia. But don't think we managed it in peace and quiet. Oh no! Bulgarians are no fools! Bai Ganyo never missed a chance to take a jab at the Serbs, to remind them of Slivnitsa. In Nish and even in Belgrade he asked all the clerks and porters, "You're really a Bulgarian, aren't you? C'mon, admit it. You're all Bulgarians, but you're trying to turn yourselves into Serbs!"[13]

As we set off through Hungary, the wheels of one of the rail cars caught fire. May those railway technicians burn in hell! We were stopped for a long time. The railway workers ran back and forth, sprayed water all over the place, and I don't know what all else. Were they fighting the flames or fanning them? Well, finally we got going again. As for the Hungarians, they just laughed. They'd seen it all before. Bulgarian travelers! Then the same car caught fire somewhere else. They left the damned thing behind to be repaired.

Bai Ganyo had traveled before, experienced man that he was. So he explained to his less sophisticated fellow travelers, "Now we're heading for Pest. After we pass Pest, we'll reach Vienna. Prague's after Vienna. I've been to all those places; I know 'em like the back of my hand."

We didn't stop at the small stations, and at the larger ones we paused only long enough for them to give us clearance. The riches of Moravia caught

---

13. Serbia and Bulgaria justified their competing claims to disputed territories by maintaining that the population in the affected regions was Serbian or Bulgarian, respectively.

everybody's attention. The beautifully cultivated valleys, the exquisite gardens, the countless factories caused even Bai Ganyo to admit that Moravia had outdone our fatherland. "Well, we work, too, but these folks aren't kidding around! They get on a job, and they get it done!" But then he realized that he had slipped into complimenting them, so he added, "Of course, it's all for nothing. They do the work, and the Germans eat up all the profits."

The trip didn't pass without some comic relief. The four of us—me, Vancho, Filyo, and Ivanitsa's son[14] (I don't believe you know him)—took a first-class compartment. Bai Ganyo settled into the neighboring second-class one, along with some traveling companions well stocked with provisions. Bai Ganyo had, in his haste, evidently forgotten to pack any food for the trip in his *disagi*. "Oh well, after all, we're all Bulgarians; we'll look after each other. From this one a little bread, from that one a bit of cheese—and a fellow can get by! You bet!" And in fact, Bai Ganyo did get by quite well. His companions treated him to food and drink; he treated them to his most fervent patriotism, seasoned with appetite and thirst. But all good things must come to an end. Finally, his companions' provisions ran out; the wine jugs were emptied. (In order to avoid an egregious error I must correct myself: the wine jugs were emptied back while we were rushing past the battlefields of Slivnitsa and Dragoman, with cries of "Long live Bulgaria! Hurraaaaaah! Here, let me just wet my whistle! Hurraaaaaah!")

Bai Ganyo began to insinuate himself into our compartment. At first he cooked up various pretexts—either he needed some matches or a glass of cognac because his stomach was upset—and so, little by little, he made himself at home, settled in, and didn't budge from our compartment. He just forgot about his friends, and why not? What good were they to him? They didn't have a morsel left; everything had been eaten and drunk up. But, thank God, we always had something to nibble on; we bought food at the stations. Bai Ganyo didn't want to let the opportunity to try various foreign goods slip by—just out of curiosity, of course.

"What's that there; is it grapes? Bravo! Lookit, give a teensy little bunch over here! Mmmmm! Tasty! Bravo!" His curiosity drove him to acquaint himself in a similar fashion with our food, our cognac, and our tobacco.

"That tobacco case there, is it made of silver from the Caucasus?" Bai Ganyo inquired as soon as he saw one of us preparing to light a cigarette.

---

14. "Ivanitsa's son" here refers to Aleko himself. His father was Ivanitsa hadzhi Konstantinov, a successful merchant from a prominent upper-middle-class family.

"No, it isn't; it's made in Vienna," answered the owner of the tobacco case.

"Is that so? Let me see it. Goodness me! And look, it has tobacco in it, too! It's Bulgarian, isn't it? Bravo! Hang on; just let me roll myself a cigarette. I've got cigarette papers. If anyone needs any, just ask—I'm here!"

We were very much aware that he was here: by the smell of his boots, by the distinct odor of his sweaty body, and by his strategic advance toward total occupation of an entire row of seats. At first, he sat on the very edge of the seat; then he started getting a little more comfortable. Later, three of us had to sit on one row of seats, and Ivanitsa's son had to scrunch up in one corner of the other, so that Bai Ganyo could stretch out horizontally. And he didn't miss a trick. We conspired to ascertain how far Bai Ganyo's need for comfort would take him, and he, candidly, began to feed our curiosity.

"Listen, move over a bit so I can put up my other leg too. Ahh! That's it! Good! Ahhh! Eh, goddamn! What a pleasure! Just listen to the locomotive: chugga-chugga, chugga-chugga. It's flying! I really like to stretch out like this. The other compartment is too crowded. And those fellows over there, they're such simple folk. How can you have a conversation with them? What are you eating over there; is that a pear? Bravo! Let's see if I can eat a whole pear lying down. Thanks. Where do you guys get this stuff?"

"We buy it," one of us answered, barely containing himself.

"Is that so? Bravo!" said Bai Ganyo approvingly, his mouth full of succulent pear. "I love pears."

Soon Bai Ganyo began to doze, lulled by the monotonous chugging of the engine. Meanwhile, I sat there thinking. How do we get rid of this guy? Suddenly, a brilliant idea popped into my head. I winked to my friends and said, "What do you say, gentlemen? Shall I make us each a cup of coffee? Pass me the Primus stove and the fuel."

"Coffee?" exclaimed Bai Ganyo, and he jumped up from the bench as if he had been stung. "What a great idea!"

"How can we make coffee? There's no water," piped up Ivanitsa's son, artfully feigning disappointment.

"Water, is it?" rejoined Bai Ganyo with the same enthusiasm. "If it's water you need, just ask me! I'll be back in a second!" And he dashed out of the compartment.

We were dying of laughter. Ivanitsa's son stretched out and took up the whole row of seats. Bai Ganyo came back huffing and puffing more than he needed to. He had to show us what trial and tribulation he had endured for our benefit. In his hand he held a small jug.

"Here, I found some, just like I told you I would! I scrounged around all the cars! Finally, I saw a jug and grabbed it. When I got it in my hand some woman started shouting after me, 'Hey, bring back that water; it's for my child!' So I'm thinking, what excuse can I dream up, what can I tell her, and then it came to me. 'Excuse me, madam, but someone back there has fainted.' 'Is that so?' she says. 'Yes.' 'Well, in that case, take the water to him quickly, but bring back the jug.' What a sucker! Phew. I'm all sweaty. Come then, let's have that coffee."

One of my friends, who could no longer contain his indignation, rebuked him. "Aren't you ashamed of yourself, sir?"

Bai Ganyo looked at him, his face drawn as if attempting to express his astonishment as clearly as possible, and then he said quite unexpectedly, "It occurred to me that you might be setting me up, but what the hell, I told myself. Well then, at least give me a cigarette and a spot of cognac."

We gave him a cigarette and a glass of cognac, and he went back to his own compartment, back to his "simple folk." Soon we heard his voice through the compartment wall. "Those educated fellows are a sorry lot. I don't know how their bosses put up with them. Just wait till your Bai Ganyo returns to Bulgaria. Then we'll see who's who."

We approached the Czech border. Traveling with us were some commissioners, sent by the government to learn how to set up such an exhibition so they could hold one in Plovdiv. One of them had pinned the Bulgarian tricolor on each passenger's lapel. During our trip a rumor had gone around that we were to receive a formal welcome both at the border and in Prague (consequently, we were prepared for the reception). But in fact, what we saw surpassed all our expectations.

So here we are, coming to the border station, the locomotive is already whistling. To the left and to the right of the tracks we see a tide of people flowing toward the station. A light rain was falling, so the men, women, and children hurrying toward the station were all carrying open umbrellas. We stopped. The platform was crowded with people. Immediately a band struck up our national anthem, "Shumi Maritsa," followed, to our boundless pleasure, by a choir singing their anthem, "Hde domov můj," in Czech. Bai Ganyo, in particular, praised the Czech people for learning the melody of the "Bulgarian" folk song "Where Is My Homeland?" so well.[15] Except, he noted, that

---

15. "Shumi Maritsa" means "The River Maritsa is Murmuring" and was the Bulgarian anthem from 1886 to the end of World War II. In 1861 Teodosiy Ikonomov

they didn't pronounce the words clearly enough, so they were a little hard to understand.

My face flushes with embarrassment when I recall the comportment we displayed at that first meeting. Just imagine, gentlemen. The city has assembled, people from the villages have come to meet their Bulgarian brothers, they have brought a band and a choir, and a bunch of young girls are lined up with bouquets in their hands. They all stand there waiting for their brother Slavs to get off the train so that they can welcome them with words, with songs, with music, with bouquets; but these "brothers" simply stick their heads out of the windows and gape! Believe you me, gentlemen. The windows of the train cars are narrow, as you know. One guy puts his head out, another squishes in over his shoulder, a third manages to peek out from underneath his arm with one eye, and they just stare! It makes you want to sink into the earth! Oh, if only there had been a photograph! The people meeting us were taken aback; they didn't know what to do, where to put the bouquets! The band stopped, the choir stopped too, and everyone fell silent as we stared at one another.

After a while, Bai Ganyo stepped off the train. All of the Czechs strained their eyes toward him. They cleared a path for him to pass by, and pass by he did. Oh, Lord! How majestically did Bai Ganyo pass by those hundreds of eyes and hands offering him bouquets! He pulled at his mustache with his whole hand and twirled its left side upward, thrust out his elbows, coughed with authority, and glanced with one eye at a young miss who held out her bouquet right under his nose. He looked at her and wiggled the upturned fingers of his left hand, as if to say, "You're welcoming, Missy, are you? You're doing a nice job; welcome away! I love it!" And he passed by, without bestowing on her the honor of receiving her bouquet. The young lady pulled her hand back in confusion. A little while later, Bai Ganyo reappeared, not very graciously buttoning up a certain part of his attire. Once again, they cleared a path for him, once again he twirled his left mustache, and once again he coughed and blew his nose, and then he climbed back on board. The locomotive whistled, and we set off.

Lest any of you think that I'm exaggerating, that I'm embroidering my story to make fun of Bai Ganyo, let me tell you that on the contrary, I'm leaving some things out, because even now I cringe when I recall them. For

---

translated "Hde domov můj" into Bulgarian, substituting references to Bulgaria for all the Czech references, and the song became quite popular in Bulgaria.

example, I neglected to tell you at the beginning what a sight our train was by the second day of the journey. I did tell you, didn't I, that our travelers had brought their infants along? As a result, apart from the constant crying and shrieking, the lavatories were soon turned into laundries where soiled diapers and baby clothes were washed, and the corridors in the cars became drying areas for this laundry. The mothers stretched out clotheslines and hung those less-than-perfectly-washed diapers out to dry. They replaced the banners that were supposed to decorate our train. And so, instead of the white, green, and red tricolor of the national flag, a host of bicolors glistened in the sun: white dappled with yellow! These charming banners adorned our train when we stopped at the Czech rail stations and when the crowd met us with bands, with songs, with bouquets, when mayors and other dignitaries greeted us with ceremonial addresses. The yellow and white banners fluttered on the lines while our leader, Mr. Vasilaki, deafened the Czech audience with his resounding, sentimental speeches, and when, at each station, Mr. Petko stoked the national pride of the fraternal Czech nation with his lofty orations from which the assembly could hear clearly only the words "Brothers! Ivan Hus . . . Oh! Ivan Hus, brothers!"[16] Bai Ganyo, indignant that these speeches made no mention of our own national giants, kept poking one of the teachers in the ribs, saying, "Hey, Teach, come on, you say something; let's show them who we are. Now's the time. Say something about Philip Totyo, about Khan Krum the Terrible, or sing a song . . ." And all the while the bicolor banners flapped away![17]

Our entire journey from the Czech border to Prague was one triumphant procession. Wherever our train passed—whether through towns, villages,

---

16. Mr. Vasilaki and Mr. Petko refer, respectively, to Vasil D. Stoyanov, director of the Bulgarian National Library, and Petko Gorbanov, a lawyer from Sofia, both of whom went to the exhibition and made public speeches there. An article in the Bulgarian newspaper *Svoboda* (Freedom) pointedly described these speeches as being within the bounds of international norms and as avoiding political (i.e., pan-Slavic nationalist) insinuations. Nonetheless, references to Jan Hus (1371–1415), the Czech national hero and opponent of German influence who was burned alive as a heretic, thus setting off the Hussite Wars, is indeed potentially nationalist here. The use of Bulgarian *Ivan* for Czech *Jan* (English John) links the two Slavic "brotherly nations."

17. Totyo was a Bulgarian revolutionary and leader of a band of insurgents against Ottoman rule during the national revival period in the nineteenth century. Krum was an early Bulgar ruler (ca. 803–14), famous for his victory over the Byzantine emperor Nicephorus I (802–11), whose skull Krum had cleaned and lined with silver and used as a goblet.

or fields—hats were flung in the air, and endless cries of "*Nazdar!*"[18] rent the air.

I caught sight of a woman working in a field, who, seeing how the men were waving and throwing their caps in the air, began to wave her hands madly and then untied the kerchief from her head, whirled it in the air, and shouted out, "*Nazdaaaar!*" And another time, we were passing through a town (I don't recall its name—we were quite overwhelmed by then, you know), there were people in the street, at the windows, in the trees, on the fences, even up on the rooftops. And in this town, I remember, I noticed a new house being built. It was nearly finished, and the beams for the roof had been raised. At the top of the roof they had set up a long pole decorated with vegetables, topped off with a flag (just as people do in our country when we build houses). There were several workmen up there, and when they saw that all along the street people were waving kerchiefs from every window and calling out "*Nazdar*," they ran along the beams to the top of the roof, took hold of the pole with the flag, and tried to pull it out so they could salute us. Evidently, it was stuck solid—they couldn't get it out—but they loosened it up at the base enough so that it could be waved with a slight swing from left to right. These two events—the woman working in the fields and the carpenters on the roof—touched me deeply. They were nothing like our pompous journalistic rhetoric: "The entire intelligentsia rent the air with a frenetic hurrah"; "Today, the entire nation rejoices."[19]

We arrived at the station in Prague. There weren't that many people on the platform, we noted, just the official delegation: the deputy-mayor, if I'm not mistaken, and members of the exhibition committee. This reception seemed too low key; we had become accustomed to triumphal welcomes. But this was clearly by design. These were people who knew what they were doing, and they realized that if there were a crowd on the platform, and then 160 people got off the train, they would all mingle together and there would be a mishmash of guests, hosts, and baggage. So they had left the arrival area empty, with only the official commission there to greet us. Once again, the welcoming words and speeches began. From the Czech side, in Czech, came, "Brother Bulgarians! The Great Slavic . . . Cyril and Methodius."[20] From our

---

18. "Hello" in Czech.

19. Aleko is quoting and mocking the rhetoric of an article in *Svoboda* published on the occasion of the birth of Boris, heir to the Bulgarian throne.

20. Cyril and Methodius were brothers who are venerated as the sainted founders of Slavic literacy and creators of Glagolitic, the first Slavic alphabet. They were natives

side, also in Czech, we heard, "Brothers, we have come to learn from the great Czech nation," and then from our side again, in Bulgarian, "Brothers! The great Ivan Hus . . . Yes, brothers, Ivan Hus is great!" Meanwhile, Bai Ganyo, not at all pleased that only Cyril and Methodius were being mentioned, jabbed the teacher again: "Hey you, say something, Teach. We have a few great people, too! Say something about Khan Asparukh, or take out the shepherd's pipe and play us a tune or something—now's the time!"[21]

They told us that we would go to Meščanska Beseda, the city club, and from there they would send us out to various lodgings. They had arranged for our baggage to be brought there, and so we started off. We entered the train station from the platform, and what a sight it was! The station was swarming with people. Literally, if you had dropped an egg, it wouldn't have hit the ground. Down the center was a pathway just wide enough for us to walk through, and along both sides were elegant ladies with bouquets. They were all in their Sunday best. No sooner had the first "*Nazdar*" thundered out than they began to hand us bouquets and shower us with flowers, and then, when we got out on the street and looked around—good God!—as far as the eye could see there was only a narrow strip clear for us; every other spot was taken up with people. And again, rows of ladies with flowers; and again, welcoming cries of "*Nazdaar! Nazdaar!* Hurrah!" and again, a hail of bouquets. A royal welcome! Amid all this shouting and showering with flowers, we climbed into carriages and set off. I leave to your imagination the grace and dignity with which we clambered in, what with families and babies and all. We were thunderstruck by this unexpectedly grandiose reception. We tipped our hats left and right, and eventually it occurred to us to take them off all together. (When it comes to getting things right, we're naturals, no doubt about it. We know all those damned picayune details; we know etiquette and all that stuff!) A smile was frozen on my convulsively trembling lips, and I wanted to laugh and to cry and to sink into the earth all at the same time.

We reached the Meščanska Beseda and sat at tables out in the courtyard. We waited for our baggage to arrive and for them to assign us lodgings.

---

of Salonika, modern Thessaloniki, in what is today Greek Macedonia, which at times during the Middle Ages was part of the Bulgarian Empire. In 863 they led a Byzantine mission to the Slavs of Moravia, an area generally accepted as having included territory of the modern Czech and Slovak republics.

21. Asparukh (ruled ca. 670–701) was a leader of the ancient Bulgars, a Turkic-speaking people who crossed the Danube from what is now Bessarabia and founded the first Bulgarian state.

Several carriage drivers waited a whole hour by the doors to be paid, poor fellows, but many of our group didn't see the need of paying. "Big deal!" said Bai Ganyo. "What would it have cost them to pay for the carriages? After all, we're Slavs. That's where they should show us their Slavic solidarity, you betcha! And how! Everything for free. Any fool can put on a show if you pay him. All that 'nazdar' stuff is just a bunch of hot air."

The luggage arrived, and they began to direct us to our quarters. Our gracious hosts had taken pains to secure us housing. I'll spare you the arguments with the cabbies, with the waiters at the club, with the organizers about the late arrival and the accidental mix-up of luggage, people's dissatisfaction with their housing arrangements, the haggling, and other stuff like that. Let me just take you up to our room for a moment. (Don't be alarmed, madam.) The four of us were staying in one large room with all the conveniences. It looked out onto a courtyard. Right across from us rose a building with the same number of floors. At one point, while moving the flower pots on the windowsill so she could close the windows, Anushka, the maid who looked after our room, suddenly turned to me and, glancing over at the facing windows, asked me in Czech, with evident embarrassment, "Excuse me, sir, is that man over there also Bulgarian? Look what he's doing! He's as dark and hairy as a savage! Ha-ha-ha ha!"

I looked in the direction she was pointing, and what do you think I saw? Bai Ganyo, standing at the open window, without having drawn the curtains or shut the blinds, had liberated himself from his clothes above the waist, and when I caught sight of him, he was leering at our housekeeper and stroking his hairy chest, evidently trying to ensnare her with his charms.

The local papers that day reported the news of the imposing (they got that right!) arrival of the dear guests, their Bulgarian brothers. They also carried the schedule for our visits to the exhibition and the sights of Prague. They reported where we had been, how we had been met, how the Czechs had greeted us, and how we had responded. The name of our leader, Mr. Vasilaki, resounded. He got the attention owing to his countless speeches, and to tell you the truth, say what you will, if it hadn't been for Mr. Vasilaki's pulling the wool over their eyes, the whole thing would have been a disaster.

Members of the committee met us by the entrance of the exhibit. Once again, there were speeches about the Czech nation and the Bulgarian nation. Here, you see, they didn't make the mistake of welcoming us as Serbs! Apparently, that kind of mistake had been made at the entrance to the Plovdiv Exhibition, when they mixed up the delegations from two rival Bulgarian towns. The people in Sliven and Yambol are constantly at odds with each other—whether out of envy or out of spite, who knows! So the delegation from Sliven presented itself at the entrance of the Plovdiv Exhibition, and a member of the committee gave them a welcoming address, taking them for the representatives from Yambol, and started praising their rivals to the hilt. "Brave citizens of Yambol! Glorious citizens of Yambol!" The Sliven delegates, meanwhile, broke into a sweat and started coughing behind their hands and giving each other looks. What a picture!

We entered the exhibition grounds. One of the committee members took us on a quick tour of the major displays. Who did he think he was leading around? Our tourists are just like the English! As soon as our folks entered the botanical pavilion, there was no getting them out.

"Ivancho, Ivancho! C'mere, c'mere, see that tulip? Look how big it is! Remember? Your auntie has a tulip like that," someone calls out from one side.

"Marika, Marika! Come over here! Look at the mimosa! That's a mimosa, see? Do you remember it from the children's illustrated encyclopedia I bought you for Easter?" another voice chimes in from another side.

"Will you look at that! Basil! Tsk tsk tsk! Look! Basil! So the Czechs have basil, too. Good for them!" puts in a third, and they all rush to look at the basil.

"Yeah, so what? I don't see any of our wonderful wild geraniums here," pipes up Bai Ganyo with a dissatisfied air. "What's the good of all this stuff if they don't have wild geraniums? Ahhh, but back home in *our* mountains! Damn!"

The committee member, meanwhile, stands there fidgeting, waiting for the "dear guests" to finish chattering!

I couldn't take it any more, so I left the botanical exhibit and went off to look around the other pavilions. In my absence, a photograph was taken of the dear guests, and the next day the entire group appeared in a newspaper photo.

They took us to Hradčany, to see the castles of the Czech kings. They showed us various historical nooks and crannies: the small chamber where the council had sat and decided to begin the Thirty Years' War, the window through which Czech patriots had been thrown to their doom.[22] They took us to the old city hall and to both the old and new museums. In our honor

22. Aleko has mixed up the throwers and the throwees. In 1419 and again in 1618, Czech Protestant patriots defenestrated their opponents, signaling the start of the Hussite Wars and the Thirty Years' War, respectively. The Czech Protestants lost both.

they performed an opera in the national theater, and they held a party for us at Meščanska Beseda. We went to Mr. Naprstek's house. He is a very well-respected citizen. At some point or other he got in trouble with the Austrian government and fled to America, where he amassed a fortune. He returned to Prague, where now, surrounded by honors and respect, he occupies himself with philanthropy. He has his own museum and library. The master of the house met us with true Slavic warmth and hospitality. Here we heard the most sincere and heartwarming speeches. In one of the rooms was a thick guest book in which visitors signed their names. At one point, when a bunch of our people were crowding around the book, and everyone was chafing at the bit to grab the pen and immortalize their names, Bai Ganyo tugged at my sleeve and asked impatiently, "What are they signing up for over there?"

Knowing that Bai Ganyo wouldn't be induced to sign if there was nothing in it for him, I told him jokingly that anyone who didn't want to do any more sightseeing could sign up in that book to dine at Mr. Naprstek's.

"Is that so?" exclaimed Bai Ganyo. "To hell with their antiquities, gimme the pen! Come on, give it here! Gimme the pen, quick! Can I sign in pencil? Gimme, gimme, I'm in a hurry!" And he began to elbow his way to the table on which the large book was lying. He stepped on someone's foot, and people were pushing and shoving. They began to fight over the pen and spilled ink on the book, but finally, the trembling, hairy, sweaty hand of Bai Ganyo decorated one of the pages of the large book with two sonorous words:

Ganyo Balkanski

Tsvyatko announced that he didn't wish to continue his story.

"Tell us something about the party. Didn't you say that they gave a party in honor of the Bulgarians?" called out one of our group.

I didn't go to that party. Bai Ganyo was there. Apropos, I went with Bai Ganyo to the barber that day. He intended to charm the Czech ladies that evening, so beforehand he took every possible measure to ensure he would appear in all his glory. He bought a necktie, he polished his medal ("You didn't think your Bai Ganyo had such things, did you?"), and we went to the barber, since his beard and hair had gotten rather scruffy. He sat in the chair. The barber carefully tied a cloth around his neck and began his work. We must have spent almost a whole hour there. It wasn't so easy to please Bai Ganyo.

"Here, here; tell him to take off a bit here," Bai Ganyo would say, pointing to his neck. "He should smooth it here; have him shave it a bit with a razor. But tell him to keep a sharp eye out so he doesn't nick a pimple, or the devil take him!"

The barber sees the angry expression on Bai Ganyo's sweaty face in the mirror and he looks at me quizzically. "What is the gentleman saying?" he asks me meekly in Czech, thinking that he has committed some affront to Bai Ganyo's taste.

"You just tell him to stop babbling!" says Bai Ganyo, turning to me, using a tone that suggested he had hired me as a translator. "Just tell him to leave me a small beard, but to make it a little more pointed, like Napoleon's; got that? And tell him to comb my mustache so it turns up like this. Like the mustache of that Italian king, heh-heh-heh! Have you seen his photo? Tell him to make my mustache like that. Go on, tell him."

I didn't have the courage to translate Bai Ganyo's humble desire literally. It would have made a lot of trouble for the barber. After all, is it an easy task to transform someone into Napoleon III and Umberto, aided only by a razor and a comb?[23] And look who we're talking about!

The coiffure was completed. Bai Ganyo took out his money bag, twirled it around on its string, opened it, reached down to the bottom, shoveled up a handful of coins, turned his back to us, rummaged around in the coins, selected one, and handed it to the barber, but he handed it to him in such a fashion as if to say, "Here you go, take it. What the heck, let it be on me." The coin was a twenty-kreutzer piece. But then it occurred to him that he was, perhaps, being too generous, and so as not to be taken for a fool, he stretched out his hand toward the barber and rubbed his fingers as if to say, "Give me change." The barber opened the drawer in a flash, threw the coin inside, picked up two ten-kreutzer pieces, slammed them angrily down on the marble counter top, and disappeared through an inner door. The coins rolled onto the ground. For a fleeting instant Bai Ganyo seemed taken aback, but before I could take stock of his expression, he bent down and gathered up the money, saying, "Let him cut off his nose to spite his face! Let's get out of here, to hell with them. Everyone just wants to fleece you. But I know them all. Slavs! Bullshit!"

---

23. King Umberto I of Italy was a popular ruler at that time.

6

Bai Ganyo at Jirechek's

"What Tsvyatko just told you happened later," said our shy Ilcho, "but I know that Bai Ganyo was in Prague on a previous occasion. He was there for a long time and sold quite a bit of rose oil. Would you like me to tell you about it?"

"If it's about Bai Ganyo, don't ask; tell!" we all replied.

OK, then listen. Bai Ganyo arrives in Prague from Vienna. He gets off the train at the station, shoulders his *disagi*, and walks out into the street. The cabbies descend on him to offer their services, and he dips his chin down, Bulgarian style, to signal no. They interpret his gesture as an affirmative nod, and a cab pulls up right in front of him. Bai Ganyo gets mad, stares wide eyed, and makes angry gestures. A policeman sees him and makes the cabbies back off. Bai Ganyo is wondering how he can find out where our famous historian Jirechek lives.[24] Jirechek has lived in Bulgaria; he loves the Bulgarians; Bai Ganyo will go to his place. "Good day." "Good day to you." And maybe he'll invite him to stay at his place. Why spend money on a hotel? While he was thinking along those lines, a porter in a red cap came and stood in front of him and offered to carry his *disagi*. Bai Ganyo asked him if he knew where Jirechek lived. The porter answered in the negative but expressed the hope that he'd be able to find him and held out his hand to take the *disagi*. Bai Ganyo didn't give them up, in part because his *muskali*

---

24. Josif Konstantin Jirechek (1854–1918), Czech historian and professor at the University of Prague and the University of Vienna, was a world-famous specialist on the Balkan Slavs. His *History of the Bulgarians* (published in Czech and German in 1876) was the first scholarly study of Bulgarian history. He lived in Bulgaria from 1879 to 1884 and served there as minister of education and in other important posts.

were inside and "might get swiped," and in part because he saw that the guy was nicely dressed, and who knew how much he'd try to fleece him for.

"Your Grace, you go in front and I'll follow behind," said Bai Ganyo politely. "Don't worry about the *disagi*; I'll carry them." This politeness on Bai Ganyo's part was calculated. He figured it would make the porter well disposed toward him and at the same time show that he, Bai Ganyo, was not some rich important man, so the guy wouldn't try to fleece him.

They walk along and ask at each cross street where Jirechek lives. Finally, someone realizes that they're looking for Professor Jirechek and tells them where to go to ask, and they keep asking till they find him. Bai Ganyo gives the porter a hearty "Thank you very much" and enters Jirechek's apartment.

"Oho! Good day. Bai Jirechek, how's it goin'? You doin' OK?" exclaims Bai Ganyo in his most friendly manner as he enters the master of the house's study. The latter shakes hands with him in surprise, invites him to sit, and curses his memory, which can't recall who this kind friend is.

"Don't you recognize me?" Bai Ganyo adds helpfully, mixing formal and informal modes of address. "Were you not a minister in Sofia?" "Yes." "Well, I'm from there, too!" Bai Ganyo concludes triumphantly. "So we're fellow townsmen, so to speak, heh, heh, heh, and how! Do you remember the article in the newspaper *Slavyanin*?"[25]

"Yes, yes, I remember," answers Jirechek in a reserved and condescending tone of voice.

"Oh boy, did they ever smear you! But don't you worry about a thing; don't pay them no never mind. I really stuck up for you. They said 'Jirechek this' and 'Jirechek that.' But I said, 'Excuse me,' I said, 'it's not like that.'"

Jirechek knows Bulgarians well, and so he's not at all surprised at Bai Ganyo's familiarity. The conversation continues for several minutes in this vein and then passes to more practical matters. Bai Ganyo praises the apartment of his host, hints broadly that "after all, there's even room for a guest to stay here." He speaks of Bulgarian hospitality and expresses sorrow that "you see, others aren't like us Bulgarians; if a foreigner enters a Bulgarian home, they'll give him food and drink as well as a place to sleep."

---

25. During the early 1880s, the liberal newspaper *Slavyanin* (Slav) published a series of articles attacking Jirechek. To avenge himself, Jirechek wrote a ludicrous attack on himself in typical journalistic style, signed *Neznanov* ("Unknown-ov" or "Son of unknown") and sent it to the paper, which published it immediately. Despite being ridiculed, the newspaper continued to publish attacks on Jirechek until he left Bulgaria in 1884.

Jirechek attempts to persuade him that the apartment is too small even for its occupants. Bai Ganyo turns a deaf ear and expands on the theme of Bulgarian hospitality. From this theme, the conversation veers to Bai Ganyo's little business. He informs his host that he has brought rose oil to sell and announces, "Tomorrow, if you like, take me to all the factories. It's fine with me. You'll take me around, since I don't know the language, OK?"

Jirechek hastens to reply that he's not acquainted with the producers of essential oils, because his occupation is of a completely different nature, and moreover, he has no free time. But he will tell him where Bulgarian students gather, and one of them will be able to help him.

"If you like, I mean," adds Bai Ganyo. "I won't force you. I'll also give the wife—is she here?—a *muskal*. I know her, too, of course." (Jirechek couldn't for the life of him figure out what wife he was talking about.) "And if you have friends and relatives here, tell 'em that I've brought rose oil—there's no shame in that. I'll hang around your place more; we'll chat about Bulgaria. And if you like, I'll even stay here at your place while I'm in Prague. What do you say?"

"I'm sorry, but . . ."

"That is to say, I mean, if you would be so kind," Bai Ganyo explains in confusion. "I'd prefer a hotel, but I said to myself, hey, I said, Jirechek, he's one of us."

"Thank you very much for your consideration; I would happily give you a place to stay here, but I don't have any extra room. Today, however, you are our guest and will dine with us."

"Let's dine, of course; why should we not dine?" agrees Bai Ganyo. "After all, Your Grace has certainly eaten his fill at Bulgarian tables, even if not at mine."

Jirechek was occupied with a very urgent matter, which had been interrupted by the arrival of Bai Ganyo. The master of the house was sitting on pins and needles and couldn't figure out a polite way to expedite the time that would be taken up by his eloquent guest. He rang, and a servant appeared, whom he instructed to tell the household that a guest had arrived from Bulgaria. After a while, Jirechek's mother entered. Bai Ganyo rose from his seat with great difficulty, moved his hand twice toward his forehead in an Oriental sign of respect, and condescendingly exclaimed, "Oh, hello, hello, howdy-do; c'mon, let's have a hug, Bulgarian style. How are you doing these days? I'm so glad."

The lady of the house greeted him kindly and by means of a series of questions displayed a lively interest in the fatherland of their guest.

"Well, now, tell me truly," said Bai Ganyo, "where is it better, in Prague or in Sofia?"

The lady was confused, since she had never been to Sofia, and Bai Ganyo, as he asked the question, looked at Jirechek with a devilish smirk, as if to imply his opinion about women. "After all, she's only a woman; what kind of a conversation can you have with her?"

"His Grace will dine with us at home today," Jirechek informed his mother, and then, in order to get on with his work, he asked her in German to take Bai Ganyo into another room. The lady of the house proposed to Bai Ganyo that they go into the next room. Bai Ganyo looked searchingly at Jirechek, looked at his *disagi* with the *muskali*, and made a calculation with his eyebrows. "They said something in German; who knows what they're up to. But I don't think so. After all, he was a minister in our country. But then ministers are no good either! But this one doesn't seem like that type to me." And then he got up hesitantly and headed in the direction of the neighboring room indicated by the lady. When he got to the door, however, he turned and tried to guess from their faces his hosts' intentions, and he observed some mute signals that his hosts were in fact exchanging. Actually, these signals meant "try to keep him busy for a long time, because I have a lot of urgent business," but Bai Ganyo interpreted them otherwise.

"These things here could get in your way," he said, looking at the *disagi*.

"Oh no, not at all. Please, don't worry about them," answered Jirechek.

"Look, I know they'll get in your way, for sure. Let me just take them into the other room." He reaches out to take them, but his hosts protest graciously. "Not that I'm afraid or anything, it's just that I thought . . ."

They pass into the living room, and the hostess closes the door behind her so as not to disturb Jirechek in the study. She does her best to find something to interest Bai Ganyo. She offers him various albums, she shows him pictures, she sets before him a whole stack of illustrations, but Bai Ganyo's mind is elsewhere, and he responds to his hostess's kindness with feigned indifference. "I'll pass, thank you; why don't you look at them yourself. I've seen many pictures and portraits! I may be young, but I've been around."

Bai Ganyo glances impatiently at his large silver watch and then introduces a rather interesting and opportune topic. "I'm very curious to know more about Europe. Take this, for example. In our country, when noon arrives, we sit down to dinner. In your country things are different. When you do eat dinner, for example?"

"We normally dine at five, but today we could eat earlier. Excuse me while I leave you for a moment," says the hostess and exits through the other door.

Bai Ganyo sits alone in the room and stares absent-mindedly at the pictures. From time to time he spits on the carpet—not because he's hungry,
but who knows?—and rubs it in with his boot. His ears prick up at the
slightest noise from the study. At one point he hears Jirechek get up from his
desk, take a few steps, and stop. "What a fool I am! Why didn't I bring my
disagi into this room?" Bai Ganyo sits on tenterhooks until he can contain
himself no longer. He tiptoes quietly along the carpet toward the door to the
study, leans down, and puts his ear to the keyhole. All he hears is his own
quickened breathing and the blood pounding in his ears. But even this doesn't
calm Bai Ganyo. He doesn't see anything through the keyhole, and pressing
the door handle hesitantly, he opens it and furtively pokes his head into the
study. He sees Jirechek squatting near the *disagi* in front of a bookshelf.

Bai Ganyo titters awkwardly at him. "Tee, hee, hee, you're working, are
you? Tee, hee, hee! I thought I'd just take a look. Don't you worry; work
away, I'll just close the door again." Jirechek looks at him in amazement. The
reason for Bai Ganyo's peculiar curiosity never crosses his mind.

Dinner is ready. They all go into the dining room and sit around the table.
Jirechek's parents, his sister, Bai Ganyo, and Jirechek himself. Before beginning the meal, Bai Ganyo starts to cross himself, but with a knowing smile.
In this manner he wants to show his hosts that he's not one of those simple
folk, and that he's not much of a believer, but it's not bad to be on the right
side of God, too (we're on good terms with the devil, so why not burn a little incense for the Lord, just in case).

"I'm a Liveral, from the Liveral Party," he explains, "but every now and
then I just up and cross myself.[26] There's no harm in it, we're people after
all . . . What's this; is it soup? I love soup. Soup is a European dish, but *chorba*
is Turkish. Nowadays, we eat more soup than *chorba*.[27] Oh, *pardonne*, excuse
me, I've soiled your tablecloth, tsk, tsk, tsk. Good grief!"

Carried away with his desire to prove himself a man of impeccable manners, Bai Ganyo had failed to get a good grip on the bowl of soup that his

26. Here, and later, Bai Ganyo butchers the terms "liberal" and "conservative." The
Liberal Party in Bulgaria favored a constitutional democracy that would limit the power
of the rich and subordinated the prince to parliament. The Conservative Party favored a
monarchist system and the limitation of voting rights to qualified property owners, and
it attempted to keep liberal provisions out of the constitution.

27. Soup and *chorba* are basically synonymous, but *chorba* entered Bulgarian from
Turkish, while *supa* (soup) entered Bulgarian from Western Europe. Aleko is mocking
Bai Ganyo's attempt to appear more "European" and less "Oriental."

hostess handed him, and he spilled a good bit of it onto the table. Before they could stop him, he gathered some of it up with his spoon and poured it back into his dish. The hostess didn't want to allow him to eat that soup, but he, out of delicacy of feeling, cupped his hands around the bowl and wouldn't let them exchange it.

"I've got peppers in my *disagi*," announced Bai Ganyo suddenly. He was burning with the desire to crush one of the small peppers into his soup, which seemed rather bland for his palate, but he was hesitant to take out the peppers, lest they think him a boor, and so he wanted to sound out his hosts beforehand.

"Oh? Do you have peppers?" replied Jirechek.

"Of course I've got peppers; what do you think? After all, as you know, 'dear Mother Bulgaria' can't manage without the hot stuff," replied Bai Ganyo ironically, and without waiting another second, he jumped up from the table, dashed into the study, hauled out the *disagi*, squatted over them, with his back to his hosts, and then brought two peppers to the table.

"Two will do for the five of us; these are really hot," he announced as he crushed half of a pepper, seeds and all, into his bowl, and then politely offered the rest to his hosts: "Here, go ahead, crumble some in, heh, heh, Bulgarian style! No, really, do crush some in; listen to me and you'll see what a treat it is. Well, as they say, you can lead a horse to water, and all that. Just a minute, I'll crush some up and I'll show you what real soup is!"

And indeed, Bai Ganyo spiced up the soup so much that a person unaccustomed to it would have been poisoned. He began to slurp it up. And when a Bulgarian slurps, it's no joke. Three hundred dogs at each other's throats can't drown him out. Big beads of sweat broke out on Bai Ganyo's forehead and were ready to gush down into his bowl. He'd slurp once from the tip of the spoon, then he'd set the spoon down and quench the spicy liquid with two or three mouthfuls of bread; again he'd take up the spoon, slurp the soup, sniffle, and again, two or three mouthfuls of bread.

"Hey, pass me another piece of bread, will ya? You people eat with no bread at all," marveled Bai Ganyo. "As for us Bulgarians—we eat a lot of bread; I don't want to brag, but with a *chorba* like this, *pardonne*, with a *soup* like this, I can eat up a whole loaf. You betcha."

They didn't bet on it, but even without the wager Bai Ganyo devoured copious amounts of bread.

"Where do you get this wine?" asked Bai Ganyo inquisitively, not that he cared about the answer but just to have a pretext for getting another glass.

"We buy it," answered his host. "Do you like it?"

"Ah, it's the real thing! You buy it, do you? Pass the bottle over here. My stomach is burning like red-hot iron from that pepper. If I drank up the whole bottle it would boil inside me. Well now, we have good wine, too; a few nickels would buy you a quart, and if you polish off a quart by yourself, you're all set! Upf, I belched, excuse me, that was a bit rude, *pardonne*, but what can you do? It's human nature; you can't hold it in."

Thanks to Bai Ganyo, dinner at Jirechek's turned out to be quite lively. Coffee was brought to the parlor. Bai Ganyo, thanks to the tasty, and above all, filling, meal, wanted to treat his host to a hand-rolled cigarette, and his tobacco just happened to be in his *disagi* again. To tell the truth, his cigarette case was in his pocket, but he needed an excuse to check on his *disagi*; he couldn't just leave the *muskali* like that among strangers. Anything is possible in this world.

Bai Ganyo wouldn't hear of his host's refusal to smoke some of his tobacco: "No, no, my good friend! How can ya not light up when it's Bulgarian tobacco?"

Bai Ganyo lit up and started slurping his coffee with gusto. Now that's what I call slurping! Should you find yourself in such good spirits, able to spend whole hours at a time talking with a companion, sitting in a room where no one can overhear what you're saying, much less understand it— under such propitious circumstances, could you restrain yourself from talking politics? It was too much for Bai Ganyo. He couldn't resist; he poured out his heart. "Well now, Bai Jirechek, so tell me, Your Grace, are you a Liveral or a Conserve? I bet you're a Conserve. And as for me, if you wanna know, I can't understand either of 'em, but come on, let 'em do what they want. It's all horse trading, y'know, it's no joke. But, do you wanna know the truth? (No one's eavesdropping are they?) Do you wanna know the truth? They're all scoundrels on both sides! You just listen to me; don't you worry! They're all scoundrels, every last one of 'em! But what're you gonna do? It's no use beating your head against a wall. A little wheeling, a little dealing, I've got some lawsuits going—it's impossible not to. If you're not on their side, your goose is cooked. Even I feel like being elected a deputy or a mayor. There's some gravy to be skimmed off of those things. People are making a bundle, y'know? That's all well and good, but you've got to go along to get along. Otherwise, the devil himself couldn't get you elected. That's the way it is. I've been in the very thick of it, so I really know the ropes." Jirechek could scarcely doubt that his guest knew "the ropes."

7

Bai Ganyo Goes Visiting

When Bai Ganyo was finally convinced that there was no chance of installing himself in Jirechek's apartment, he picked up his *disagi* and, refusing to listen to the urging of his host to leave them until he found a place, set out, escorted by the servant, for Národny Kavárna—the café where Bulgarian students congregated. It was already seven o'clock when he entered the café with his *disagi* in his hands and his *kalpak* on his head. How could anyone not know who he was or where he was from? To the left of the entrance several Bulgarian students sat around a table.

One of them saw their compatriot enter and nudged the others. "A Bulgarian, a Bulgarian!" Everyone turned to look at exactly the moment Bai Ganyo stopped a waiter carrying a tray with cups of coffee and asked in a loud voice, trying as hard as he could to twist Bulgarian words into something comprehensible to a foreigner, "Where be Bulgar boys hereabouts?" accompanying the question with movements of his head and his free hand. A friendly burst of laughter from the left side put an end to the waiter's mystification. Bai Ganyo turned and recognized his own dark-eyed, dark-haired compatriots clustered together.

"Oh! Good day! So this is where you've been?" he cried out heartily, putting down his *disagi* and beginning to grasp the hands of the students. "What are you looking at me like that for? Don't be afraid; I'm a Bulgarian. Come on and make room for me to sit down."

"What's your name, sir?" inquired one of the students.

"Me? Why do you ask? Ganyo Balkanski. I brought a little rose oil to your Prague. It's here in my *disagi*."

"Really?" exclaimed one of the younger students in patriotic ecstasy. "Come on, let's see it."

55

He had, in fact, only heard about rose oil.

"What's there to see? It's just an oil like any other," answered Bai Ganyo. "It's got nothing to do with you. Forget about the oil, and tell me something. Where can I stay? I was just now at Bai Jirecek's."

"Really?" the ecstatic student exclaimed again.

"What do you mean, 'really'? Why shouldn't I go see him? I did. I was thinking that he'd show me some kindness, invite me to be his guest. But damn it all, 'My apartment's crowded,' he says, and so on and so forth. He says he loves Bulgarians. Him? If there's something for nothing in it, even your Bai Ganyo can love you. Is that how you treat a Bulgarian? A Bulgarian! To tell the truth, the fellow did feed me. But as for the food, never mind, forget it. Bulgarians are much more hospitable. Even if a Bulgarian has only one room, he'll still invite you to stay."

Some of the students figured out where Bai Ganyo was going with all this, and they waited from one moment to the next for him to show his cards. Only the ecstatic student reacted sympathetically to his words and clearly shared his outrage at the lack of hospitality of foreigners.

"Really, we Bulgarians are very hospitable," he affirmed with the greatest of certainty. "People here don't want to give you the time of day. Here we have to hang out in cafés."

The student who uttered these words was quite advanced in terms of being civilized, but for some reason, he didn't have a particularly good reputation among his comrades. Apparently, several sins lay upon his soul. Among other things, they said that he really liked to get something for nothing. No wonder. That cursed sin—stinginess—infects a young person in his home environment and takes root early in childhood; it shrivels his soul, turning him into the coldest of egotists. Nothing tender, nothing noble, is left in him. Material interest governs all the actions of a miser and defines his relationships with those around him; no moral incentive precedes and no repentance follows his actions, all of which are directed uncritically toward obtaining some kind of gain. Even when these actions lead to disaster or disgrace for someone else, even then, instead of remorse, the egotist and miser feels satisfaction, as if others' losses were his gain, others' unhappiness his happiness. The only thing that could embarrass our young egotist would be someone's outwitting him. While for other nations the word "sly" is a synonym for "crafty" and "perfidious," and if applied to a person would lower him in the opinion of society, in our country we bestow the epithet "sly" as if it were the most honored decoration. "Wow! He turned out to be a sly fellow.

What a chip off the old block. He put one over on all of us. We couldn't fool him. Well done. Bravo!"

No actions or relationships made sense for Bodkov—that was his name— unless they resulted in some unearned profit, something for nothing, what we call in Bulgarian *kyoravo* or *kelepir*. (Are there any expressions in the European languages that can express the true meaning of these words?)[28] If he paid a visit to local families, he did it not out of sociability, nor out of a desire to become acquainted with the life of more civilized circles; the intel- lectual and moral interests of this society not merely were of no concern to him but were even a burden to him. They were like boring intervals, unbear- able pauses, which stood between him and the goal of his visit: the windfall, be it some kind of meal or some outing at their expense. He couldn't imag- ine relations with women without some ulterior motive. He kept a whole list of girls, of who had how big a dowry; nothing else interested him in that quarter. In the same way, self-interest defined his relations toward his friends. Flattery, slander, intrigues, and betrayal were the tools of his trade. Even such things as national and tribal sympathies and antipathies served him only as a means of extracting personal benefit. More than once he had had his hand in the purses of different Slavic committees: now he's a "refugee from Batak,"[29] now he's an "emigrant." But then, in such matters Aslanov is the greater master.[30]

---

28. The words *kelepir* and *kyoravo* both entered Bulgarian from Turkish and have the sense of the English "windfall," "free lunch," "pork barrel," "boondoggle," or "undeserved riches." In modern Turkish, *kelepir* means "cheap bargain," while the adverb *kyoravo* is derived from Turkish *kör* (blind).

29. Batak, in the western Rhodope Mountains, was the site of a terrible massacre in the Turkish reprisals that followed the April Uprising of 1876. The April Uprising and the reprisals were followed by a Great-Power conference at which autonomy was sought for Bulgaria within the framework of the Ottoman Empire. Owing to conflict- ing interests among the Great Powers, Turkey rejected the proposal, and on 12 April 1877 Russia declared war on Turkey. In March 1878 Turkey signed a treaty with Russia at San Stefano (modern Yeşilköy) under the terms of which a Bulgarian state was cre- ated that stretched from the Danube to the Aegean and from the Black Sea to Mt. Grammos—that is, all of what is today Bulgaria and the Republic of Macedonia plus northern Greece, eastern Albania, southern Kosovo, and eastern Serbia—to be admin- istered by Russia for two years. Alarmed at the prospect of such a large territory in southeastern Europe under Russian control, the Great Powers convened the Congress of Berlin in June of that same year. The autonomous Bulgarian princedom that emerged from that conference and that was to be administered by Russia for nine months cor- responded roughly to the northern half of modern Bulgaria. Most of what is today the

Such was the ecstatic student who supported Bai Ganyo's view regarding foreigners' lack of hospitality. "Yes, we hang out here in cafés; no one invites us over," he repeated, to please Bai Ganyo.

A student with a jaundiced air, smiling scornfully, spoke up. "But where do you want them to let you hang out?" It seems he had long harbored a dislike for this young egotist. "Do you want them to carry you around on their shoulders? Why should they? Is it because even before you've managed to cross their threshold, you'll make a pass at the servant girl who meets you in the hallway? Is it because in their society you're either as silent as a stump or you open your mouth only to jabber banalities and stupidities? Is it because to their faces you praise them to the skies but behind their backs you slander them? Is it because you pull the wool over their eyes and pass yourself off as the son of a millionaire industrialist or shipowner, when your father has two looms for making carpet fringe or two leaky boats, just so that you can charm the parents and sweep their daughter off her feet? Why should they accept you with open arms? Who are you? What are you to them? Just whose nose are you rubbing in your hospitality? And what is this vaunted hospitality of yours? Is it that a Bulgarian will lay out greasy bedding for you and then wrap you up in a dubious blanket? Oh, for God's sake, lay off the wild boasting! Isn't it time for us to open our eyes?"

"What's got you all hot and bothered?" asked one of the students. "Is now the time to pick a quarrel with him, when we have a guest?"

"Let the man talk. After all, he's not asking for money, is he?" Bai Ganyo soothed him with this typical argument: *after all, he's not asking for money.* He can say whatever he wants, he can do whatever he wants, as long as he isn't asking for money, as long as he isn't digging into our pockets, going after our interests. He can even lie, as long as he isn't asking for money.

---

southern half of Bulgaria was constituted as Eastern Rumelia, an autonomous province of Turkey with a Christian governor appointed by the sultan every five years. It was unified with Bulgaria in 1885. The territory from the eastern Pindus to the western Rhodopes and from Mt. Shar to Mt. Olympus (which was called Macedonia—much of which had been included in the Bulgaria established by the San Stefano treaty) as well as Thrace remained Ottoman territory with promises of reforms. Turkey retained these territories until the First Balkan War (1912). See 138n85 regarding Macedonia. Thus, as a result of the 1877–78 Russo-Turkish war, Russia became Bulgaria's liberator. At the same time Russia looked after its own interests, sometimes to the detriment of Bulgaria's. This is a recurring theme in Bulgarian politics of the period, and therefore in *Bai Ganyo* as well.

30. See 77n37.

But after this chance incident, a conversation among them could no longer be maintained. The company fell silent, and one by one they began to drift away. Finally, the only Bulgarians left were Bai Ganyo and the ecstatic student, who didn't want to let slip this opportunity to extract some profit from his chance meeting with a Bulgarian merchant of rose oil. Birds of a feather flock together.

Not an hour had passed, and the student had been so successful in tearing down his friends in front of Bai Ganyo that Bai Ganyo was driven to exclaim with all his heart, "How awful! What sons of bitches!" One more hour and Bai Ganyo was already in the room of the student, who was able to exploit quite masterfully and for his own benefit the arrival of the guest, whom he recommended to his landlords as his fellow countryman, a millionaire, who "had loads of factories for rose oil." He managed to borrow from the landlady—to whom he had not paid his rent for some time now—ten gold pieces. While in one room the student was singing the praises of Bai Ganyo's riches, in the neighboring room Bai Ganyo had already taken off his padded jacket and was rooting around very carefully in it for something, mumbling under his breath, "Those damned lice have shown up again." Bai Ganyo's concept of hygiene was not very highly developed. "Is there anyone alive who doesn't have lice?" say our old folks back home. And reassured by that adage, they don't interfere too zealously with the proliferation of the little creatures. And why should they deny themselves a pleasure such as this? The sun is beaming down, and what's the point of that sun if you can't go out onto the veranda, stretch out on a straw mat, and sneeze two or three times from its dust? And then your granny comes out, and you lay your head on her knee, and she thrusts her bony fingers with their dirty nails into your hair, and just like cleaning rice, she starts in. Pop! from here, pop! from there, and then those little creatures really get scared and they start swarming all around your head, and it's quite a pleasant tickling sensation, and then old granny starts up singing, and you're basking in that beaming Balkan sun. How idyllic!

After he had completed his entomological excavations, Bai Ganyo repaired his toilette and without knocking entered the neighboring room but immediately cried out, "*Pardonne!*"—and with good reason: he had barged in on a pretty tender vis-à-vis between the student and the daughter of the proprietress. They were wrapped around each other as befits two young hearts in love. The girl, embarrassed, ran out into the next room.

"What did you come in like that for? You embarrassed the girl," said the student with an ironic wink.

"You've hit the jackpot!" Bai Ganyo whispered conspiratorially, eyes aglitter, as if to a tomcat in a convent. "Nice looking, the devil take her. Is she a maid?"

"What do you mean, 'a maid'? She's the landlady's daughter."

"Is that so? You can't figure out who's a maid and who's a mistress here; they're all so shiny, all dressed in clean clothes. One will plant herself in front of you, simper at you sweet as pie; you think she's a maid, you catch hold of her, and you've gotten yourself in trouble; another one turns up, pretty, modest; you think, huh, this must be the lady of the house; you stand up, invite her to sit down; she gets embarrassed—why sure—you talk to her about politics, and then you see that she's cleaning your boots."

From the student's stories, accompanied by a variety of gestures with which he embellished and gave more emphasis and significance to his words, Bai Ganyo discovered that the young man had been, for several months, under the guise of pure love, laying siege to the daughter of his widowed landlady with an irresistible doggedness.

"And she, the silly fool," explained the student, "is hoping that I'll marry her. Let her go on hoping, and let her feed me well; let her mend my shirts. If she were some rich girl, I could understand why a man would take her, but she's a pauper like me. She's hanging around me because she thinks I've got money to burn. If she knew what I was, do you think she'd be lusting after me? The local girls are awful con artists. But, of course, I know how to handle them!" And he explained at great length and in great detail how he handled them.

"Good for you!" exclaimed Bai Ganyo with gleaming eyes, delighted by his young companion.

"But wait a minute. That's not all. If that were all there was to it, it wouldn't be worth anything. There's another girl, too, and I've got my eye on her, but who knows? Now, if I could turn her head, there'd really be something in it for me. She's rich. I'm invited to be their guest tomorrow. They're taking me on an outing to some village."

"So when will you take me to the factories?" asked the ever-practical Bai Ganyo.

"No problem; the next day. Tomorrow, you stay here, hang out with them. As soon as they see that you don't know the language, they won't let you go to a hotel; they'll invite you to stay, and you'll eat your fill for free."

And in fact, the next day early in the morning, the student went visiting, and Bai Ganyo was left alone in the apartment with the proprietors. As was his habit, he got up very early that day. He woke up and saw his friend off and waited another hour until the ladies of the house woke up. This waiting was very hard for him. He kept feeling that certain pressing need, just like anyone else, but he had forgotten to ask the student where that place was. And like it or not, he had to wait for the members of the household to get up—no matter how awkward it was—before he could ask them. It's very bad when a person abroad doesn't know the language; they can't understand you even regarding the most basic things. You have to explain to them using your hands, point with your fingers. And it's not like everything can be acted out. Bai Ganyo knew several languages. He could speak Turkish like a real Turk; he understood Romanian; he had a smattering of Serbian and Russian, but the Germans and the Czechs didn't understand a single one of these languages. You couldn't say that Bai Ganyo didn't know any German at all; he did know a word or two.

In the neighboring room the family members had gotten up and were moving about. Bai Ganyo took a peek through the keyhole, not out of some inappropriate curiosity but simply to see whether they were dressed yet, and then carefully, holding his breath as he familiarized himself with their toilette, he mentally composed a phrase in German that would correspond to our "Where is the you-know-what for number two?" and finally cobbled together as a translation the phrase "*Wo ist diese für gross Arbeit?*" Knock! knock! knock!

"Enter, please!" answered two female voices from the neighboring room.

Bai Ganyo opened the door, uttered a single "*pardonne*," and rather shyly got out in German, "Where is for big job?" and he waggled his fingers about to emphasize the question.

"What, sir?" the bewildered girl asked in Czech, as she tried to see through the outward appearance of the man presented to her by her lover as a millionaire.

"For a big job," the even more embarrassed Bai Ganyo repeated in German, and again he motioned with his fingers and head but could see that they didn't understand him.

They understood him all right, but not the way he needed; the women thought that he was informing them that he had come to complete a big job, a major sale of rose oil.

"The devil take it!" Bai Ganyo thought to himself. "What do I do now?" And so that at least the daughter wouldn't be a witness to his difficult position, he motioned with his hand for the mother to come into his room. He shut the door and then repeated his question again in German, this time supplementing it with a desperate pantomime that forced the woman to make her escape into the next room, choking with suppressed laughter. The maid appeared and relieved Bai Ganyo's curiosity. An uninterrupted trio of female laughter shook the walls.

The aroma emanating from the open doors of the kitchen into the hallway whetted Bai Ganyo's appetite, and out of curiosity he went to see what they were preparing. The landlady and the maid were in there.

"*Was ist das?*" Bai Ganyo asked in a condescending tone not so much out of a desire to familiarize himself with the culinary arts of the Czechs as to show that he'd been around Europe and knew about such things, and that he knew German to boot. "Is that soup? Are you preparing soup? I know. *Ich fersten supa!*"

And Bai Ganyo, with a mixture of German, Bulgarian, and fractured Bulgarian, assisted by impressive gesticulations, gave the lady of the house to understand that he wouldn't refuse a sampling of their cuisine. When he saw that the women were more inclined to express themselves in Czech, Bai Ganyo also switched to "Czech" and reinforced his condescending request with the words "I wants let's eat" while translating these words by repeatedly touching his fingers to his open mouth, and finally, showing three fingers, he poked his chest with his index finger, poked the same finger at the chest of the proprietress, and then pointed it into space, as if indicating the invisible daughter of the proprietress; in other words, "Let's all eat together, the three of us!" It was also important for Bai Ganyo to know what time dinner would be, since he was planning to take a stroll and didn't want miss the meal and wind up "throwing money away on food when it could be had for nothing, a free lunch," and so he pulled out his huge pocket watch and holding it under the nose of the lady of the house made her point with her finger at the hands in order to show him when they would "let's eat." As soon as he was persuaded that everything was in good order, Bai Ganyo went into his room, stuffed the *muskali* into his sash, and went out onto the street, both to take a stroll and maybe to come upon a customer for his rose oil.

Bai Ganyo looked about. There were streets intersecting each other all over the place; one could get them mixed up and get lost. Being a practical person, he took a look around to find some landmark by which he could recognize the house. On a rear wall that was across from him, he saw a sign with big letters; he took out his notebook, and wetting the tip of his pencil with spit, he wrote down an exact copy of the sign, and absolutely sure that he had in his hands the exact address of his apartment, he embarked along the narrow streets of Old Prague. Hmm, let's have a look at this; hmm, let's have a look at that; hmm, here's a customer; hmm, there's a customer. He was completely carried away. And not only did he get carried away, but he got lost as well. So now what? The harder he tried to retrace his steps, the more entangled he became in the streets of the Jewish quarter; first an hour passed, then two; he dead-ended at some house. No way out there. He set off in another direction, walked and walked, and found himself on the banks of the Vltava River. "What the devil, what now?" To make things worse, dinnertime came and went. Our Bai Ganyo really got down to business now; he walked for all he was worth, drenched in sweat, out of breath. This simply wouldn't do! The people he met, especially the police, regarded him suspiciously; this flustered him even more. "What the devil do I do now?" Moreover, he was hungry, his stomach was in revolt, but why the hell should he throw money to the wind when he was invited to dinner?

But, you will ask, why is Bai Ganyo wandering the streets when the address is in his pocket? Eh, that's just the problem. You don't really think that Bai Ganyo is a dope, do you, that he didn't remember to pull out his notebook, stop one person after another on the street, and, showing them the address written down there, ask each one with his fingers, "Where?" He knows about these things. He stopped both men and women, but no matter whom he stopped and asked, it was the strangest thing. As soon as he showed them what was written, they would either look at him in amazement and burst into laughter, or they would turn away from him in disgust. One lady, probably some hysterical old spinster, as soon as he showed her the address, lit into him so that even Bai Ganyo lost heart. "The devil take it, either I'm nuts or all Prague has gone crazy," he thought to himself, and he couldn't stop wondering about the effect produced by the address he had written down. He thought and he thought. He looked all around, and suddenly, as luck would have it, coming up before him he saw Národny Kavárna, the café where the Bulgarian students hung out. Bai Ganyo went inside and found the splenetic student.

"Good day! C'mon and tell me, Your Grace, am I crazy or are the people here crazy?" asked Bai Ganyo out of breath, with wet hair plastered to his forehead.

The student looked at him quizzically, and Bai Ganyo told him how he had lost his way, how he had asked for his house by the address, and the answers he had received.

Knowing that the Czechs were rude and fanatical only when it came to Germans and were otherwise fairly polite, the student couldn't understand how it was that they didn't help Bai Ganyo.

"Here, please read what it says here!" Bai Ganyo proffered his notebook.

The student read it. At first he frowned, and then he simply exploded with laughter.

"Did you show this address to any lady?" he asked through his laughter.

"Why? Sure, I showed it. What of it?"

"What of it? Do you know what's written here?"

"What?"

"It says: '*Zde zapovědeno* . . . Here it is forbidden to . . . ' You must have copied this off of some wall."

"I don't believe it! Lookit. Tsk tsk tsk! Are you telling me the truth? Imagine that," said Bai Ganyo, clucking his tongue, and even he began to laugh.

The student didn't know where Bodkov's apartment was—they didn't visit each other—and so he advised Bai Ganyo to wait for a bit, as some Bulgarian would come along who could show him the house. It's easy enough to say "wait a little," but let's see, was Bai Ganyo's stomach of the same opinion? It was not only not of the same opinion but demonstrated this overtly with continual rumbling.

"You aren't hungry, are you?" the student asked him when he heard these signs of revolution.

"Who me? Not in the least!" Bai Ganyo prevaricated, because if he were to tell the truth, this guy would show him to the hotel, and it would simply not do for him to admit ("After all, how could I tell such a pigheaded kid!") that a free lunch was waiting for him at the landlady's.

Bai Ganyo and the "pigheaded kid" just couldn't strike up a conversation. From their very first meeting they had somehow instinctively known that they wouldn't get along, because according to the Bulgarian proverb (eh, and what exquisite proverbs Bulgarian genius has created), mangy donkeys can smell each other from across nine hills. The one came from Bulgaria; the other had been living in Europe. Surely there ought to be something for them to talk about, since after all there must be some sort of difference between the West and our homeland. Bai Ganyo, however, didn't perceive this difference, and how could he? Wherever he goes, he brings with him his own atmosphere, his own manners and customs; he looks for lodging according to his own tastes, he meets with his own kind of people, those he's accustomed to and in whom, of course, he sees nothing new. If he goes to

Vienna, he'll stay at the Hotel London. It's just as stuffy there, it has the same smells of cooking and hydrogen sulfide, as at home; he meets with the same Turks, Greeks, Armenians, Serbs, and Albanians that he's used to meeting every day; he won't go to the Café Hapsburg, since he's afraid that they'll fleece him. Instead, he'll go to the Greek coffeehouse, where it's just as dirty and stuffy from eternal smoke as in our own coffeehouses. If he's traveling on business, he'll go to Bulgarian merchants, and because they are his intermediaries, he doesn't even realize that he's coming into contact with Europeans. And that it is precisely outside of this circumscribed sphere that European life begins is something he neither knows nor even cares to know. The upbringing, the moral world of the European, his domestic situation, the fruits of centuries of tradition and the gradual refinement of intellectual movements, social struggles, and manners and customs, the museums, the libraries, the philanthropic institutions, the fine arts, the thousands of displays of progress do not burden Bai Ganyo's attention.

"It's not as if my father was always listening to opera," says Bai Ganyo, and bewitched by this principle of fossilization and ultraconservatism, he isn't terribly impressed by the "new fashion," that is, by civilization. But for all that, Bai Ganyo doesn't have the fortitude of the Chinese, who surrounded themselves with a wall against the forces of civilization, and although he is inspired by the principle "My father didn't do it and I won't do it," before you know it, he has put on a clean shirt and donned gloves, and when they force him, he even wears a frock coat; he's angry, he laughs, but he wears a frock coat. You can hear him say "*pardonne*," talk about the "costentution," boast wherever he goes that he loves "soup," when in fact he'd prefer a spicy *chorba* over any European specialty.

"Here comes a young Bulgarian. He knows where Bodkov's apartment is," announced the "pigheaded kid."

"Come on, take me home." Bai Ganyo addressed the Bulgarian, in a tone that shouldn't even be used with lazy servants; but the words "politeness" and "courtesy" in Bulgarian are newly stolen from the Russian language, "tact" has been borrowed from the French, and the closest thing we have to a term for such concepts is the word "fawning." Those gentle, tender, cordial forms of address that characterize relations between civilized people and make life more kind and more pleasant are incomprehensible to Bai Ganyo; he says, as the Lord intended, "Hey there, you, listen here, take me home." And why should he say something like "Please, be good enough to, be so kind as to"—what kind of fawning behavior is that?

The Bulgarian youth took Bai Ganyo to the entrance of his building and left. Bai Ganyo looked at the unfortunate sign on the opposite wall, shook his head at it menacingly, clucked his tongue, and entered the house. He didn't run into anyone in the hallway. He poked his head into the kitchen: the fire had already been put out, the dishes washed and put away. "Pfui, what a shame, I missed a free lunch," grumbled Bai Ganyo as he went back to his room, crouched over his *disagi*, pulled the *muskali* out of his sash, thrust them inside the *disagi*, pulled out a greasy piece of hard cheese, cut himself a chunk of dry bread, and began to put down the revolution, all the while chomping away so voraciously that even the most indolent Swiss cow would have envied him. In order to stimulate his salivary glands, which were exhausted from fruitless labor, he sent down his esophagus one thoroughly chewed hot chili pepper, which brought tears to his eyes, and loud sniffles joined in with the smacking sounds. The maid, who was doing her housework in the neighboring room, when she heard the strange sounds accompanying Bai Ganyo's snack, opened the door and popped into the room. Embarrassed, Bai Ganyo hid his *disagi* behind his back, turned his tear-streaked and sweat-soaked face aside, said "*Pardonne!*" and snorted energetically, and dismissed the maid. That is to say, he didn't tell her to leave, but she hurried away, since she thought that the millionaire must have received some sad news.

Bodkov didn't return that evening. Toward nightfall, the ladies returned home; once again, the fire was lit in the kitchen, and they began to prepare supper. Bai Ganyo already felt at home. "After all, what's the point of standing on ceremony with women," he thought, and without any warning, he entered the kitchen and related more with gestures than with words that he had gotten lost in the streets and missed dinner, but nonetheless, they still owed him a dinner and he should be compensated with a supper. Bai Ganyo was a devotee of the culinary arts, and not only was he an expert but any malpractice in that craft upset him. He saw, for example, that the landlady was preparing to place a fresh fish in boiling water, and he reared up with all his might, grabbed the landlady's hand, and with his other hand pulled the fish out and made a sign with his hand and head by which he meant to say, "Stop, don't make a move, just watch how fish is prepared!" "Salt!" commanded Bai Ganyo. They gave him the salt, he rolled his sleeves up to his elbows, exposing his hairy arms, thrust his far from delicate fingers into the salt cellar, and began to massage salt thoroughly into the (already salted) fish, both inside and out. "Red pepper!" As if these silly fools would have red pepper! "Black pepper!" commanded Bai Ganyo. He grabbed the pepper and rubbed it over the fish. "Grill!" proclaimed the triumphant chef, but at this

point they couldn't understand him, for all his gestures. Why, even he himself had a look around and couldn't spot a grill; but was this going to stop
Bai Ganyo? He's an old hand at it. Taking up a pair of tongs, he raked all the
coals to the opening of the stove, left the other dishes to rest (it was a good
thing that they were already done), spread the tongs apart, placed the fish
between them, and tried to put it into the stove, but the doors were too narrow; the fish got caught, slipped out, and plop! onto the coals. "Oh no!" cried
out the landlady. "Never mind, it's nothing!" Bai Ganyo calmed her, grabbed
the fish, blew off the ashes and embers that were stuck to it, and put it back
to grill. Smoke and the smell of fish filled the entire kitchen. The proprietors were in despair. Bai Ganyo was beaming. He was in his element. He
was both grilling the fish—inhaling, sniffing, inspired by the appetizing
smoke—and issuing commands with his free hand, which was filthy—as a
result of the fish's somersault—that the table be set, so that his dish would
not get cold. "If fresh fish isn't hot, you have to throw it out!" The baked fish,
with its head and tail coated in ashes, was placed on a plate under Bai
Ganyo's magnanimous supervision. "Quickly! Quickly! While it's still hot,
give me some lemon and wine; without wine it's not worth a plugged nickel."
They all sat down around the table, while they sent the maid running out
for some lemon and wine. What else could they do? The millionaire wasn't
going to change his habits to suit them, after all! The landlady reached out
to cut the fish. "Please, please, please! Don't!" yelled Bai Ganyo and grabbed
her hand, then turned the fish on its back, pressed down on it here and there
with two of his fingers, and it split into two halves. Eh, how could you not
celebrate! The maid brought lemon; Bai Ganyo cut it, took one half in the
cup of his hand, and squeezed it over the plate with such diligence that even
the pulp of the lemon fell on the fish. So what do you think; did Bai Ganyo
have an appetite? It was a close call as to whether there was as much lemon
juice on the plate as there was saliva in Bai Ganyo's mouth. They brought the
wine, too. The supper commenced.

The Aesculapiuses recommend Carlsbad, and I don't know what other
"-bad," for those suffering from digestive disorders. Let them take those
patients by the ear and set them down at the table in front of Bai Ganyo, and
even if their stomachs are in worse shape than the streets of Uchbunar,[31]

31. Uchbunar was an extremely poor, ethnically mixed neighborhood at the edge
of Sofia where thugs were recruited by crooked politicians (see 94n52 and "Bai Ganyo
Does Elections"). For a different view of the neighborhood, see the novel *Moyat Yuch-
bunar* (My Uchbunar) (Sofia: Bŭlgaski pisatel, 1979), a memoir for children by Salis
Tadzher, a Jewish author who grew up there.

you'll see what effect this spectacle has on them! Bai Ganyo ate, Lord I'm not kidding. The way he ate, even his ears were flapping. Every organ in his body was in motion, but his teeth, tongue, and nose were in first place. This is when a fellow realizes the lack of color and the poverty of language. With what words, with what interjections, with what punctuation marks, or even with what musical notes is it possible to describe the chomping, the grunting, the snorting, smacking, tongue clucking, and sucking that came raining down like hail out of Bai Ganyo? What lucky hostesses! It's not every Czech housewife who has the good fortune to take pleasure in such a sight.

They finally ate their fill. They moved to the parlor. Bai Ganyo, as red as a lobster, was alternately twirling his mustache and burping into his cupped hand, then mumbling *"pardonne."* They settled themselves into chairs. Bai Ganyo rolled himself a cigarette, smeared with grease from his fingers, and began to draw on it and blow clouds of smoke through his mustache. Wouldn't this be the most appropriate time for a treat? For some music, for songs, for love? The young lady guessed the mood of the millionaire and asked him whether he liked music. Who? Bai Ganyo? Well now, if Bai Ganyo doesn't love music, who does? Who else could inspire such respect in the Gypsies, that is to say, the musicians, as Bai Ganyo? All he has to do is wink at them, and then just you watch what happens. They're on fire. Let that fiddle twang! Let that clarinet squeal:

> Your body's like a slender tree,
> A sharpened stake that pierces me.
> Your sweet skirt's hem is my desire
> It has my insides all on fire![32]

"Shut up now, you *Chingene*![33] I don't want any love songs. Play me some drinking songs!" exclaims Bai Ganyo and raps on the table with his glass. They start to play "Car-carnation," but Bai Ganyo raps his glass. They stop. They begin "We don't want riches"—again he raps his glass. They switch to

---

32. Aleko is mocking a genre of Balkan urban popular music associated with Turkish and often played in taverns. Aleko's Bulgarian parody is a mixture of stock phrases and awkward similes: *"Snagata ti e topola, / na moyto sûrce kat' dva kola. / Na fustanya ti tegelya / izgori na mene dzhigerya . . ."* The parody is based on a Turkish popular song of that time referring to a Bulgarian barmaid.

33. Çingene, Turkish for "Gypsy," is derogatory in today's contexts. The description here is typical of a certain class of taverns in southeastern Europe and is intended by Aleko to suggest a contrast with the atmosphere of a refined drawing room in the West.

"Green Leaves." "Aaah, that's more like it. Hey, hey, c'mon, let's have some fun, c'mon," and crash! the bottle smashes on the floor or through the window. So, who is the master of such things? And did they happen only once, or even twice? Well now, how were these women supposed to know what kind of man your Bai Ganyo was? Even if you explain to them just how much glass you've broken to music, they can't understand you!

"I love music!" Bai Ganyo announced patronizingly. "I love music!" he repeated and shook his head, which in his opinion expressed the sad necessity of listening, for the sake of women, to the pitiful jangling of a piano. "What do you understand about playing, about good times?" Bai Ganyo thought to himself.

The young girl opened the piano and began to play some of those endless songs from *The Bartered Bride*, by Smetana. From her fingers poured forth the sounds that transport every Czech soul into ecstasy. Her mother, who was undoubtedly hearing these songs for the thousand and first time, was basking in bliss, and her gaze, which was turned toward Bai Ganyo, sparkled with national pride and self-satisfaction; she moved her head in time to the tempo of the piece, now adagio, now allegro, as if marking the grace notes with her nose. From time to time she'd give Bai Ganyo a sign with her eyes, alerting him to the approach of some favorite moment in the song, but the millionaire answered with his eyes, "Take care, Your Grace, don't look at me; I've heard my fair share of these things!" And in order to turn his signals into deeds, he rose from his chair at precisely that moment when his hostess was expecting to enjoy the effect that Smetana would have on Bai Ganyo and quickly, with a plan in mind, went into his room, took the *muskal* open for sampling from his *disagi*, and returned to the parlor. He winked at the mother, thinking, "Look who is going to make an impression," tiptoed up to the young girl engrossed in the music, and—what a devil that Bai Ganyo is!—uncapped the *muskal* of rose oil and very slowly slipped it under the young girl's nose. As soon as she caught the scent of Bai Ganyo's sweaty hand, stinking of fish, she turned away in revulsion, and distracted by the music, she at first frowned at him but then instantly realized that before her was standing the millionaire, and so she simpered, and he asked her, "Which is better, your Smetana or what you're smelling, eh?" and he tucked the *muskal* into his sash. The girl stopped her playing. Bai Ganyo began. (What's that, you say? I couldn't understand you.) He started to play carelessly, with one finger, without sitting down. "Just enough to get them to understand that we also know thing or two about this kinda crap." An accordion had fallen into

the hands of one of Bai Ganyo's relatives, and every once in a while, when
he found himself in the mood, Bai Ganyo would pound his fingers on it trying to bang out some song. Now he began a startling pizzicato, which in his
opinion corresponded to the song "Granny's favorite, sla-slanin-kaa, slaninka,
kidnapped-oh-my-pet-slaninka," which was "Slaninka" lifted in its entirety
from the Czech song "Slaninka."

"The gentleman is playing 'Slaninka,' Mommy!" the young girl said, coming out with her discovery.

"'Slaninka' it is indeed!" answered Bai Ganyo. "Where do you know it
from?"

Delighted with his success, Bai Ganyo sat down at the piano in order to
play, now with some justification, something more serious. And what could
be more serious than "Terrible Is the Night"? Bai Ganyo began to play but
stopped, dissatisfied with his performance. And with good reason! "Terrible
Is the Night" was not composed for the piano; the sounds get cut short. Hit
a key on "Terrr-" and the sound doesn't last. The accordion is a completely
different matter! As soon as you push your finger down on " . . . ble . . ."—
squeeze, by God, let it drone for half an hour, squeeze, let it throb in waves
as long as your heart desires! But with a piano—tinkle, tinkle, nothing.
Nothing! Bai Ganyo saw that the effect of "Slaninka" was weakening—he
thought and thought, then decided, "Well, just wait until I start singing 'Terrible Is the Night' to those petticoats!" He stopped and grew thoughtful;
he wanted to get in a sorrowful mood, in keeping with the spirit of the sad
song, so he sighed once very deeply, and placed his right hand over his ear.
His eyes grew drowsy, and how he gaped!

Grandissimo maestro Verdi! You don't have, you can't have, enemies! But
if, God forbid, such a monster were to appear, he would be Satan himself.
God is great, *Esimio Maestro*, and all the arrows of the Evil Spirit are pow-
erless against you! One means alone, just one, can the Tempter use and . . .
and the entire musical world will be covered in mourning. We will pray, you
pray, too, *Divin Maestro*, to the Almighty Creator, lest Satan be allowed to
lead you into the salon where Bai Ganyo is singing "Terrible Is the Night."
And when your delicate hearing has been touched by these wild, inhuman
sounds, which you can't understand, the Evil Spirit will reveal to you the
horrible truth with his satanic laugh: Ha ha ha! Verdi! This is a song from
your divine *La Traviata*! Ha ha ha ha-a!![34]

---

34. The aria "Oh qual orrenda notte" is not in fact from *La Traviata* but from Verdi's
Macbeth. In 1897 Aleko referred to Verdi as his favorite composer.

"It's late now, gentlemen," said shy Ilcho, as he looked at his watch. "Midnight! Come on, let's go home; God willing there'll be another time for us to tell some stories about Bai Ganyo."

"Hey, Ilcho, tell me now, why do you detest Bulgarian songs so much?" asked Dravichka as they left. "Who, me? You think I detest them? I'm sorry, my dear friend, that you misunderstood me. I'm capable of taking delight, of losing myself, of being transported into ecstasy by our beautiful, melancholy folk songs, by true Bulgarian songs, and not by those disgusting parodies of foreign popular songs that the Bai Ganyos of this world pass off on us distorted beyond recognition by those Gypsy grace notes and vocal contortions of drunken trills and embellishments . . . We have songs, but we don't have singers. I'm ready to embrace my enemy if he sings to me, as it should be sung, the song 'O Bogdan, May God Strike You Dead' or 'Hey, Vela, My Girl, Roll Up Your White Sleeves' and to look askance at my friend when I see that he's taking delight in 'Green Leaves,' 'Little Carnation,' and other such Gypsy treats."[35]

---

35. Here Aleko is expressing an attitude shared by many nineteenth-century nationally oriented urban elites in Eastern Europe. They romanticized the "pure" folk songs of the countryside and denigrated songs associated with professional musicians, who were often Roms (Gypsies). The first two song titles are Bulgarian rural songs, whereas the second two were popular in many lands of the former Ottoman Empire.

8

Bai Ganyo in Switzerland

"So, what about you, Dravichka; why are so quiet? Don't you know anything about Bai Ganyo?" one of our company asked our merry friend Dravichka.

"Sure I do, pal; I know lots of things, but how can I tell them?" answered Dravichka with false modesty.

"What do you mean, 'how can I tell them'? If only I had your way with words!"

"Well, all right, listen."

One summer I was taking a stroll in Genlaus, you know the place, in Switzerland. I had gotten myself a room in a hotel and had gone out to walk around the city. The city is beautiful; the surroundings are picturesque and magnificent. I'm just walking about, no particular place in mind, staring left and right, wandering from street to street, and I come out onto the square where the opera theater is. Right across from me I see an elegant café. Wait a minute, I say to myself, why don't I stop in and take a break. To the right of the entrance I see a glass partition with a clear view of the square, and I go inside both to drink a coffee and to watch the passersby. And what do I stumble upon in there? Three entire tables occupied by Bulgarian students! Now just try to tell me that Bulgarians don't have a taste for luxury. In such a beautiful city, in the prettiest part of town, in the most elegant café, they have taken the best seats. Noise, smoke, matches and smoldering cigarettes on the floor; clatter, shouts, quarrels . . . Here they're playing backgammon, there preference, across the way twenty-one. And from all sides I hear, "Six and a five! Hearts! Hand over the money! Four and a one! Quit looking at my cards! Garçon! Hit me! Double fives! Liar, you don't have double fives! Thirty-one! Spades! Garçon! You don't know anything about preference!

I don't take advice from socialists! Double twos! And I don't want advice from the bourgeoisie! Trump! Bastard! Garçon! Proud of your medals now, are you? Clubs! So are you with those Russian *Chifuti*, then? Gentlemen, here comes the 'sucker'! Garçon! A beer! Hey, lend me one more franc! You're a deadbeat! Get a loan from the waiter! Double fours!"

The personage who had been branded with the less-than-affectionate epithet "sucker" entered the café and greeted the students, who met him, as they say, with open arms, and he couldn't decide which group to join, since each table was trying to lure him in. Such fondness for a sucker seemed to me, at first, inexplicable, but it wasn't long before my perplexity was dispelled by the words that traveled from table to table at that person's expense. Then I realized that the sucker was the son of a landowner from Argentina, in South America, a rich young man. His father was apparently sending him five hundred francs a month, half of which, with the help of twenty-one, was being regularly distributed into the pockets of our "young scholars." And because he good-naturedly let himself be fleeced—since it gave him the pleasure of observing the curious (to him) greed with which our boys tried to coax his pocket money from him—he had been awarded the title of "sucker."

No matter what hour of the day I visited that café, starting from nine in the morning until late in the evening, I always found the same faces at the same pursuits: backgammon, preference, twenty-one. When these youths did their reading, by what means they acquired European culture remained a mystery to me. The one thing that was clear was that almost none of them spoke French even passably well. As soon as one of them so much as opened his mouth in that language, the crudeness of his intonation, his diction, and the construction of his sentences gave him away as Oriental.

After another day or so, the group was joined by several bitter, nihilistic young Jews who snarled at the capitalist tyrant from the dark corners of the taverns. I don't understand the sympathy for these dark heroes, who were capable of being simultaneously nihilists and agents for the secret police, at the same time anarchists and the lowest sort of abusers of social funds, libraries, and other institutions. Instead of making friends with the French, the Germans, and the English, always exemplary models both in their diversions and their studies, instead of being imbued with their spirit of decency, work ethic, honesty, and chivalry, these boys of ours found their ideal either among the Jews, the Greeks, or some Armenians, who exploited their resources and energies in the most despicable manner, drawing them into the suffocating atmosphere of their malevolent, crude, and sterile verbiage. Later, I discovered that there were other young Bulgarians in that city who didn't visit that café and who dedicated themselves most seriously to their studies.

One day, at the peak of a heated game of twenty-one, when the Argentinean had lost about one hundred francs, a person with a *kalpak* cocked on his head, a walking stick under his arm, and *disagi* in his hand entered the café.

"Oho! Bai Ganyo! Welcome!" cried out the entire group.

"Good to be here. How are you?" answered the newcomer, who, benevolently refusing polite offers to make room for him at their tables, came and sat at mine, overturning my cup of coffee as he sat down. A natural bully.

"*Pardonne!*"

"Never mind; don't worry about it," I hurried to say, although I observed he didn't appear overly worried.

"Aha! Are you a Bulgarian? Eh, in that case, good day. I'm Ganyo Balkanski. Where might Your Grace be from?"

I told him. We got acquainted.

"I'm going around the world with this damned rose oil," Bai Ganyo announced to me in a discouraged voice.

"What, isn't business going well?"

"Eh, to tell you the truth, sir, it isn't."

"Why not?"

"Why not? We've outsmarted ourselves. There was a time when if you said Bulgarian rose oil, they'd fly like bees to honey, but now, damn it all! You go into some soap maker's shop and as soon as you open your mouth and say you're Bulgarian, the moment you say '*bondjour*,' he asks right away, '*essence de rose?*' and even while he's asking he's smirking. Now, who cares about the smirking as long as you can make a deal, but they don't want to! 'Give me a gram as a sample,' he says. He's toying with you! How can you give him a gram? If you pour out one gram, you'll spill two. 'But my friend,' I tell him, 'this rose oil isn't the kind you think. This is pure essence.' 'Eh,' he says, 'you all say that; you all sing the same song.' He says it just like that, right to your face. He doesn't even want to get to know you. It's all that geranium oil, damn it to hell!³⁶ The Anatolian mafia has chewed us up and spit us out!

---

36. Owing to a poor rose harvest in 1893, rose oil adulterated with geranium oil was manufactured in Bulgaria and Turkey.

And you see, pal, it's not just one or two of them. They came swarming through Europe in hordes: Anatolians, Armenians, Turks, Greeks, and they lie, they cheat people, and they've burned someone here, put the touch on someone there, and people are sick of them. If you smell of roses, they run for cover."

The innocent Orient appeared before me with all its charms. To complete the picture, on all the tables around us backgammon pieces clattered, cards were slapped down—noise and smoke to high heaven!

"I'm very pleased with our boys," Bai Ganyo told me, watching the game players. "Good for them! Some of them are so bold they give the professors down payments. Take, for example, let's say, that guy there, the older one; see him? The one playing blackjack. Do you know, he has three medals! For the Serbian war, for merit, and for I don't know what else. He was an examining magistrate; he knows the law by heart. So why did he need to study further? Well of course—he has money to burn. He got here only three months ago, but if you could hear him—he speaks French like nobody's business. His mind is so sharp (knock on wood). He should've been a doctor by now, but people here are stubborn. The rector, he says, won't let him. It's not possible, he told him, to earn a doctorate in three months. Well, how can it not be possible when the lad knows everything? Stand him up right now, he'll tell you all the laws; he has them down pat. The rector told him, he says, you can't read it all in three months, he says, so how can you learn it? Bold as brass, he says, 'Nope, I'll be a doctor in three months.' That guy says, 'Nope, can't be done.' 'Can't?' 'Can't!' So then one day our fellow flies off the handle, shoots his mouth off, and mops the floor with them. It's true; go ask him if you like." I took Bai Ganyo's word for it and didn't go ask the holder of the three medals.

He continued: "And do you know how that business ended up? It wasn't enough that the rector dug in his heels and wouldn't let the kid become a doctor, but the dean, he says, took the same line. Your Grace knows what a 'dean' is—that whatsit that they have here, whatever, you know. Our boy showed them a pile of certificates from the municipal council, from the prosecutor, and a service record, you name it. But the man is stubborn, do you understand? And he's not just some regular Joe but an examining magistrate! And with three medals on his chest on top of it! The rector began to harp at him that in order to be of use to himself and his people—what business was it of his!—he needed to go through the whole course in the normal way, that living abroad a little more would also be good for him—

nonsense!—and other such old wives' tales. And not just the rector—monkey see, monkey do—the dean also weighed in. 'Yes,' he says, 'I also recommend that you follow the advice of the rector!' Eeh! And then our boy blew his top and opened his mouth. 'But,' he says, 'why are you interfering in this; what are you, the rector's lawyer or something?' So he ticked off the dean. Those people tucked their tails between their legs; they couldn't even say boo! Hey, *garçon! Yun kavé.* No, say what you like, Your Grace, but we've got some fine boys. Good for them!"

"Hey, you, *garçon! Yun kavé!*" called Bai Ganyo.

"*Monsieur!*" responded the bustling waiter.

"*Yun kavé e aport gazet bulgar,*" ordered Bai Ganyo and then, turning toward me, he added, "I haven't forgotten that damned French stuff."

The waiter brought him coffee and a stained folio in which were fastened several dog-eared Bulgarian newspapers.

"Let's see what news there is, what's happening in the world," said Bai Ganyo, opening the folio and immersing himself in politics. I observed from the side how he thirstily, eagerly devoured the news articles, smiled, and now and then, his eyes shining, let out a 'Bravo!' At one point, bursting, it seemed, with delight, he turned toward me.

"Eh, they really got them. Listen, let me read it to you."

"Excuse me, Mr. Balkanski. At least here I'd like to give my ears a rest from such politics," I said, getting up from my chair. "Good-bye."

"But just listen to this. 'That piratical mob of pimps, thieves, and scoundrels who poke their snouts into the filth . . . ' Wait, it gets even better further on!"

"No, no! Good-bye, Mr. Balkanski," I called out resolutely, and left.

9

Bai Ganyo in Russia

"Dravichka tells a story so well, gentlemen, that it will be difficult to satisfy you with any kind of tale after his. But still, to tell the truth, I know some things about Bai Ganyo, too," Vasil announced. "From Moscow and St. Petersburg!"

"C'mon, get started. Don't beat around the bush," replied Dravichka.

"The expression 'beat around the bush' doesn't seem very poetic to me," Mato said jokingly.

"Be quiet, gentlemen. Vasil, c'mon, my friend, get started!"

On the way to St. Petersburg we stopped at the station in Vilna. We were traveling together, the two of us, Bai Ganyo and I. We went into the station restaurant. Bai Ganyo wanted me to treat, since on the way I had supposedly smoked some of his tobacco. I ordered beer and snacks. The restaurant manager listened in on our conversation, apparently recognized that we were Bulgarians, and asked us in Russian, "Excuse me, gentlemen, are you by any chance Bulgarians?"

We answered in the affirmative.

"Do you happen to know a Mr. Dimitrov, a student?"[37]

"I don't know him. Do you know him, Bai Ganyo?"

"Dimitrov? Hang on. Aha! I remember Dimitrov; yes, I know him. A bright lad; I know him, of course."

---

37. The actions attributed here to Dimitrov, as well as those ascribed to Aslanov, who is introduced on page 58, are based on allegations against A. Mitrov, the Plovdiv district attorney, that were published in a letter to the editor of *Svoboda* on 30 August 1891. Mitrov committed suicide nine days later. The veracity of the allegations and the identity of the author of the letter were never established.

"Might you be able to tell me where he is now?" asked the restaurant manager.

"He's in Constantinople now," answered Bai Ganyo. "In a week he'll get married there. He found himself a sweetheart deal."

"What the . . . ?" exclaimed the thunderstruck manager. "He's getting ma-a-a-rried? But he's married here, gentlemen!"

"You don't say! Well, whadaya know about that, heh-heh-heh," Bai Ganyo snickered heartily. The manager stared at him in amazement.

"You don't know him," continued Bai Ganyo, turning to me. "He's a real bright kid, that Dimitrov."

The manager told us the following story: "One day, gentlemen, Mr. Dimitrov arrived by train with a deaf-mute boy who was about thirteen or fourteen years old. I had known Dimitrov from the year before. He lived in our city, he fell in love with a girl, they got married, and they left either for Moscow or Petersburg, I don't know which. When he showed up this year with the deaf-mute, he told me that the kid had a brother in your country, in Bulgaria, an official or an army officer—I don't remember—who was supposedly going to send him one hundred francs a month so that he could live in one of the Petersburg institutions for deaf-mutes. Since Mr. Dimitrov was going to some other city, or so he said, he asked me to take the boy in, feed him, and look after him in the meantime. He assured me that he'd come back in ten days. I agreed and took in the unfortunate child and cared for him as if he were my own. Ten days passed, then a month, then another, and there was no word from Dimitrov. I try to find something out from the child, but the poor thing was deaf and dumb; he couldn't explain anything. And I could tell that the child was depressed. I wrote to Petersburg and to Moscow. No one answered. During the third month, gentlemen, the child disappeared. We made inquiries, we tried searching, we went to the police, we sent telegrams out in several directions—nothing. The unfortunate child had dropped off the face of the earth. To this day, I don't know what happened to that child. Let Mr. Dimitrov bear the sin; I'll bear the one hundred rubles it cost me. And you say that he's going to get married next week? Dear God, how is such a thing possible? For God's sake, gentlemen, inform your authorities, warn that unfortunate girl he is going to marry."

I promised the manager that as soon as I arrived in St. Petersburg, I'd inform a certain gentleman, who, I was certain, would immediately send a telegram to the Exarch of the Bulgarian Church. I paid up. We got on the train and set off for Petersburg.

"Why did you have to stick your nose in?" said Bai Ganyo with reproach. "How do you know what kind of woman his wife here is?"

We were traveling in third class. Bai Ganyo took up two seats and lay down to doze. At the next station, several more travelers came into our car, and the extra places had to be given up to them, but Bai Ganyo is no simple-minded fellow. He pretended to have fallen asleep, and boy, how he snored. A huge German, a peasant, came up to Bai Ganyo with his bag in his hand and tried to wake him up, tapping him lightly on his boots. Bai Ganyo rolled over and just kept on going hrrr pffff hrrr pfff, and hiding his face from the German, he winked at me as if to say, "See what a devil I am!" "Come on, get up!" shouted the German in Russian and began to prod my traveling companion quite roughly. "Hrrr pfff." "Come on, stop pretending, damn you!" growled the German, and with one swipe he knocked Bai Ganyo's legs off the seat then shoved him onto his *disagi* and sat down next to us. Bai Ganyo pretended that he had been startled awake, rubbed his eyes, and, as if nothing had happened, immediately pulled out his tobacco tin, opened it, and offered it to the German. "Bulgarian tobacco!" he said in Russian.

"Aha! So you're Bulgarians! Pleased to meet you," the German said amiably and began to roll himself a cigarette. "You're going to St. Pete. Me too. So we'll be traveling together."

As soon as we arrived in St. Petersburg, I hastened to keep the promise I had made to the restaurant manager in Vilna. I met my acquaintance and described Dimitrov's exploits. He sent a telegram to Constantinople at once and succeeded in stopping the wedding. In turn, he told me the rest of the story of the deaf-mute boy. When and how he was put up to running away from Vilna is unknown, but one day, he turned up in St. Petersburg and for a long time was the victim of the most base exploitation on the part of Dimitrov, who not only kept for himself the money sent by the unhappy boy's brother but even forced the poor child to go from door to door begging money from the most influential people and best-known philanthropists of St. Petersburg. And not only in St. Petersburg but also in Kronstadt, where he forced him to go to John of Kronstadt, the famous saint of the common people.[38]

Since I had practically nothing to live on, I was forced to live in the Deshovka, a cheap hostel that was the refuge of the poorest of students.[39] Bai Ganyo insisted most energetically that he come with me to the Deshovka.

---

38. Ioan Ilich Sergeev, a priest at the St. Andrew Cathedral in Kronstadt, used his popularity among ordinary people to accomplish many good deeds among the sick.

39. "Deshovka" comes from the Russian word *deshëvyj* (cheap).

"But that's impossible, Bai Ganyo. This establishment is only for students."

"So what if it's for students?" Bai Ganyo said, attempting to convince me. "Aren't students people, just like me? After all, what's the big deal if they take in a Bulgarian?"

"But you're a rich man, Bai Ganyo. You can afford a hotel."

"Don't be a jerk," Bai Ganyo scolded. "I thought you were smarter than that. C'mon, my fellow Bulgarian, why should we give money to the Muscovites? If you stumble on a cheap deal, grab it with both hands. How are they going to know what kind of guy I am?"

"It's impossible, Bai Ganyo. The poor students will protest. They'll get mad at me and might even kick me out of the dorm."

"You pig-headed Bulgarian," continued Bai Ganyo. "Don't you have a mouth? Doesn't your little brain work well enough to think to tell 'em that I'm your brother, fallen upon hard times? Heck, it would be enough just to say I'm a Bulgarian; you know what suckers the Russians are!"

"No, no, I can't," I exclaimed decisively, and set out for the Deshovka.

"Oho! You think that you'll get rid of me so easily? Just you wait. You ain't seen nuthin' yet," growled Bai Ganyo as he set off after me. "Bulgarian! Some Bulgarian he is. He doesn't have a nickel's worth of patriotism. Hang on, man, don't rush off like that. I can't catch up with you; my *disagi* are heavy. Hang on, my Bulgarian friend!"

At that moment, we must have presented a strange sight, since people passing by on the sidewalk stopped and stared at us. Bai Ganyo was ten paces behind me, his *disagi* slung over his walking stick on his shoulder; his *kilim* draped over the other arm, which he raised from time to time to wipe his sweaty forehead. His *kalpak* barely stayed on top of his head. Bai Ganyo stumbled along after me and growled, "Hang on, for God's sake, man, at least take the *kilim*; it's tearing my arm off. You think you'll get rid of me. You don't know what kind of a guy your Bai Ganyo is!" I lunged on in a panic, wondering how I was going to show up with Bai Ganyo at the Deshovka and how I was going to excuse such an unjustifiable act. I'd have to lie. I saw that it would be impossible to get rid of him. After all, it was only a matter of a few days, and like it or not, I had better resign myself to the situation. And Bai Ganyo kept following me; he grumbled all the way but left off his bullying talk and began in a minor key. "Listen, Bai Vasil, wait a little, can't you, please, Bai Vasil? After all, we're Bulgarians."

And imagine, gentlemen. At that instant, I felt sorry for Bai Ganyo! Believe it or not. I acknowledged that his actions were reprehensible, that he was a disgusting miser, an egotist, a sneak, a hypocritical exploiter, coarse and vulgar to the marrow of his bones, but I pitied him; in the delicate vibrations of the tone of voice in which he said those last words, my ear caught a tender note that was hidden and still hides in Bai Ganyo's heart but rarely— Oh, God, how rarely—makes itself manifest. I don't know, maybe it will seem funny or weird, but I'm telling you, gentlemen, that at that moment I saw Bai Ganyo differently, as if someone had whispered to me, 'Don't despise this crude, sneaky, miserly wretch. He's the product of coarse circumstances. He's the victim of crude tutors; the evil does not reside in him but in the influence of his environment. Bai Ganyo is energetic, level-headed, observant—especially observant. Put him under the guidance of a good leader and you will see what deeds he can do. Until now, Bai Ganyo has shown only his animal energy, but hidden within him is a tremendous supply of potential spiritual strength that only awaits a moral impulse to be transformed into a living force.'"

We arrived at the Deshovka. Most of the students had not yet returned from their vacations, and so there were plenty of free places. My bed had been kept by my faithful friend Kocho, an Albanian, an utter pauper, who received a stipend of three rubles a month for tea and sugar from the Slavonic Society.[40] He had registered at the university and taken courses for two years, but when he became convinced that it was not for him, he dropped out and entered the seminary. This Kocho was a good fellow. He'd give his life for a friend, but God forbid that you make him angry; in an instant all his Albanian tribal passions would boil over, he'd go pale with rage, and his eyes would become completely bloodshot: a real beast! As Bai Ganyo and I entered the room we found Kocho in a horizontal position on his bed; on this bed it was hard to distinguish the pillow from the sheet from the blanket. Kocho jumped up from the bed with the agility of a panther, hugged me, kissed me, introduced himself to Bai Ganyo, and, all cheerful and smiling from ear to ear, had us sit down on the bed and on a trunk, all the while apologizing for the slight disorder in the room. Then he opened the door and gave a wild Albanian yell: "Van'ka, old friend, put on the samovar." "What do you need the samovar for when there's no tea or sugar?"

---

40. The Slavonic Benevolent Society was founded in Russia to combat the influence of the Roman Catholic Church and the Greek Patriarchate, especially among Orthodox Christian Slavs in the Balkans. In this respect Orthodox Albanians had common cause with Orthodox Slavs, hence Kocho's stipend.

answered the old friend from the depths of the corridor. Kocho clutched his head with both hands, crossed the room, grabbed his hat, and without listening to our pleas for him to stay, that we would buy tea and sugar, he went out, shouting, "Right away," and disappeared. Bai Ganyo and I waited for half an hour, then an hour—Kocho didn't return. Something must have happened to him.

So as not to waste the beautiful day, I proposed to Bai Ganyo that we go for a walk. "Oh, let's keep waiting; the guy is going to give us tea," answered Bai Ganyo. He couldn't pass up anything free, no matter where it came from. Nonetheless, I insisted. Bai Ganyo stuffed the *muskali* into his sash, and we went out. As we approached the Anichkin Bridge, we heard a bestial howl, mixed with the most desperate curses and insults. We went out onto the bridge, and what did we see? Kocho, like an enraged tiger, was squeezing his iron fingers into the neck of an unknown gentleman, whose hat had rolled onto the cobblestones. He had bent the man's head back and was trying to throw him off the bridge. The victim was making every effort to get away, but it was not so easy to escape the hands of the maddened Albanian. "Crook!" roared Kocho. "Bastard! Scoundrel! You're the spy, not me, you spy, you son of a bitch! I'll kill you, you wretched scum!" I rushed to separate them. Bai Ganyo shouted after me, "Leave them alone. Why should you get yourself in trouble? Let them get into their own mess. Leave them alone. They'll drag you to the police station as a witness." I didn't pay any attention to Bai Ganyo's advice and set off toward the Albanian, who kept on yelling and screaming the foulest epithets at his victim, who had already been dragged to the edge of the bridge and who, it seemed to me, in another moment would fly head first into the clear waters of the Fontanka. "Crook! Bastard!" roared Kocho, digging his bony fingers even deeper into the thick neck of his opponent.

When I was just a few steps away from them, the victim, alarmed at his impending doom, made a desperate lunge and pulled free of the grip of the Albanian, grabbed his hat as it rolled, and set off at a run. "Stop, crook! Filthy coward, scum!" Kocho grabbed a rock and hurled it after him. The unknown man ran up to a passing tram, jumped in, and vanished. But the Albanian didn't calm down. "I'll kill you, you rotten crook!" he continued to snarl, shaking his fist toward the spot where his enemy had disappeared. I called Kocho by name; he turned and didn't recognize me! There was something savage in his look. His eyes flashed; his face went alternately red and pale with rage; his teeth chattered as if he had a burning fever; his lips twisted convulsively, letting out a low growl. "G-r-r-r, C-c-c-r-r-o-o-,

Sunuvab-b-b-b-i-i, b-b-b-bastard, sc-sc-sc, Crook!" he cried out again, turning to threaten his invisible enemy.

"Kocho, my friend, what happened to you; who was that gentleman?" I asked with friendly sympathy. He stared at me with blank malice and still didn't recognize me! "I'll kill you, you wretched creature! I'll show you who's a spy!" Kocho snarled and shook his fist at a passing tram, as if his enemy were riding in every streetcar. "Kocho, please, tell me what happened," I begged my friend, who was enraged to the point of madness. "Who was that gentleman?" Kocho looked at me again and shouted, "He's the biggest scoundrel in the world! Do you understand? The big-gest scoun-drel!" and again he rolled his eyes and again began to spew curses. I realized that my friend had been the victim of some sort of foul play perpetrated by his enemy, but just what sort I did not guess, nor could I have done so.

What Kocho told me was so base that it could not have been an object of speculation. This is what he said after he had come to himself a bit: "Imagine, gentlemen; after I left the Deshovka I went to the Slavonic Society to get my stipend so I could buy tea and sugar to treat you. You know, my dear Vasil, what kind of stipend I receive. Three rubles a month. Three miserable rubles! And just imagine; there is a scoundrel who envies me and covets my wealth. And who is it? Your compatriot. I congratulate you. I'm going to knock that crook's teeth out! Imagine, gentlemen; I go up to the cashier and ask him to give me my three rubles, and he addresses me in an angry tone of voice: 'Aren't you ashamed of yourself, young man? Here you are a student and you're mixed up in such a dirty business.' 'What "dirty business"?' I exclaimed, alarmed. 'We have evidence,' he continued, 'that you're a spy for the Bulgarian government.' 'What? Me, a spy?' 'Yes. We have conclusive evidence. Your stipend has been taken away and given to the brother of Mr. Aslanov.' 'For God's sake, who gave you this evidence?' I asked through tears of rage that were choking me. 'Mr. Aslanov himself,' he answered calmly. 'A-r-r-g-g-h-h, *besa ta besa!*'[41] I roared like a madman and rushed out into the street to the Anichkin Bridge. You know the rest . . . Oh my God! Gentleman, can you imagine anything more foul? The crook! I'll, I'll, I'll . . . I've sworn my oath and I won't forget."

We comforted Kocho as best we could and went to a tavern to drink some tea. We lingered there for quite a while, engrossed in the Albanian's stories

41. This is Aleko's rendering of an Albanian oath, "Besa-besë," roughly "I swear on my honor." *Besë*, definite *besa* (oath, honor, truce), is a central concept in traditional Albanian law and culture.

of Aslanov's despicable actions. Even Bai Ganyo refrained from exclaiming his usual "Bravo!" and "Good for him!" but rather, on the contrary, clucked his tongue, shook his head in amazement, and said, "What a beast that guy is!" We left the tavern and set off down Nevsky Prospekt. A mixed crowd from all parts of the world filled the sidewalks of this glittering thoroughfare, and we could barely make our way through the passersby. All sorts of cabs moved along the roadway in two lanes. Store after store, each more luxurious than the last, tempted the eyes of the public. Bai Ganyo even went so far as to offer the opinion that "in the end, even Petersburg isn't all that bad." For an entire hour we pushed our way through the crowd until we reached the Neva. We came out onto the quieter English Quay and had not gone ten steps when Kocho pulled roughly at my sleeve and exclaimed in a strangled voice, "That's him!"

"Who?"

"The crook!"

"What crook?"

"The biggest. Stop. Let's hide so he doesn't see us," he mumbled and pulled us by our sleeves so that we stood behind the columns of a doorway. Bai Ganyo stuck his nose out from behind the column and looked in the direction that Kocho was pointing.

"Who do you see?" asked Kocho.

"I see a person," whispered Bai Ganyo conspiratorially. "Hey, Vasil, look! That person looks a lot like our Dondukov-Korsakov."[42]

"That's who it is," answered Kocho. "Who else do you see?"

"I see two other people, kneeling before Dondukov. Hey look! Tsk tsk tsk! They're kissing his boots, weeping, begging him for something, beating their chests. Look! Tsk tsk tsk! He's trying to get away from them, but they're not letting him. They're holding onto his legs, one from one side and one from the other."

"Look more carefully. Can you recognize either of them?" demanded the Albanian.

"I can't. How can I recognize them when they keep banging their heads on his boots? Hey, wait a minute," said Bai Ganyo. "Hold on. I know him. It really is him. It's him! The one you were going to throw off the bridge. That's him."

---

42. Prince Alexander Mihailovich Dondukov-Korsakov was appointed imperial high commissioner for Bulgaria at the end of the Russo-Turkish War.

"Yes, he's the one, the swine. You are now witnessing one of his miserable comedies," growled the Albanian through clenched teeth. "OK, come on
now, let's make our way back onto Nevsky Prospekt."

"Wait, let's see how the scene ends," I declared.

"There's no need to," said Kocho decisively. "We know the end. They'll
hang onto his legs and weep until he gives them a few rubles or some letter
of recommendation for another victim or makes some other intercession.
Those scoundrels are capable of fouling the name of an entire nation."

"Goodness, what a beast that guy is!" exclaimed Bai Ganyo and clucked
his tongue.

"Hey, why did you stop, Vasil? Keep going!" said one of our company.

"Tell the story about Ermolova."

"Forget it. I'm disgusted," said Vasil.

"Or about Princess Belozerskaya."

"Really, lay off. I can't go on."

"But do you know the story of Bai Ganyo and the tripe *chorba*?" said
another.

"Well, do you know the one about the shaven mustaches?"

"That's enough, gentlemen! There is no end to stories about Bai Ganyo.
C'mon, let's start the second part of the evening. C'mon, Marcus Aure-
lius, sing us something. Or you, Kalina-Malina, start up a song.[43] C'mon.
'Zapretni-i-i, Velo mome-e-e, beli rûkavi.'"[44]

The second part of the evening started, and the party didn't break up till
after midnight.

Farewell, Bai Ganyo! Travel around Europe. Bring the products of our
beautiful Valley of Roses to every land, and please, Bai Ganyo, gaze more
deeply into European life, and may you see its face. Its wretched backside has
been forced on you enough.

---

43. Kalina-Malina refers to Alexander Malinov, who headed the Democratic Party
in 1902.

44. This is the beginning of the Bulgarian folk song that is also mentioned in "Bai
Ganyo Goes Visiting": "Hey, Vela, My Girl, Roll Up Your White Sleeves" (see 71n35).

PART TWO

10

Bai Ganyo
Returns from Europe

"Have you heard the news?" cried Marcus Aurelius, flinging the door open and bursting breathlessly into the room.

"What news?" we all asked.

"Bai Ganyo is back from Europe!"

"Impossible!"

"What do you mean, 'impossible'? Gentlemen, I saw him. I talked with him. His first words . . . Ha-ha-ha! His first words were, 'We've made . . .' Ha-ha-ha! 'We've made a mess of it,' he says. Ha-ha-ha!"

"Quit giggling, man," cried Arpakash impatiently. "Tell the story. You want some tea?"

"Arpakash, come let me kiss you right between the eyes."

"Blockhead," said Arpakash with a good-natured smile and handed a glass of tea to Marcus Aurelius, tugging him by his curly mustache with his free hand. "You über-blockhead."

"Captain, please don't rock the boat," Marcus Aurelius joked in Russian. He took a slurp from the glass and related the following:

"Imagine, gentlemen; what luck, a few days ago, on the twenty-second (your favorite number, Alyosha), on Sunday, Gervanich and I were making the rounds of the little inns on the River Iskûr, over by Vrazhdebna, and we ran into a whole lot of people there."[45]

"I'll bet the Urvichers were there."[46]

---

45. Vrazhdebna is a village near Sofia that was popular with Aleko's circle.

46. Urvich is the name of a monastery in an extremely picturesque location. It became a preferred destination for people in Aleko's circle, who spoke of founding an Urvich Club, the members of which would be known as Urvichers. Aleko was a passionate advocate of nature excursions, which is reflected in the opening of this chapter.

"No, they weren't; they were over at their beloved Urvich. Don't inter-rupt me, Arpakash. There were tons of people there, mostly foreigners—Germans, Czechs, and not one, absolutely not a single one of our local hill-billies, paralyzed as they are by apathy. Only Grandpa Hadzhi passed by, heading for his farm.[47] The weather, you know, was wonderful—such mead-ows, such fields, such fresh greenery in the woods, you couldn't get enough of breathing that air. The foreigners had come with their whole families, hauling in provisions, blankets, swings for the children. Folks had planted themselves here and there like bouquets in the shady patches, and they were feasting. It was a treat to see them. They weren't, as you might think, fancy, rich people, no, just craftsmen, tradesmen, regular working folks—tinsmiths, blacksmiths, carpenters. Work six days—play on the seventh. And not like Your Graces crowding into smoky coffeehouses with your damned card games like *bachka*."

"Marcus Aurelius! Is that you I hear, my dear friend? Saint John the Golden Tongued, let me kiss you!"

"Shut up, Arpakash. Don't interrupt me."

"Hey, Amonasro, don't interrupt the man," put in Moyshe.

"But truly, friends," Arpakash said, carrying on his joke with an unctuous look, "tell me, isn't Marcus Aurelius sweet, especially when he pronounces that lovely little word '*bachka*'? That 'ch' is absolutely musical."

"Will you shut up, Amonasro, king of Ethiopia?"

"And have you noticed, gentlemen, what a bottomless hatred our sweet Marcus Aurelius nurses for *bachka*?"

"Listen, Amonasro, shut up or I'll have Moyshe pour a whole glass of cognac down your throat."

"Our jo-kers are quite a-pair, they saw gran-ny's un-der-wear, ev'-ry-bo-dy teased them so, to the girls they could-n't go, taa-ra-ra-boom-dee-ay, ta-ra-ra-boom- . . ."[48]

"You're crazy, Arpakash; honest to God, you're crazy," Marcus Aurelius said somewhat reproachfully. "Be quiet a minute, I beg you."

"Enough already, Arpakash," put in Ozhilka.

---

47. Grandpa Hadzhi refers to hadzhi Bonyo Petrov, father of the writer Georgi hadzhi Bonev. His estate, Vrana, was later confiscated by Ferdinand (see 154n110). Among Balkan Christians, the honorific *hadzhi* referred to those who had made a pil-grimage to Jerusalem.

48. The Bulgarian reads "*No kakvi zevzetsi nashti, kat' videli baba s gashti, vsichkite go podigrali, i momata mu ne dali.*"

"*Et tu, Ozhilka? Et tu, Brute?* Come on and sing 'Last Night I Passed by Sevlievo.'"

"Down with Arpakash!" shouted Moyshe, and after him the whole company began roaring, "Down with him!" and they finally forced the Ethiopian king to shut up.

Marcus Aurelius continued:

"No, really, friends, this thrice-cursed *bachka* is deplorable. It has paralyzed us. It has coated our minds with mold and cobwebs. I tell you I know some guys who've spent ten whole years—ten years, my friends, that's no joke—doing nothing at all but rotting in the smoke-filled corners of the Café Panah with cards in their hands,[49] and right in front of their noses blooms this lovely, this picturesque, urban garden, whose breezes and freshness they are incapable of enjoying; and then outside of Sofia, in the surrounding area, there are such wonderful places. We sit in the coffeehouses and sigh for Switzerland, but all we need is a little energy, and Switzerland, a Bulgarian Switzerland, is right here before us—Mt. Vitosha, Rila, the Rhodopes.[50] Even the most miserable pauper among the foreigners living in Sofia has enjoyed the magnificent view from the Black Peak of Vitosha, but go on and tell me, is there one local—just one, for God's sake!—who has ever climbed Vitosha? We know of Italian workers who have left steady jobs here just because they were sick of the monotony and risking everything set out to wander, to see the world; but then, on the other hand, there are cases like, let's say, the shepherd of the Dragalevtsi monastery, who has observed Sofia from on high his whole life.[51] He watched it for years before the Liberation. He watched its destruction, its renewal and growth. He continues even now to peer down at its sparkling façade while sitting in the shade of a walnut tree, but to this day he has never had the will to come down from the mountain, to take a look around, to see up close the utterly fascinating transformation of the capital city. Actually, I exonerate this unique philosopher and even, to tell the truth, envy this child of nature. But what can I say about the majority of our wealthy citizens who spend their whole lives suffocating in

49. The Panah was a well-known café in the center of Sofia.

50. Mt. Vitosha is just south of Sofia. Mt. Rila is in southwestern Bulgaria, and the Rhodope Mountains are in the central part of southern Bulgaria. Vitosha was and is a popular spot for outings, and Cherni Vrûh (Black Peak) is its highest point.

51. The village of Dragalevtsi is now a suburb of Sofia on the lower slopes of Mt. Vitosha. The monastery serves as the summer residence of the Patriarch of the Bulgarian Church.

the dust, smells, and fumes of Sofia's old streets, who have looked out at the beautiful hills of Dragalevtsi all their lives but have never felt the desire to get up and go there and enjoy the clean, cool air, the enchanting music of the bubbling stream and the nightingales?"

"My! You're a regular poet, Marcus Aurelius. Imagine that. But tell me, why are you prattling on and on? Weren't you going to talk about Bai Ganyo?"

"I'm 'prattling on and on' because it just makes me so mad when I see the apathy that has paralyzed us. You might say we don't understand the beauties of nature. No, it can't be that we don't understand. It's a natural feeling; even cattle understand it. But the fact is we're bound by an Oriental languor. If I grab you by the collar, Arpakash, and drag you toward the Urvich monastery, as soon as I lead you beyond Kokalenski hill, over the chasm of the Iskûr, and you hear the mysterious speech of the meandering, foaming river, you'll start clucking your tongue and you'll shout, you'll definitely shout, 'Wow, this is a real Switzerland! Look at it. Our Bulgaria is gorgeous, and we, like idiots, know nothing about it but would rather spend our holidays hanging around in coffeehouses.' But as soon as you get back to Sofia and breathe its suffocating atmosphere, you'll fall back into lethargy. Apathy will turn you back into a stone until someone else drags you off by the collar."

Now, about Bai Ganyo. Gervanich and I hiked around all day in the woods, lolled in the grass among the trees, ate, drank, gazed at the jolly groups of foreigners who had given themselves over body and soul to merrymaking; they had set up all sorts of games; they were singing, running, jumping—you had to envy them! Toward evening, after a tasty snack, Gervanich and I went into the tavern for coffee. Suddenly, from over by Orhaniysko Road, we heard bells, and a little bit later a carriage full of travelers appeared in a cloud of dust. A traveler stepped down from the carriage, then a second one descended, and from behind the cabby's back we heard the voice of a third. "Bai Mihal, here, take these *disagi*; careful you don't bang them around; let's not break the *muskali*. Y'know, we don't want to be embarrassed in front of *him*."

And with these words, guess who jumped down from the carriage? Bai Ganyo. The same old Bai Ganyo, just as you knew him before he left for Europe. The only difference was that he had a necktie on; also, he's got a more imposing look now, shows a sense of his own worth and his superiority over those around him. The man knows Europe like the back of his hand. Europe has become old hat to him. He tugged on the left side of his mustache, coughed a bit into his hand, and surveyed the groups of merrymaking foreigners with the kind of look our policemen give their prisoners. Then, casting a glance and shaking his head at his ignorant fellow travelers, as if to tell them, "What a bunch of losers," he sighed and with depth and great significance uttered, "Oh, the Prater, the Prater."

"What did Your Grace say? I didn't quite catch it," said the one called Bai Mihal.

"What a bunch of losers," Bai Ganyo pronounced, with deep sympathy. "Eh, the Prater, the Prater! Has it occurred to you what a wonderful thing Vienna's Prater Park is? But how could it occur to you? And if I were to try explaining, you wouldn't understand."

And in order to demonstrate to his simple companions who was in a position to understand him, he approached a group of carousers who were surrounded by empty beer kegs, and putting on an ironic smile, he indicated the woods with his eyes and said, "*Das ist bulgarische* Prater, ha-ha-ha!"

The whole group, their eyes cheerfully befogged with beer, looked our "German" up and down, and one of the company, paying no attention to Bai Ganyo's ironic utterance, presented him with a glass of flat beer, saying half in Czech, "Please, sir, did you want some beer?"

"These guys don't understand me either," Bai Ganyo thought to himself, and, returning to his comrades, added, "They're as drunk as, as Cossacks."

After that, his group entered the inn and seated themselves near us. My back was toward them, so Bai Ganyo couldn't recognize me, and the fact that he didn't recognize me was obvious from the words he uttered at our expense. "Those fellows must have gotten themselves pickled, too. Bunch of Germans!"

The waiter approached the travelers and began wiping off the table.

"Can I get you anything?" he asked.

"Nothing. We've got our own. But hey, anyway, bring us some water and a light, pour us some fresh water," ordered Bai Ganyo.

Among the travelers there began a cryptic, serious conversation, not all of whose words reached our ears.

"This evening, we surely won't see the big shot. It'll be late," whispered Bai Ganyo. "We'll send him the gifts and let him know about tomorrow, and then he'll arrange the time for us to go before the prince."

"But what about a gift for the prince?" Bai Mihal asked warily.

"Not necessary," answered Bai Ganyo authoritatively. "All that matters here is the big shot. Pull the wool over his eyes and you're home free. We'll give him what the lawyer wrote for us, let him read it, and if something needs correcting, that's his business. And in front of the prince, stand firm; don't be frightened. You just watch what I do. I'll say, just as we were told to say, 'Your Royal Highness, don't do it, don't accept his resignation. Think of the Transdanubian Province,' and you repeat after me, 'Don't do it, Your Royal Highness!'"[52]

"Naturally, what else would we say?" Bai Mihal answered obediently.

"As for you, Bai Mihal, you've got a whiff of Russky. I'm not so sure about you. Watch your step!" warned Bai Ganyo sternly.

Bai Mihal pleaded innocent. "Who, me? Don't talk like that, pal. Someone will hear. Even the walls have ears. When I hear the word 'Cossack' I get the shivers."

"You get the shivers, eh?" whispered Bai Ganyo softly with a wink. "But when the Russians came, who was it that cleaned out the cattle from the Turkish villages, eh? Since when do you have those riches, eh? Speak up!"

"Well, but you, too, Bai Ganyo," whispered Bai Mihal. "Truth to tell, you've had the water mills since the Russian occupation, haven't you? Tell me; isn't that so?"

"Come now, one can't even have a simple conversation with you. What's done is done. It's not that way now. Now it's the Transdanubian Province, you understand?"

"How could I not understand?" said Bai Mihal, and he winked impishly at his comrades.

All three of them burst into muffled laughter, trying not to be heard.

---

52. In 1886 Stefan Stambolov came to power and Bulgaria broke off relations with Russia owing to Russian interference in Bulgarian internal affairs. Anti-Russian parties, especially Stambolov's, accused czarist Russia of aspiring to annex Bulgaria as its "Transdanubian Province." At the beginning of 1894 Prime Minister Stambolov's position had become untenable, owing in part to the disintegration of the anti-Russian bloc among the Great Powers and in part to pressure from elements dissatisfied with his cautious approach to the Macedonian question (see 138n85). Prince Ferdinand went to Vienna, unbeknownst to Stambolov, and initiated contacts with the Russian ambassador there to prepare the way for reconciliation. Stambolov learned of this, and when Ferdinand returned to Sofia, Stambolov's government resigned, assuming that the resignation would not be accepted. To their surprise, Ferdinand accepted the resignation, and in response Stambolov attempted to organize a national movement to force Ferdinand to reverse his decision. On 18 May 1894 a motley crowd of thugs and Stambolov supporters set out from Uchbunar (see 67n31) intending to hold a demonstration in Alexander Square in the center of Sofia to force Ferdinand to retain Stambolov. Hearing of this, a huge crowd of ordinary citizens occupied the square and shouted things like "Down with Stambolov." The next day Konstantin Stoilov was appointed prime minister.

"Well, watch your step. Be on guard, because if anyone hears us, we'll really be in hot water. Hey, boy, what's that newspaper there? *Freedom?*" Bai Ganyo turned to the waiter.

"*Free Speech*, sir."[53]

"Eh, I'd like to read it," Bai Ganyo whispered to his comrades, "but I'm scared, damn it. The big shot will hear of it——then go try to straighten things out."

But just then a scene occurred that froze the travelers in their seats. A five- or six-year-old little boy was wandering idly about the entry of the tavern, improvising various songs to himself, and, obviously under the influence of the "down with Stambolov" heard constantly in Sofia for the last three days, he abandoned the standard text to the tune of "Shumi Maritsa" and, carried away by his song, used the words that had been impressed on his mind: "Down wi-ith, down with, down wi-ith, down with, do-own with, do-own with, down with Stambolov!" Approving laughter from the groups of revelers interrupted the child's improvisation, and, excited by his unexpected success, he started singing again in a louder voice, almost shouting, and instead of "Ma-arch, ma-arch," he cried, "Do-own, do-own, down with Stambolov, dow-dow-dow-do-own with, down with Stambolov." This time, in addition to the friendly laughter, you could hear applause and shouts of "Bravo," "Down with him," "Down with the lecher," and "Down with the tyrant" from a group of young people returning from a hike.

I turned to the table of the three travelers.

Bai Ganyo and his comrades sat motionless like statues. Open mouthed and glassy eyed, their faces expressed such a pitiful mixture of fear and wonder that I could only be sorry I didn't have a camera. Bai Ganyo was the first to recover; he turned his eyes toward the demonstrators and instantly shuddered, as if struck by an electric current. A mounted police officer passing on the road heard these terrible shouts, and instead of drawing his sword and waving it with a maddened howl like a cyclone over the heads of these outrageous rebels, these evil souls, these bandits and traitors, instead of this, he watched them calmly, with a good-natured smile on his face. If a volcano had erupted on Vitosha at that moment, it could hardly have astounded our travelers more than that scene.

---

53. *Svoboda* (Freedom) was the newspaper of Stambolov's National Liberal Party. *Svobodno slovo* (Free Speech) was that of the opposition coalition (the so-called legal opposition).

"We've made a mess of it!" Bai Ganyo pronounced with a despairing sigh. "Hey, Bai Mihal, please, go over by the counter and sneak a look at *Free Speech*. See if you can figure out what's going on."

"Well, fine and dandy; why don't you go yourself? Let's see how brave you are," answered Bai Mihal.

"Eh, you're so simple minded! After all, how hard is it to take a peek? Just go by the counter as if you're looking at the *rakia*, whistling to yourself like this, then with one eye, zip, like that, look to see if by chance there's a new minis . . . Simple!"

"Impossible, keep your wits about you."

"But didn't you see the officer? Well then, hang on, I'll have to take the bull by the horns—I'll look at the newspaper, the hell with it."

Bai Ganyo rose from his seat, began whistling "Green Leaves" through his teeth, and, looking around as if distracted, circled like an eagle toward the counter, approached, grabbed a bottle of cognac by the neck, and, pretending to read the label, swiveled his eyes to the right so far that someone facing him would have seen only the whites, until his gaze fell on the folded newspaper, of which only the masthead, *Free Speech*, was visible. He slid out his right hand and, whistling "Green Leaves" louder in order to cover the newspaper's noise, unfolded one part of it and, with eyes horribly slanted to the right, read, "News from the court. Presented to H.R. Highness today was the prime minister and minister of the interior, Dr. K. Stoil . . ." Something caught in Bai Ganyo's throat; he coughed, licked his lips, which had suddenly gone dry, and cast a sideways glance downward to read the large letters of a headline: "Fall of Stambol . . ."—and Bai Ganyo's heart fell into his boots. He let the cognac bottle slip and to cover up the resulting noise began to cough loudly. Bai Ganyo turned toward his comrades and uttered portentously, "It's happened."

"Don't even say that, Bai Ganyo!" cried Bai Mihal.

"It's over," added Bai Ganyo, and as he drew near the table, he whispered softly to his comrades in Turkish, "Stambolov *efendi* is down the toilet; now it's Stoilov."

"It can't be. What are you saying? In the paper did it . . . ?"

"Of course."

"But could it be some kind of trick?"

"What do you mean, 'trick'?" burst out Bai Ganyo, and gathering all his courage, he banged on the table and called out, "Hey, lad, bring *Free Speech* over here."

The friends instinctively lowered their heads and began looking around nervously.

The boy brought the newspaper and by chance happened to hold it out to Bai Mihal, who pulled back his hand as if being offered a piece of red hot iron and signaled with his eyes toward Bai Ganyo. Bai Ganyo took the paper and, of course, turned this way and that to see who was and who was not at the tavern; after all, how could Bai Ganyo get up the nerve? But in the end he had the guts to do it! He unfolded *Free Speech* and began: "Fall of Stamb . . ."

Bai Ganyo began to cough, and his comrades began coughing even harder. Bai Mihal looked out of the corner of his eye toward the paper to see whether his brave friend was reading correctly and assured himself that there was no mistake. The third comrade also bent his head toward the paper and read, and a tremor shook him, and his world began to spin. So many of his lawsuits and hearings that had lain dormant for years under the prosecutorial robe would be dragged out into the light of day by those three little words!

With much huddling, whispering, and coughing, they picked their way through the lead article, and glancing here and there through the paper, they finally discerned and understood that the deed was done.

"We've made a mess of it!" said Bai Ganyo. "What now? Now it's too late to beg for his resignation not to be accepted. Oh, the hell with it. Eh, Mihal, why are you so quiet? Tell us. What's to be done?"

"That's for you to say, Your Grace. I'm as taken aback as if I'd been whacked on the noggin with a club," replied Bai Mihal despairingly.

"And you, Gunyo, why are you silent? You say something, too! What do we do now, huh?"

"Eh, what do I know? Whatever you say, Your Grace," muttered Gunyo, his spirit broken.

"But don't you have a brain, you dolt? Is it always up to me to fix things up for you?" Bai Ganyo shouted, almost weeping with despair. "Never mind. I'll tell you what to do this time, too. Y'know what?"

At this point Bai Ganyo pondered a bit, frowned, scratched his head even though it didn't itch, coughed once or twice in his fist, groped in the pocket of his frock coat, pulled out a paper folded in four, and gave it to Bai Gunyo.

"Here, read this damned thing one more time. And then I'll tell you what we're going to do."

"But Your Grace, why don't you read it?"

"Hey, Gunyo, don't get me riled. You know why I don't read it. You're better at reading these highfalutin words."

Gunyo unfolded the paper and read, more or less as follows: "Your Royal Highness! Heavenly storms have broken over our unfortunate heads! Our five centuries of enslavement are a pleasant dream in comparison with this cruel blow that the northern foe has dealt us through the resignation of our—Oh! Are there words?—most sagacious leader, that Cicero, that Newton of the Bulgarian firmament. *O tempora, o mores!* Nay, Your Royal Highness! We still believe in the good sense of the valiant Bulgarian people and trust that it will not part with a man who personifies its aspirations and ideals—in all things honest, noble, chaste, progressive, liberal. We shall not believe that Your Royal Highness will entrust executive power to those depraved traitors, to those ignorant and ill-bred nonentities who strive night and day to undermine the foundations of our system of government and to hurl our beloved fatherland under the stinking boots of the Cossack.

"Your Royal Highness! *Timeo Danaos et dona ferentes!*[54] The resolution above has been adopted by eleven thousand eminent citizens, and Ganyo Balkanski, Mihal Mihalev, and Gunyo Kilipirchikov have been delegated to carry it to Your Royal Highness's feet. Hurrah!"[55]

"What a good-for-nothing people we are," said Bai Ganyo, with much head shaking and tongue clucking. "When it comes to lying, those old Gypsies can't hold a candle to us. Was it anywhere near that many? Eleven thousand eminent citizens, they say. Ha, ha, ha! Take away the thousands; how many are left?"

"Eleven people," answered Mihal.

"Were there that many?"

"There were, Bai Ganyo. It's the truth. Didn't I go with an officer to round them up myself?"

"Good-for-nothings! Now, y'know what? Going back now is out of the question. Gunyo, you're a bit of a lawyer. Get to work, please, and let's all of us concoct another address, for the new one. Here, I've got paper. And let's hope they don't find out that we came to beg on behalf of that scoundrel, because then our game is up, especially your game, Gunyo. If there's another prosecutor . . ."

---

54. "I fear Greeks bearing gifts."

55. The name Kilipirchikov is based on an eastern Bulgarian pronunciation of *kelepir*; see 57n28.

Gunyo coughed. "Give me the paper and pencil," he said anxiously. "You watch; I'll write."

And he began writing: "Your Royal Highness! Heavenly storms have broken over our unfortunate heads!

"Now we have to write it all the other way around. How will we write it? Wait! How's this: 'The heavens have opened and poured blessings on our fatherland.'"

"Only 'fatherland' sounds too plain," declared Bai Ganyo. "Put in 'our beloved fatherland.'"

"Me, too. I think it's no good without 'beloved,'" said Bai Mihal.

"All right, I've put in 'beloved.' Next: 'The five centuries of enslavement are a pleasant dream in comparison with this cruel blow.' Now backwards: 'Our liberation from five centuries of enslavement is nothing compared to the splendid events that have broken the shackles of cruel tyranny.' Do you agree?"

"You should've added 'fiends from hell,'" said Bai Ganyo. "But never mind, go on."

"... which the northern foe has dealt us through the resignation of our— Oh! Are there words!—most sagacious leader, that Cicero, that Newton of the Bulgarian firmament."

"Now, how to turn this around? Wait! Like this: 'And which is due solely to Your Royal Highness, most gracious sire and father, since you accepted the resignation of that—Oh! Are there words?—most cruel torturer, that Caligula, that Tamerlane of the Bulgarian firmament.'"

"Bravo, Bai Gunyo!" cried Bai Ganyo, his eyes shining with enthusiasm.

"How do you think all that up, Gunyo?" Mihal flattered him.

"'*O tempora, o mores!*' can stay as is. That always fits right in, no matter where you put it. 'Nay, Your Royal Highness!' Let's put in 'Yea, Your Royal Highness!'

"'We still believe in the good sense of the valiant Bulgarian people and trust that it won't part with the man.' Now instead of 'will not part' we'll put in 'and will obliterate from the face of the earth' and instead of 'the man' we'll put in 'the savage beast.'"

"No, better put in 'the rabid monster,'" corrected Bai Ganyo.

"But I think we should put in 'flames of hell,'" said Mihal.

"Eh, that's pushing it. Ha-ha-ha! But why 'flames of hell'? It would be better to put in 'filthy bloodsucker,'" said Gunyo.

"Yeah, look at it now! Excellent!" approved Bai Ganyo.

"'...who personifies its aspirations and ideals—in all things honest, noble, chaste, progressive, liberal.' Now let's turn it on its head. '...who personifies the nation's misfortune in all things dishonest, undependable, corrupt, obscurantist, and tyrannical!' Next: 'We do not believe that Your Royal Highness will entrust executive power to those depraved traitors, to those ignorant and ill-bred nonentities.' How to reverse it, now? Hold on! I've got it! Here's how: 'Allow us, Your Royal Highness, to count ourselves blessed and to express our most boundlessly loyal sentiments, since you have entrusted power to the hands of those noble patriots, to those educated and well-bred statesmen, who strive night and day to undermine the foundations of our system of government.'"

"What? You've made a mistake!" said Bai Ganyo in alarm.

"We'll turn it backward right away, like this; instead of 'to undermine' we'll put in 'to fortify.' 'And to hurl our beloved fatherland under the stinking boots of the Cossack.'"

"Let's see now," said Bai Ganyo. "This is the tricky part. We don't know, damn it all, what position these new guys will take toward the Russkies. If we knew that they wanted to make peace, it would be child's play, a piece of cake. There's all sorts of things we could write. 'Czar liberator, Czar protector, true-born brothers, mangy German *Chifuti*,' and so on; but we don't know which way the wind will blow. All right: 'Slavic brothers,' but if *those guys* are also against the Slavs, then it'll be, oops, Bai Ganyo the traitor! No, you know what; let's throw out that bit there about the 'stinking boot.'"

"Eh, but then what do we put in?"

"Ho-old on. Don't rush. Let's think a bit. Y'know what? Now, since we don't know yet how the wind will blow, we can put it in both ways and let them interpret it as they will. Let's put this in: 'And to embrace fraternally the Russians and the Germans to boot.' Pfui! May God strike them dead!"

"No, that doesn't fit at all! What's this 'to boot' business? Does one talk like that to a prince?" the lawyerly Gunyo protested.

"Well, how does one talk, you scum?" Bai Ganyo erupted. "Are *you* going to teach *me*? Do you know who I am? Do you know that I've been all over Europe? I'm not a blockhead like you. Do you know that those Jirechek–Schmirechek types hung on my every word when I spoke to them? The English, the Americans, they all honored me in Dresden, and you want to teach me my business? Do you know that I . . . ?"

"I know, Bai Ganyo; how could I not know?" said the astonished Gunyo, excusing himself.

"Eh, well, if you know, what was all that about? Never mind. Write it down as best you can."

"Let's write it like this: 'And to place us, if not higher, then at least on the level of the great European powers . . .'"

"Whatever, agreed," approved Bai Ganyo.

"'. . . of the great European powers, restoring us to the grandeur of Asparukh and Krum.'"[56]

"Agreed. Good."

"Now, to continue: 'Your Royal Highness! *Timeo Danaos et dona ferentes!*' Instead of that it will be best to put in 'Vox populi, vox dei.'[57] Do you agree?"

"After all, why not; put it in. It's not entirely Bulgarian, but if it's needed, what can we do about it?" Bai Ganyo agreed.

"'The resolution above has been adopted by eleven thousand eminent citizens, and Ganyo Balkanski,' and so on; all of that can stay the same, right to the end."

"Shall we leave it just eleven thousand people or shall we increase it in honor of the new guys by another thousand or two? Shall we butter them up?"

"It's enough, Bai Ganyo. In our town even if you rounded up the blind and the beardless they'd barely add up to eleven thousand. But never mind; it's for their sake, isn't it?"

"I agree, but still in place of 'Ganyo Balkanski' wouldn't it be more elegant to put in 'Mr. Ganyo' and so on? So the prince can see that we aren't some kind of low-class people, huh?"

"I'd say it that way, too," put in Mihal.

"Gentlemen, it's getting late. Let's go!" called the Turkish cabby from the threshold of the inn. The travelers left for Sofia.

———

The next day, gentlemen, I read in one of the local papers that a delegation from the town of P., consisting of Ganyo Balkanski and others, had presented itself before the great gates of the palace to express thanks for liberation from the tyrannical regime.

Two days later in that paper, I read a dispatch from the same town, signed in the name of "thousands" of citizens, notifying those in power that Bai Ganyo and his comrades were a false, self-appointed delegation and that the

---

56. See 41n17 and 43n21.
57. "The voice of the people is the voice of God."

true representatives of the people had already left for the capital to present their thanks.

I knew the hotel where Bai Ganyo stays when he's in town and set off to see him. I didn't want to express indignation at his base deed, because no degree of indignation would suffice to condemn it, but I wanted to test whether it was possible to make this unfortunate product of circumstances recognize the full horror of his action.

On the board in the hotel I looked up which room Bai Ganyo was in and went up by the stairs. I knocked on the door. No one answered. I turned the handle, and the door opened. The room was empty. They had left. On the table I noticed a scrap of paper on which was written in Bai Ganyo's hand, "To the editors of the newspaper *Free Speech*." The latter name was crossed out and it its place was written *Freedom*. It continued, "The subterfuges of Stambolov"—and this also was crossed out and in its place was written "Anarchy."[58] It was clear that the author of the letter had long debated which path to take, because in many lines there were crossed-out words replaced with their complete opposites. For instance, "patriots" was written and crossed out, and over it was written "highway robbers," and this was also crossed out and overwritten with "patriots." The whole letter was littered with x-ed out words, scratched by an angry hand. Because in drawing the second line, the ink had run out, the pen had been dipped again in the ink, and a line twice as thick had been drawn. Under the crossed-out lines stood the following words: "You made monkeys of us, damn you, you stinkers!"

---

58. On 18 May 1894 *Svobodno slovo* published an editorial under this headline, detailing Stambolov's transgressions. Meanwhile *Svoboda* accused the government of unleashing anarchists and socialists.

11

Bai Ganyo Does Elections

This selection is dedicated to my inestimable friend Tsvetan Radoslavov.[59]

"Cut the chatter, I tell you; we need to elect representatives," cried Bai Ganyo as he banged hard on the table.[60]

"But how can we elect representatives? Where will we dig up voters? And anyhow, you, Bai Ganyo, aren't you supposed to be a liberal?" said Bochoolu, daring to object.

"Who told you I'm a liberal?" Bai Ganyo asked sternly.

"What do you mean who told me? Don't you remember how you were beating up on the conservatives, how you were cursing them; how could you not be a liberal? Don't you know? You said it yourself—you even bragged to Jirechek about being a liberal," retorted Bochoolu.

"Eh, you're a fool," answered Bai Ganyo with a condescending smile. "What if I did say something to Jirechek? Does saying it make it true? Ah, you sucker, if I can't take in a Jirechek, who can I take in?"

Gochoolu spoke up. "You're right, Your Grace. Bochoolu, keep quiet, don't harp on it. I'm a conservative too."

---

59. Tsvetan Radoslavov (1863–1931) was born in Svishtov. He completed a degree in philosophy at Leipzig and taught psychology at the University of Sofia.

60. Four months after the fall of Stambolov, general parliamentary elections were held. Aleko was a candidate for the opposition in his native Svishtov. Stoilov put together the National Party consisting of his own partisans, former conservatives, people from Stambolov's party, and careerists. This party made use of the same electoral methods as the previous regime: intimidation, fraud, and violence. Aleko writes here from personal experience.

"Well, what am I, a bump on a log? I'm absolutely a conservative myself," blurted Dochoolu.[61] "Come on, Bochoolu, you be a conservative too, and we'll fix it so those others can't do anything."

"All right, but I don't know whose side the provincial governor will be on," answered Bochoolu.

"The governor? He's with *us*, of course," announced Bai Ganyo. "And the chief of police is with us. The standing commission isn't legitimate, but who's going to challenge its legitimacy? It's ours. The election bureau is ours. The city council is ours. The mayor is a little wishy-washy, but we'll keep him in line. The councils in the villages haven't been confirmed yet, on purpose, understand? If they're with us, we'll confirm them, if not, the hell with them. I tell you again: as for the governor, don't worry. He's ours."

"But the porters?" questioned Bochoolu.

"The porters are also ours, and the Gypsies, and Danko the Thug is ours."

"But isn't he in jail for robbery?" asked Bochoolu in surprise.

"Oh, come on now, are you stupid or something? We got him out. He was the one who got us the porters, wasn't he? He went to them the day before yesterday, rounded them up, and showed them who was boss. They froze in their seats when he roared, 'I'll smash your teeth in if you don't vote for Bai Ganyo!' And the porters came on board. Danko bargained them down to two levs apiece and one whole night of eating and drinking on election eve."

"What an incredible bandit!"

"And how much do you think he charged us? Only fifty levs. He went to those guys on the other side to ask for one hundred levs, and they told him off and kicked him out. You'll see him now on Sunday. He'll break their bones!" said Bai Ganyo in a self-satisfied tone.

"Bochoolu, go call Gunyo the Lawyer to come and write us a proclamation. Tell him, 'Bai Ganyo wants you.'"

As soon as Bochoolu had gone, Bai Ganyo leaned forward and with a secretive voice turned to his comrades. "Keep quiet. Right up to election day

---

61. "B," "G," and "D" are the next three letters in the Greek alphabet after "A" (in Cyrillic, for historical reasons, "V" comes between "B" and "G"), and *olu* is from the Turkish suffix *oğlu* (son). The image conjured up by the names Bochoolu, Gochoolu, and Dochoolu is that of a nineteenth-century Bulgarian equivalent of Tweedledum and Tweedledee. It is also worth noting that the characters of Bobchinsky and Dobchinsky from Nikolai Gogol's comedy *Inspector General* are of the same type, and their names could well have been an inspiration to Aleko. (I am indebted to David Kramer for this observation.)

we'll make that idiot think that we're going to make him a candidate; we'll write up a few ballots with his name just for show, but the other ballots will be made by the clerks in the city council and from the regional government. Now listen to me. The minister definitely wants me to be a candidate. You, Gochoolu, do you want to run too?"

"Yeah, sure, I'd like that, Bai Ganyo," answered Gochoolu.

"Well, I'd like that, too," said Dochoolu.

"Ah, you'd like that, would you? Well to tell you the truth, you've made a complete fool of yourself in public. Why did you have to be so obvious? Who was it squawking in the public squares, 'Long live the great patriot!' 'Down with the vile tyrant!' 'To the gallows with Kliment!' 'Long live Kliment!'?"[62]

"But we were all in it together, weren't we, Bai Ganyo? Why are you talking out of both sides of your mouth?"

"Together, sure, but *we* always kept our activities hush-hush. Well anyway, never mind, since you want it so much; all right, I'll get you elected, even though the villagers hate you. After all, you've been robbing them blind with your high interest rates."

"As for that, don't bring it up, Bai Ganyo. We all know about you, too," said Dochoolu warily.

Bai Ganyo was just about to explode, but at that moment Gunyo the Lawyer came in. Bai Ganyo explained what kind of proclamation was needed. Gunyo sat down at the table, took up the quill, and sank into deep thought. On Bai Ganyo's orders the waiter brought a bottle of *mastika*. Gochoolu, Dochoolu, and Bai Ganyo drank. Gunyo wrote. Half an hour later, the following text was ready:

Appeal to the Voters of Our District
In view of the great importance and significance of the forthcoming elections of national representatives for the present and future of Our Fatherland, our citizens, numbering more than seven hundred souls,

---

62. The first two slogans refer to Stambolov, the second two to Metropolitan Kliment (the writer Vasil Drumev), an implacable opponent of Stambolov and Ferdinand. In 1889 Stambolov ordered that Kliment be imprisoned and sentenced to death. Stambolov fell from power before he could have his orders obeyed, however, and so the first and third slogans and the second and fourth slogans were shouted by the same crowds, depending on who was in power.

gathered today in the courtyard of the school in the Ragpickers' Quarter, and having considered the question of the candidacies of various individuals for representatives, we have reached agreement and unanimously decided to recommend to the distinguished voters of Our Region as their national representatives their fellow citizens:

Ganyo Balkanski, merchant, renowned throughout Bulgaria

Filio Gochoolu, merchant in finances

Tanas Dochoolu, merchant in the wine industry

That is, the very same people who were also recommended to you last month by the committee of the National Party in its declaration of 27 August.

As we proclaim this unanimous decision of Ours to the rest of the distinguished voters of our city and district, who hold dear to their hearts the good of the Fatherland, material improvement for the farmer, alleviation of the condition of the taxpayer, in a word, the interests of Our District, we urge them to cast their votes in the election on the 11th for our three afore-mentioned fellow citizens, who we are fully confident will represent our country in the National Assembly with dignity.

Distinguished Voters,

Several citizens have already presented you with a slate containing the names Nikola Tûrnovaliyata, Lulcho Doktorov, and Ivanitsa Gramatikov, persons not from Our circle, persons foreign to Us, who do not and cannot hold Our trust.[63] Perhaps others will also appear and try to persuade you to vote for their candidates. We advise you, distinguished voters, not to be deceived by their seductive words and not to be taken in by their flattery and not to believe in the various rumors and inventions they spread and the allegations of various circular dispatches and so on. Nikola Tûrnovaliyata is originally from Tûrnovo, and therefore he's so stubborn he'd burn the quilt to get rid of the fleas. Lulcho Doktorov is devoted body and soul to the Transdanubian Province, and as for Ivanitsa Gramatikov, nobody knows him, and, nota bene, he is Russian-educated and thus a traitor to Our Dear Fatherland.

Distinguished Voters,

We are convinced that the aforementioned persons, namely those below:

Ganyo Balkanski

---

63. The references here are to the three actual opposition candidates: Nikola Kon-stantinov, Dr. Vankov, and Aleko.

Filyo Gochoolu

Tanas Dochoolu

who are totally loyal and subservient to the THRONE AND DYNASTY
OF HIS ROYAL HIGHNESS OUR BELOVED PRINCE
FERDINAND I and who will faithfully uphold our present patriotic
government, led by the current prime minister, will gain your support.

"Bravo, Gunyo!" Bai Ganyo exclaimed. "You're a veritable Bismarck!"

"Well, did you think I was stupid?" said Gunyo complacently.

"Now go and give this to the printer; have him print it in great big
letters."

"What about the money?"

"There is no money, just tell him to print it. If he doesn't, let him know
we'll tell the city council and the other departments not to have their print-
ing done at his shop. Got it? Now get going," commanded Bai Ganyo.

"Do you know," continued Bai Ganyo, "*those guys* sent a telegram to the
minister complaining to him that the governor was going around the villages
campaigning?"

"Those idiots!" said Gochoolu.

"You said it!" agreed Dochoolu.

"It's not as if the minister is the Holy Mother of God who has to listen
to every little thing they say. Apparently he answered them, 'The elections
are free,' ha ha ha!"

"Heh heh heh!" snickered Gochoolu and Dochoolu.

"He's a real devil, damn him. Free, eh? I'll show them freedom! On
Sunday they'll see a freedom that they'll remember the rest of their lives.
Especially Gramatikov! That poor bastard hasn't seen our elections yet.
Just let those Vlahs[64] of ours come out to meet him, those Gypsies with
their bloodshot eyes bulging out an inch, with their gravelly voices, those
sashes up to their necks, let them stare right at him, then let that wild boar
Danko the Thug come up behind him and just shout, 'Grab him!'"

"Heh heh heh!" snickered Gochoolu and Dochoolu, their eyes glowing
with satisfaction.

---

64. Here the reference is to Romanian speakers living in Bulgaria. At that time,
Romania and Bulgaria had conflicting claims to Dobrudja (the region of the Danube
delta), and so Romanian speakers in Bulgaria were viewed with suspicion and as a kind
of fifth column.

"Li-be-ra-als! Cos-ten-tu-tion! I'll give them a costentution. They're still pinning their hopes on the circular dispatch. They've numbed people's ears with that circular dispatch. If they're not reading it, then they're showing it to the whole world. The governor and I had a good laugh yesterday at the coffeehouse. Just for appearances, he had them print that damned dispatch and then had sent it around the coffeehouses. Yesterday, we were sitting in the coffeehouse, watching *those guys*, with their heads all bent over a table like sheep at lunchtime, reading and rereading the dispatch. They were so happy; we heard them whispering, 'Free! The elections are free! The police won't interfere!' And the governor and I, hee, hee, hee! I give him a look and I tell him, laughing, 'We're a sure thing.' He starts to chuckle and hup! drinks down a *mastika*. He pats his pocket, meaning here's *that* letter, about the *freeness* of elections,[65] winks, and says, 'We're not a sure thing'—and heh, heh, heh, hup!—another *mastika*. We got ro-y-ally drunk! And then Danko the Thug came in, and some others, and still more people, and then we shut ourselves up in the coffeehouse, and I called to the fiddlers, 'OK, boys!' The strings were smoking! Georgi's *mastika* is no good. The snacks are lousy. Why does he serve you pickled okra instead of pickled cucumbers? Ugh! I've got a headache from yesterday. Gochoolu, pour us each another *mastika*!"

"Here's to the hangover!"

"Forget it. And tonight, we'll have to drink again. Starting tonight, we have to get our people set up in the taverns."

Dochoolu spoke up. "Isn't it too early, Bai Ganyo?"

"It's not too early. Tomorrow is Saturday. They have only thirty-six hours left for drinking. It's not too early. It's just right. And after all, they won't all drink the whole time. They'll take turns. Some will drink for five or six hours. They'll rest, and others will start in. One group after the other! Once they get together, they won't leave. They'll drink there, eat there, sleep there. Got it?"

"We know. This isn't the first time we've done elections!" put in Gochoolu.

"You, Gochoolu, when you pass by the Albanian's, tell him to bake three hundred *okas* of bread for this evening and to send one hundred *okas* to Topachoolu in the Gypsy Quarter, one hundred *okas* to Gogo's tavern in the Ragpickers' Quarter, and one hundred *okas* down to the porters. You, Dochoolu, drop by those bars and tell 'em to start giving out wine and *rakia*

---

65. When voters in Svishtov protested to the district attorney, he answered that he had had instructions.

as of this evening. Tell 'em to go heavy on the *rakia*, you hear? And you tell 'em not to overcharge too much, or there'll be hell to pay. The year before last, they swindled us out of two thousand levs for nothing, the bastards. Tell 'em to watch their step, because the city council is ours. Drop by the butchers, too. Tell 'em to collect a couple of baskets of whatever scraps they have—liver, tripe, bones—and we'll send them to the taverns so they can each cook up a kettle of *chorba* for our boys. Tonight, the governor and the chief of police will return from the villages. I'll take them with me to make the rounds of the other taverns and coffeehouses. We'll get the clerks from all the departments to write up ballots; we'll make them write all night. I chose the paper myself, sort of a grayish, yellowish color. We'll fold our ballots like amulets."

"Three-cornered," clarified Dochoolu.

"Three-cornered. And we'll need to get hold of some of their ballots to see what their paper is like and how they fold them, so we can have the clerks write up one or two thousand ballots on their paper with our names."

"You're a sly devil, Bai Ganyo. You've got all those tricks down pat," said Gochoolu reverently.

"Well, naturally. How could I be Ganyo Balkanski and not know the ropes in this business, too? You, my dear sir, can drop me in any district you like and tell me to get anyone you like elected. If you pick a donkey as the candidate, I'll damn well get the donkey elected for you. Just give me the police chief and his men, and give me one or two thousand levs. For you, my friend, I'd get those fine fellows together, the rabble and riffraff, say forty or fifty jailbirds, and set 'em up in two or three taverns around the outskirts, give 'em a keg apiece, and then shout out to them, 'Hey, you guys! Come on! Long live Bulgaria!' He-ey! Now you'll see! Their bulging eyes turn bloodshot. They begin to pull their knives out of their sashes and stab them down into the tabletops. They raise a hullabaloo with their rough, gravelly voices. You'd be terrified! Then, during the night, you up and lead these monsters through the town. Opposition? The devil himself couldn't stand up against you. Take them past the house of some opponent. Man, oh man! When they open up those mouths of theirs! If you heard them from three miles away, it would make your skin crawl; your hair would stand on end like a hedgehog's bristles. Then call the village mayors and clerks and flash your eyes at them and gnash your teeth and point out those jailbirds. Voters? You won't even see their shadows. When twelve people from each village have shown up, regional councilmen and mayors together, you gather the officials and clerks, post police in the outskirts to turn back the other villagers, surround the bureau with those forty or fifty cutthroats, create some kind of confusion, stick a few bundles of ballots in the box, and voilà, your donkey is the national representative, ha ha ha!"

"Ha ha ha," responded Gochoolu and Dochoolu. "Bravo, Bai Ganyo!"

"That's right, but the police alone aren't enough. The election bureau also has to be yours," added Gochoolu.

"I think so, too," chimed in Dochoolu. "It's ours now, but speaking hypothetically. Seriously, Bai Ganyo, please explain to us. How did you get control over the bureau?"

"How?" answered Bai Ganyo with a self-satisfied smirk. "Very easily! Didn't we elect the district council? Eight came out *theirs*, four ours. We forced an appeal of four of theirs, the most important ones. Now, you'll say that they raised a fuss. Rubbish! By the time they get it sorted out, the elections will be over. We ended up with four of theirs and four of ours. But those we left them with were all the worthless ones. We held a meeting to elect a standing commission. The messenger boy couldn't locate one of theirs—do you remember?"

"Tsk tsk tsk," clucked Dochoolu. "What good is Bismarck? Bismarck couldn't hold a candle to you."

"Just wait; you haven't seen anything yet. After all, should only the Germans have a Bismarck? Anyway, we were left, gentlemen, with three of theirs, and our four, the majority! Eh, of course! We weren't born yesterday. The commission ended up completely ours. Not only that, but ours received more votes, because we had promised two of theirs separately that we would elect them secretary of the commission, and they, the suckers, voted, and voted for ours. Ha ha ha! Now they walk around the streets in a daze. Especially one of them, an influential, wicked guy. We took him around the villages to campaign with us, promising to elect him secretary, and he, the blockhead, up and quit his job. He counted his chickens before they hatched. Sucker! Dochoolu, pour us each another *mastika*."

Bai Ganyo strained the *mastika* through his mustache, wiped it with his palm, twirled up the ends of his devilish mustache, and continued.

"Now, let me tell you how one chooses an election bureau. It's done by drawing lots. The chief judge of the court pulls them out. They call it 'the luck of the draw,' but I can make them pick whoever I want. And very easily: if you put the slips in a glass, so they can be seen from outside, you have to scratch a little mark with ink on each of the filled-in slips, or, if they're in a box, you have to use a deep box so that the slips can't be seen from the outside. You have to arrange the filled-in ones on one side and the blank ones on the other. Then all you have to do is whisper to the judge that 'he's in for it' and therefore he'd better watch his step. They call out, 'Ivan, Stoyan, Pûrvan!' Do you need Pûrvan? Take a filled-out slip. You don't need Pûrvan? Take an empty slip. In other words, the judge draws the lots."

"What a devil Bai Ganyo is! Those simpletons sure did pick the wrong person to oppose! Too bad for them!" proclaimed Gochoolu.

"With a head like yours, how come you're not a minister already?" marveled Dochoolu.

"Cut it out. That's enough," said Bai Ganyo modestly. "You know what Bulgarians are like!"

In the east, dawn is just beginning to break, and a pale light spreads into the interior of Gogo's tavern in the Ragpickers' Quarter. Some thirty select troops are strewn about on the tables, on the ground, over the chairs; their snoring, like thirty tigers attacking one another, can be heard from the street, and it catches the ear of the police guard. From time to time one of these heroes arises with half-closed eyes, stumbles through the motionless bodies, grabs the jug, and thirstily quenches the alcoholic fire burning his stomach, throat, mouth, and cracked lips; the bodies on which he has trod in the dark awaken and spew curses and oaths from their hoarse, dry throats. What a stench! Their breathing emits a hellish odor and poisons the air of the tavern, which even without that would be foul, infused with the fumes from this mass of dismal characters.

Gochoolu and Dochoolu are already awake and drinking coffee in Nasty Hasan's coffeehouse. The last tactical maneuver lies before them. It is time to wake the sleeping camps of the electoral army. Here they are already in front of Gogo's tavern. They open the door, and a wave of suffocating stench knocks them backward.

"Pfui! Damn them all!" cries Gochoolu in a choking voice and holds his nose.

"Did they eat garlic or what?" Dochoolu's words are strained through a sour grimace and he also holds his nose.

Through the open door fresh air swept into the tavern and made it possible for the not-overly-sensitive duo to venture inside.

"Are you still sleeping, you oxen? Come on, get up," commanded Gochoolu authoritatively, and he began prodding the members of the drunken brigade with his foot.

"Gogo, give them each a *rakia* to help open their eyes," added Dochoolu.

Gogo got up sluggishly from his bed, stretched, yawned, scratched the sweatier parts of his body, and began rummaging reluctantly among the bottles and glasses. The *rakia* poured, he addressed the unroused men.

"Get up, you donkeys, here, guzzle it down! That's enough yawning like dogs. Just look at your eyes—bulging like boils! Drink up now!"

With such pleasantries, assisted by energetic kicking, Gogo made the rounds of his drink-sodden guests, offering them *rakia* to bring them to their senses. Here and there someone would growl in protest at Gogo's kicks, another would stare at him with wide open, ferocious, and blood-shot eyes, and some even attempted leaping up and grabbing the handle of the fisherman's knife tucked into his sash. These terrifying movements filled Gochoolu and Dochoolu with delight. They whispered to each other:

"Dochoolu, just look at that big tough guy there in the corner, with the bandaged eye. Do you know him?"

"How could I not know him? It's Petrescu, the one who drowned his father in the swamp! I know him. God help you if you get on his wrong side. Look at the knife he's carrying! But do you know that one there, under the counter?"

"That fat one? The one bandaging the wound on his leg?"

"No, the other one, with the ripped up mouth."

"I can't remember. Well, wait, wasn't he Stupid Petse's kid, the one who robbed the church?"

"No, Stupid Petse's boy is that one there, lying beside Boncho the Bandit. That other one is Danko the Thug's grandson. Bai Ganyo sent him here to follow these good-for-nothings, to make sure the *others* don't fool them. A terrific outlaw! The night before last he actually stole a bundle of *their* ballots."

"Bravo!"

"Do you know what we've delegated him to do? As we're infiltrating the bureau, if some of theirs should arrive, that lad will grab Nikola Tŭrnova-liyata by the collar and start yelling, 'Hold him! He cursed the prince! He insulted the prince; hold him!' Then Petrescu and Danko the Thug will grab Nikola and throw him outside. The police will take him and—into the pokey. Their guys will try to rescue him, our guys will oppose them—there'll be a dustup. The police will rush in and sweep them away like chicks. It's all arranged."

"But who will take care of Lulcho and Gramatikov?"

"Do you take them for real men? Let someone like Topachoolu stare at them. They'll just evaporate."

This is the conversation Gochoolu and Dochoolu held while watching with delight the sluggish awakening of these thirty dark personages assembled from the rabble and riffraff whose task today is to terrorize, to drive away, to sow horror and fear around the polling place, and to force already timid Bulgarians to give up their right—of which they are barely aware—to exercise their free will in determining the government. This is the conversation Gochoolu and Dochoolu held while watching these thirty horrible figures, deformed, bloated, with bulging bloodshot eyes, covered with scars and scratches, with wide sashes and knives stuck in those sashes, with savagery in their faces, with criminal convulsions in their movements. They watched them and anticipated the sweetness of the electoral victory.

All of the mercenaries were already on their feet when music was heard coming from the Gypsy Quarter. Music! Shall I describe this music, which had been going all night at Topachoolu's tavern, to which even the tavern keeper himself had swayed his hips and sung, "Vangeli, she sewed a sheet, / and got down on it for the deed. / O dear God! just clap your thunder, / strike me down and take me under"?[66] Shall I describe the fiddler, asleep on his feet, with the fiddle barely supported, almost resting on his stomach? Shall I tell you about the clarinetist, who either doesn't play at all or overblows the clarinet like a madman, his face puffed up, the veins in his neck standing out, his bloodshot eyes bulging, it seeming that with just a little more pressure an epileptic seizure will amaze his listeners? No, I won't describe the music to you, because I think it suffices to tell you that these musicians were à la Bai Ganyo.

The band played the Polovtsian March. Amid the intermittent sounds, a wild, inhuman roar split the air. A whole cloud of birds took fright and left the trees and eaves of the Ragpickers' Quarter. If an army of hungry lions were facing an army of maddened tigers and at a signal these armies were let loose at one another, the roar, which would shatter the battlefield, would be similar to the wild roar that now terrified the inhabitants of the Gypsy Quarter and Ragpickers' Quarter. This was a "hurrah" from the mercenaries gathered by Danko the Thug. There they are, coming into sight over by the bend in the road and pouring into the square.

---

66. In Bulgarian this reads: "*Vangelito chevre shilo i na chevreto súgreshilo, ya gúrmi, bozhe, udari me i po-skoro priberi me.*" This is another mock tavern song.

The band is in front. Behind the musicians come the Gypsies and the porters. At their head, carried aloft, with twirled mustache and a jauntily cocked hat, who do you think? Your own Bai Ganyo Balkanski himself. Even at this festive moment Bai Ganyo didn't forget himself. He kept his hands in his pockets. "Certainly, some pickpocket will reach in there, and good-bye purse. I know the ropes, don't I?" A second "hurrah," capable of waking even the dead, assaulted the ears of Gogo's gang, which poured out of the tavern into the square and answered with a cannonade: "Long live Bai Ganyo!"

"Good morning, boys!" called the modestly beaming Bai Ganyo.

A cacophony of thirty hoarse "g'morning"s answered his greeting.

"Courage, boys; power is ours," Bai Ganyo exhorted them, in the tones of Napoleon at Austerlitz. "Listen here, you, Danko's grandson. Do you remember what I told you? When you see trouble, grab Tûrnovaliyata by the collar and yell, 'He insulted the prince!' Get it?"

Danko's grandson spoke up gleefully from the ranks. "I know."

"And then you, Danko, and you, Petrescu . . ."

"We know it upside down and backward," said Petrescu, fully conscious of the importance of his task.

"Bravo! But now listen, Petrescu. I want you to pull off one more job. When you're all fighting with the voters, you cut just two or three of them with your knife, enough to cause some confusion, toss the knife to the side, then tear the front of your shirt, and then afterward get some blood on yourself, understand? Then go and smear your face and clothes with blood, understand? Then after that, start yelling that the citizens are trying to butcher you because you shouted, 'Long live the prince.' Get it?"

"Got it. But you'll have to give me an extra five levs blood money."

Bai Ganyo reassured him. "Money is no problem; you just do what I tell you."

Those sent out on reconnaissance from the Gypsy Quarter to the voting place—the scouts Adamcho the Chickenthief, Spiro the Bloodhound, and Lame Mustafa—rushed into the square and informed Bai Ganyo that about three thousand villagers had arrived in the city by various paths and that Tûrnovaliyata's people had given them ballots. "The chief of police said to hurry, because everything's going wrong."

"God damn your chief of police!" screamed Bai Ganyo. "What the hell did we make him an official for if he can't even scare off a few peasants! Official? Horsefeathers! He only knows how to pick up village girls! Idiot! Why didn't he send the police to the outskirts? He got sloshed and forgot what he was supposed to do, the jackass. Run quickly and tell him to gather the mounted police and send them galloping through the middle of town, understand? Have them fly like a whirlwind right through the middle of town, you hear? And we'll give him a 'hurrah' from here, and then let's see which peasant is going to stand up against us. Run quickly!"

"Gogo, give us some *rakia* here," commanded Bai Ganyo. "Drink up, damn it all. I'm paying. Why have the fiddlers stopped? Play, Gypsies! Blow that clarinet, you. Why are you gaping at me like an ox? Hah, that's the way! Yee-ee-ee-ha-ah!"

"Danko, give out the ballots, a bundle to each man. Let's go now, boys. Forward! Courage! Long live His Royal Highness! Hurraaah!"

"Hurraaaah!"

And the "voters" set off!

Ivanitsa Gramatikov, the opposition candidate, woke up at six o'clock in the morning. He got dressed, drank his coffee, and went out onto the high balcony in front of the house. The sun, which had just barely risen, reflected off the cupola of the church and the eastward-facing windows. All of nature appeared to be celebrating. Actually, nature remained as disinterested as it always is, and it was just the candidate's spirit that was celebrating.

Young, educated, a bit of an idealist but really more of a dreamer, with love in his heart, faith in goodness, hope for the future, he was not yet hardened to reality, to life. Carefree to the point of arrogance, an incurable optimist, accustomed always to be looking for the silver lining, he was trusting to the point of naïveté, even of stupidity.

Some of his friends had suggested that he run for national representative. A citizens' gathering received his candidacy sympathetically, and Gramatikov thought that everything was set. He floated along on dreams of future activity in the National Assembly. Everything was coming up roses for Bulgaria. But some nagging details, some of his friends' preparations for the elections—actions unforeseen in the election law—seemed to cast shadows over his sweet daydreams from time to time. Why was it now necessary for him to set his program before the voters? Couldn't he have done without that? Why did he have to be subjected to so many awkward moments: giving answers, promising assistance on issues of concern perhaps only to the individual petitioners? It was as if he had entrusted his entire intellect to his staff of friends surrounding him! They told him that he needed to give a speech, so he gave a speech. They told him that he needed to receive the village mayors and talk to them politely, so he received the mayors and clerks in his house and spoke to them with such politeness that the peasants looked at their feet and barely understood him. They expressed their needs, and he took notes and candidly stated which could be satisfied and which could not, to the extreme dissatisfaction of the villagers, accustomed to being promised mountains of gold. He had to take part in gatherings of prominent citizens, at which campaigners were designated and then distributed among the villages and city wards. The citizens argued loudly. He sat to the side and was silent, as if it had nothing to do with him. This stupid passivity worried him. He opened his mouth to say something, to object, but one of the staff always grabbed him by the hand and told him in a patronizing, fatherly tone, "You just be quiet. Stay on the sidelines. You don't understand these things yet." And he obediently closed his mouth and listened to the solid and self-confident conversations of the respectable citizens. "Elections aren't always like this, are they?" he thinks. "Or perhaps this is something that's starting now, in this new era." He lightly taps one of the people arguing and whispers in his ear, "Excuse me, do elections always work this way?" The person, distracted by another conversation, looks at him as though through a fog and laughingly admonishes him. "Don't worry about that now. Some other time. You don't understand these things. You just stay out of it. Everything's under control."

Everything's under control! Gramatikov got used to the idea that "everything's under control." Wherever he sat, wherever he stood, whomever he met, be it merchant, craftsman, or peasant, he heard the same thing, that everything was under control; if he went into the coffeehouse, friends surrounded him and hurried to inform him of the latest reports from the town and the villages. "Oh, g'morning Mr. Ivanitsa. How are you? Everything is finally under control now." "Oh, Mr. Ivanitsa, it's all set! The whole region is in your pocket. Don't worry about a thing. Everything's already entirely under control." If he goes for an evening walk in the city park, he encounters friends on every path, and from afar they signal him with gestures meaning "It's all set." "Everything's under control."

Everything's under control! But then again, an event that he witnessed on the eve of the elections gave him to understand that there is a difference between elections as described in the election law and elections in reality. A friend reminded him of this incident in a letter, with the following words: "Law, order, freedom, our success. Do you remember, do you remember? What a joke! Remember the invasion of the Huns in the coffeehouse the evening before the elections? Remember that 'Bulgarian citizen' with the Russian hat on the back of his head, bare-chested, barefoot, with holes in the knees of his pants? Or that one with the red eyes, in shirtsleeves, bareheaded, with the big stick in his hand? Or the Vlah outside, in front of the door, in a heroic 'intoxication' of patriotism, in deep awareness of his civic rights and duties, ripe, that is, already overripe with political wisdom, who was barely able to stand on his feet; do you remember how he, with chest puffed up by the most noble and philanthropic ideas, worthy of making an entire world happy, with his tongue thickened by the pressure of the inexpressible and lofty thoughts that roiled in his brain, declaimed about freedom and the people's rights, but when an older citizen coming out of the coffeehouse yelled at him, the freedom and people's rights stuck in his throat, just as they had stuck somewhere in the noble soul of his moral comrade-in-arms and leader? And that scum, that dregs of the slime of a savage, bestial, utterly uneducated and uncultivated layer of urban society, capable of a sort of brutality that I couldn't even imagine existed in our city, which prides itself on its 'civilization' and 'Europeanness,' this unprincipled mob, led by its various ignoramuses and weaklings, who neither possess nor are capable of possessing any principles, that scum, I tell you, has its representatives in the National Assembly, while thousands of voters . . ."

And so, on Sunday, the day of the elections, at about seven o'clock in the morning, Gramatikov stood on the high balcony of his house and lightly, joyfully breathed in the morning chill. The election law, brought to life in his dreams, sketched for him in succession the various moments of a constitutional election. The town clock, proclaiming the half hour with two strokes of the gong, cut off the candidate's sweet dreams and reminded him that it was time to leave for the polling place. He got dressed and took his walking stick but then remembered that it was forbidden to enter the polling place with any sort of weapon, so he left the stick, and set off. The streets were almost empty; people had already moved toward the schoolyard. On the square in front of the church a group of friends greeted him warmly:

"Oh, Mr. Ivanitsa, good morning. Did you see them?"

"Who?"

"The voters. Just counting villagers there're three thousand. We already distributed ballots to them. Everything's taken care of. Let's go to the school now."

They wended their way through a narrow, crooked street and emerged near the polling place. Indeed, a whole mass of city folk and villagers were peacefully and quietly buzzing in the courtyard and the adjacent street. The campaigners walked back and forth among them and half openly, half secretly distributed ballots to the new arrivals. Here and there were heard people exclaiming that they hadn't voted in years.

"Well, hell, it's been eight years since I voted."[67]

"Same with me."

"Me, too."

Such confessions were heard from all sides.

The polling place was already set up in the main hall of the school. Some voters, as well as one of the opposition candidates, were hanging around. The election began. It seemed strange to Gramatikov that the courtyard next door to the school, and also the courtyards facing it across the street, were crawling with masses of heavily armed police, among whom two officers circulated, whispering some kind of instructions. "But isn't it forbidden by the election law to have an armed force next door to the polling place? Strange!"

But he didn't have to wonder long. Before Gramatikov's eyes, such a storm of horrors and violence began erupting, swirling, roaring, and thrusting that he was paralyzed, as if struck by lightning. Here's what happened: Before he could recover from the strange impression made on him by an armed force so close to the polling place, he saw Adamcho the Chickenthief run over to one of the police officers, all breathless and excited, and whisper something anxiously in his ear. The officer called a policeman, spoke a few words to him, and sent him away. A minute later, the chief of police appeared. Adamcho whispered something to him. The chief gave some orders to the officers; they ran off in all directions, and shortly thereafter, policemen began to emerge from the courtyards of neighboring houses leading horses behind them. They mounted the horses; the chief in the lead, saber drawn, gave the order "Advance!" and twenty mounted police, armed to the teeth, surged through the narrow street thronged with voters. They surged and began to use the horses to break through the wall of humanity. Screams, yells, shouts, protests, orders, sabers glittering in the sun, waves of people raging back and forth; the horses charged at random into the crowd. The living wall split to make way for them. New waves from the rear lines swept in, and the mass

---

67. From the time Stambolov assumed power in 1886 until his fall, he was the de facto dictator of Bulgaria. He ordered that only people who would vote for the government be let into the polling places during elections.

pushed the police back. But the weapons prevailed. The living wall wavered. The Turkish voters began to evaporate one by one, saying, "Why should I get myself beat up?" The villagers began to exchange looks. The police succeeded in pushing the main part of the voters some distance away.

The other, much smaller, part remained in the schoolyard. Tûrnovaliyata and Gramatikov were there. From the other side of the street the shrill sound of a clarinet began to rend the air. Fiddles were heard, and so was the rumble of an approaching crowd. Then a wild thunderclap smashed the area. There they all are: the fiddlers; behind them, with lightning flashing in his eyes, Bai Ganyo Balkanski; there's Gochoolu and Dochoolu; there's Petrescu, Danko the Thug's grandson, Spiro the Bloodhound, Lame Mustafa; there are the Gypsies, the fishermen; and there's Danko the Thug himself.

"Long live the respected government, hurrah!" cried Danko's grandson in a high-pitched voice.

"Hurrah-rah-raaaah!" roared the fearsome hundred-mouthed crowd.

Gramatikov began to tremble. The year 1876 flashed through his mind. The bashibazouk hordes were resurrected before him. The name of Fazli Pasha froze on his lips.[68]

The wild horde of drunken monsters poured into the school courtyard. My God! What crudeness, what arrogance, what mindless ferocity in those bulging, bloodshot eyes, in those bullying gestures, in those aggressive looks! Bai Ganyo, accompanied by his retinue, who forced a path for him, went up the stairs and pushed his way into the main hall of the school, near the polling place. Through the windows came a noise, a hollow growl, and propelled by the onrushing wave, Nikola Tûrnovaliyata appeared on the steps. Danko's grandson immediately swooped down on him like a bird of prey, grabbing him by the collar, and began bawling in a hoarse voice, "Hold him! He cursed the prince. He insulted the prince. Hold him!" Petrescu and Danko the Thug didn't hesitate. The two of them set upon him like wolves, grabbed him by the arms, and dragged him down the stairs. Bai Ganyo pushed his way into the hall, took a note from the chairman of the election board, and gave it to Danko's grandson, who squeezed through the crowd

---

68. Bashibazouks were Ottoman paramilitaries noted for their ferocity. At the time of the April Uprising of 1876, Aleko was a high school student in Gabrovo. The high school teachers were arrested and sent to Tûrnovo, and on 11 May, the feast day of Saint Cyril and Saint Methodius (see 42n20), Fazli Pasha and his army suddenly occupied the school. The school wardens managed to spirit the students away to private houses and then, secretly and at great risk, the students escaped to their homes.

and pushed into the courtyard next door, and a minute later, when the foot and mounted police burst into the courtyard, they found Bai Ganyo's army pressed into a corner by the indignant voters who had remained in the courtyard. Petrescu, with bleeding chest and blood smeared on his hands and face, howled like the most innocent of babies. He had already jostled two or three voters and succeeded in carrying out the plan in good time— getting himself all bloody, climbing onto a heap of stones, and screaming at the top of his lungs for help. "They're killing me, Mr. Chief of Police! They were going to kill me. I said, 'Long live the prince,' and they went after me with knives!"

The police began its part. "Sabers out!" They unsheathed their sabers and began wielding their whips. Protests were heard. Curses silenced them. The police, assisted by Bai Ganyo's army, carried off Nikola Tûrnovaliyata and carried off his more prominent comrades; the mounted police flew into a rage and swept the courtyard bare.

Even Gramatikov, dragged along by the current of the crowd, found himself out on the street. He was stunned, as if struck by lightning! In his ears rang the words of Bai Ganyo, who shouted from the top of the stairs, "We've been around Europe a bit, too, and we know about these damned things, these elections. I've been to Belgium!"[69]

The words of Grandpa Dobri also rang in his ears. Poor Grandpa Dobri! Shoved into the street, hit hard on the head, weeping from pain, or anger, or grief, he kept saying, poor fellow, in a cracked voice, "Well, Mr. Chief of Police, well, it's like this, you know, somehow, they were supposed to be free, somehow or other." Poor Grandpa Dobri![70]

Several days later, Gramatikov read the following dispatch in one of the capital city's newspapers:

To the Prime Minister in Sofia. The elections were carried out in absolute calm and orderliness. Elected: Ganyo Balkanski, Filio Gochoolu, and Tanas Dochoolu, all ours. The opposition candidates went down in disgraceful defeat. As soon as the voters appeared, with musicians in the lead, their gang fled in disorder. The whole city is celebrating. Long live His Royal Highness.

GANYO BALKANSKI.

---

69. In his speech before the throne on 24 October 1894, Prime Minister Stoilov made frequent reference to Bulgaria's being the Belgium of the Balkans. See 15n2.

70. The adjective *dobri* means "good" in Bulgarian.

The letter to Gramatikov of which we spoke earlier closed with these words: "But what will the people say; what will they do? A curious question! You told me once that you still believe in the Bulgarian people. Come now! Don't fool yourself! What do you believe in? In a servile tribe that puts up with all this? Behold it, reflected in its representatives!

"The people you believe in are slaves, I tell you. *Slaves.* Slavery is a blessing for them, tyranny is a boon; servility is heroism; a contemptuous curse from above is music! And yet this nation is wretched and unlucky, thrice unlucky. Beaten down by fate, condemned to suffer and to depend on others, tormented by enemies, and even more so by friends and saviors, it has no fixed point to rest its gaze on, nothing to hang onto. It has lost faith in itself and in its fate and has become too 'practical' and sober, sober to the point of unconsciousness. Look at it—without aid, without counsel, shattered and torn apart inside and out, a pitiful, storm-tossed remnant of the past.

"Is there anyone to revive it, to pull it forward? Ideals?—Vanity! Wind!"

12

Bai Ganyo the Journalist

The orchestra was playing the Romanian melody "Doina."[71] Or more precisely, the one playing was our Annie on solo flute; the rest were just chiming in. We listened from the inner salon. But, you will ask, who is this "we" you're talking about? Who? Everyone knows who: the senator, Othello, Stuvencho, and me. A tall bottle of white Chateau Sandrovo stood before us, and next to it another of Giesshübler. We were lolling around a table, cigarettes in our mouths, catching the musical flourishes of "Doina," and we had surrendered ourselves to a pleasant *far niente*, the business of doing nothing. The next day was Sunday. We didn't have to work, and we could stay out a bit later. The music was decent, the *fräuleins* were pretty; we were confirmed bachelors. Perfect!

So there we were, when all of a sudden, the flute went off key, and at the same instant, the whole orchestra fell out of tune. Just then, Stuvencho laughed out loud and said, "That damned Othello! He's such a joker! Just look at him!" The senator and I immediately turned around, and what do you think we saw? That devil Othello! I don't know how he comes up with those pranks of his! He had stolen away without any of us noticing, asked the waiter for a lemon wedge, and, catching the eye of the flute player, without the others noticing, started nibbling the lemon right in front of her.

---

71. This chapter first appeared when *Bai Ganyo* was published as a book in 1895. The remaining chapters were not part of the original edition, and all but two of them appeared in the periodical *Zname* (Banner) as inserts (see the preface for details). As noted in the preface, all the stories featuring Bai Ganyo were only gathered together for the first time in Chipev's 1929 edition of Aleko's work. The dates that appear at the end of chapters 15–18 are the dates that Aleko completed the stories, which differ from the dates of publication listed in the preface.

She was a young girl, impressionable, so naturally, her mouth watered, and her lips puckered up in anticipation of that tart lemon juice. Well, just try to play the flute under such circumstances. We laughed till tears rolled down our cheeks.

The music stopped. From the street we heard a kid shouting, "Hot off the press! Get the la-test news-pa-per! Get the *National Grand-eu-eur!*" Huh, what's that? The *National Grandeur?* They've got to be kidding! Still infected with laughter from the lemon joke, we all started laughing again. Just then Gedros arrived.

"Hey, Gedros, how's it going? Sit down! Want some wine?"

"Ah, Othello, my good man. Why are you crying? Here, wipe your little nose," teased the ever-cheerful Gedros.

"Gedros, what's that newspaper, the one they're shouting about on the street?"

"What? You mean you don't know about Bai Ganyo Balkanski's paper?"

"You're pulling my leg!"

"No, I'm serious! Ganyo Balkanski is the editor in chief and owner of the newspaper the *National Grandeur.* Aaah, it's quite a story. You really don't know anything about it?"

"Come on, do you really mean it?"

"Indeed I do! Just wait till I tell you all about it. I got the whole story today in great detail, and I'll tell it to you as if I had been there myself."

We had them close the door to the inner salon, and Gedros began. This is what he told us.

A meeting was set up at Bai Ganyo's. Those present were the master of the house himself, Gochoolu, Dochoolu, and Danko the Thug. They put their heads together and began to mull over what kind of business they should set up in order to make the most of the current situation.

"We need to get in on the action, too," said Bai Ganyo. "Patriotism without payoff is for the birds. Now tell me, given how things stand these days, how can we get on the gravy train? What do you say, Gochoolu?"

"Who, me? To tell you the truth, Bai Ganyo, I still haven't changed my mind. We should open a Russian *traktir*—a little Russian restaurant."

"We should what?!"

"I'm telling you, we should open a Russian *traktir*," insisted Gochoolu.

"What's the matter with you? Are you running to Mother Russia again?" asked Bai Ganyo in amazement.

"Let's get one thing straight here. This whole business isn't about Mother Russia; it's about which way the wind is blowing."

"Blowing where? In your head?"

"In Bulgaria. Only a fool would miss this chance. Now is the time. A Russian *traktir*.[72] I've been around Moscow. I know what I'm talking about. A *traktir* with two dining halls: one for the noblemen, the other for the *muzhiks*—for the peasants, that is."

"Where are you going to find any *muzhiks* here?" asked Bai Ganyo in amazement.

"We're not exactly all noblemen here, Bai Ganyo, are we?"

"Well, OK, and then what?"

"Then, we'll need some music, a barrel organ perhaps? Surely, you've seen those, haven't you, Bai Ganyo?"

"If I haven't, who has?" replied Mr. Balkanski haughtily.

"Right. We'll have an organ and, of course, tea. We'll round up about ten young kids, make sure they're blond, so they'll look like Russians. We'll dress 'em up in some boots and red shirts, we'll give 'em each a Cossack haircut, and there you go, a real *traktir*! We'll bring in some Russian newspapers, vodka, *zakuski*, you know, appetizers, and out front there'll be a sign saying "*Russkiy Traktir*." And then we're on easy street. What do you think?"

"I don't approve," Dochoolu announced majestically. "I don't approve. If the plan is to take advantage of which way the wind is blowing, then the best thing would be to open a *kvass* factory."

"Now, that's a great way to make money. So you want to open a bakery?" said Danko the Thug, laughing.

"No, no, I mean Russian *kvass*, the drink, not Bulgarian *kvas*."[73] It's that weak fermented stuff like beer, like our *boza*."

"Oh, terrific. So now we're going to become *boza* peddlers!" The Thug was insulted.

"No, my friend. The hook isn't the drink itself. It's the name! All you have to say is 'Russian *kvass*' and people will be stampeding to try it. Haven't

---

72. Bai Ganyo is reflecting the ambivalence of the new government concerning relations with Russia. The government did not want to rush into a reconciliation, which would not only acknowledge that the previous policy had been mistaken but would also strengthen the position of its primary Russophile opponents, Petko Karavelov and Dragan Tsankov, leaders of two wings of the Liberal Party.

73. In Bulgarian, *kvas* means "yeast."

you heard what the French are up to these days? They've made a killing on it, no joke!"[74]

"That's nonsense. I don't want this *kvass* stuff," stated Danko unhappily.

"What do you want us to do?" Dochoolu asked angrily. "Tell us what you have in mind!"

"We should open a bank!" blurted out Danko the Thug.

"You're an idiot!"

"Why?"

"Quit your arguing," Bai Ganyo cut in.

"Why am I an idiot?" continued Danko angrily, shooting a bloodthirsty glance at Dochoolu.

"Be quiet now and sit down. Tell us what you have to say about the bank."

"Yeah, well, first make him tell me why I'm an idiot."

"He wants to open a bank! That's not just gravy that you can slurp up!" muttered Dochoolu under his breath, upset by Danko's glower and menacing tone. "So a bank is gravy, is it?"

"Of course it's gravy," roared Danko the Thug.

"What do you mean, gravy? Where do you get gravy from?" snarled Dochoolu.

"Shut up, all of you. We didn't come here for this!" Bai Ganyo tried to smooth their ruffled feathers. "Dochoolu, sit down."

"But where does he get gravy from?"

So one word led to another, and it seemed the whole thing was getting out of control. As you know, Danko the Thug is always spoiling for a fight, and Dochoolu wasn't taking any of his guff. They would have come to blows, but Bai Ganyo, conceding a little to one and then a little to the other, finally managed to calm them down.

So Danko sits down and begins to lay out his plan for founding a bank. "It's a piece of cake. We'll sell five or ten million levs' worth of shares, we'll get the cash, and we'll start passing out loans right and left, at a good interest rate, of course. We'll lend to merchants and to municipalities, and if the government finds itself in a tight spot, we'll give a million or so to it, too. And there you have it! We'll have the statutes drawn up so that one-half of the profit would be for us, the other half for the shareholders. What's

---

74. A Russo-French agreement signed in 1891 was strengthened with a new agreement in 1893, which greatly improved Franco-Russian economic relations.

more, we'll keep some shares for ourselves, whether we invest any money in it or not. Bai Ganyo, you're an influential man. Just knock on a couple of doors, and it's all set!"

"Don't bite off more than you can chew! There are people who are better at this sort of thing than you are. Let them start up the business, and then we'll skim some off the top," said Bai Ganyo didactically.

Gochoolu and Dochoolu nodded their heads in agreement.

"Hold on, now, and I'll tell you what I've come up with," exclaimed Bai Ganyo with authority, standing up. "You know what? We're not going to make it with a *traktir*, nor are we going to get anything going with a bank, and as for your Russian *kvass*, Dochoolu, that's just plain nonsense. So shall I tell you what I've got in mind, huh?"

Gochoolu, Dochoolu, and the Thug were all ears and impatience.

"So, should I tell you, huh?"

"Well, tell us already. Stop torturing us," said Danko irritably.

"Sh sh! Don't rush me! Haste makes waste. Should I tell you? Well? GENTLEMEN! WE WILL PUBLISH A NEWSPAPER!" announced Bai Ganyo, his face glowing with triumph.

If at that moment a sea monster had slithered into the room where they were sitting, it could scarcely have produced a greater effect than Bai Ganyo's last words. At first, they were dumbstruck; then, a moment later, Gochoolu, Dochoolu, and Danko the Thug began exchanging furtive glances, as if to say, has he, God forbid, gone off the deep end? It wouldn't do to laugh or to pity him. He'd explode. Finally, Gochoolu, hesitant though he was, decided to test the waters in a roundabout way:

"Bai Ganyo, every now and again, Your Honor likes to, heh-heh-heh, forgive me, what I mean is, you like to, um, you like to have your little joke, that is to say, heh-heh."

"What!?"

"Uh, well, no, Bai Ganyo, I just said this to . . . It's just, Your Honor, some sort of a newspaper? Are you serious?"

"What do you mean, 'are you serious'? What else would I be? Of course I'm serious. Is it a big deal to publish a paper? You just spit on your scruples (if you have any) and then start slandering right and left. That's all there is to it."

"If that's all there is, then I agree to it," said Danko the Thug.

"OK, then, it's settled! We'll call Gunyo the Lawyer. He's a master of editorials, and as for us, one of us will do the news reports, another the columns, and someone else the dispatches. The whole point is to smear anyone and everyone, and you don't need a degree for that sort of thing. Danko, head down to the office and get Gunyo the Lawyer."

"See that rascal?" said Bai Ganyo after Danko the Thug had left. "When it comes to slander, he's your man. He always goes for the jugular. He can tear some poor son of a gun to shreds and not give a hoot whether it's true or false. He's a real bum!"

One couldn't say that Gochoolu and Dochoolu were enamored of these particular qualities in Danko the Thug, nor could it be said that Danko seemed to them a suitable editor, for all they knew about journalism. They still recalled another era, and even the Ottoman days, when the press could really stir things up, but it had never spewed such an eruption of infernal insults and curses. However, the storm of wild passions that raged during the intervening years, the demoralizing influence of the demoralized press, the raw all-consuming materialism, the possibility of getting rich quick if you were willing to put your conscience to sleep, the example of the ruling elites—all these phenomena had buried their nobler feelings under such a thick layer of muck that only a new era, qualitatively different from the previous one, and as long lasting, could do away with the alluvial layers of vileness and unearth those pure feelings, like relics of past greatness.

And now, when Bai Ganyo laid out for them his plan for the newspaper—its orientation and those who would take part—Gochoolu and Dochoolu sensed a vague unease stirring in the deep recesses of their hearts. They felt that there was something amiss in this business, that there was something here that should not be. And yet, on top of the heavy sediments that covered their nobler feelings, Bai Ganyo added a new layer, which smothered them completely. He eloquently laid out for them, with passion and convincing enthusiasm, the material advantages that would accrue to them from the enterprise. Gochoolu and Dochoolu needed no further persuasion.

The door opened, and there, on the threshold, appeared the sharp foxy muzzle of Gunyo the Lawyer; behind him came Danko the Thug.

"Well then, Gunyo, what do you say?" Bai Ganyo addressed him amiably. "We want to publish a newspaper. What do you think?"

"Why not? Let's do it. Is there some sweetener in it?" asked Gunyo with a wink, rubbing his fingers together suggestively.

"Don't you worry about that!"

"Well, is there?"

"There is, there is! I told you not to worry about that."

"Fine. What sort of paper should we put out? One for the government or for the opposition? Hurry up! My clients are waiting for me."

"Ah, there's the rub! Should we be for the government or for the opposition? Drat it all, we don't know how long these guys will stay in power."

"Well, what do you say? My clients are waiting."

"You know what we'll do," put in Bai Ganyo, without paying any attention to the Lawyer's remarks. "I think for the time being we should run with the government."

"That's right. That's the way. It would be best to go with the government," Gochoolu and Dochoolu hastened to add.

Bai Ganyo looked at them angrily for interrupting and then continued. "And later on, when we get wind that they're on shaky ground, we'll give them a shove and go with the new government. What do you think?"

"Sounds good. Did they promise you anything?"

"Of course. It wouldn't be possible otherwise."

"Since that's the case, let's begin," declared Gunyo the Lawyer. Thus began a discussion of how they would publish the paper and what sort of position their paper would take on certain issues. They decided to take into account the times and the circumstances, and of course, also, "God willing," the windfall. "As for Russia," Gunyo said, "sometimes we'll bring up 'our brothers and liberators, the fraternal Russian people' and 'Long live our Liberator, the Russian Czar, God rest his soul!' But on the other hand, if need be, we'll drag out the old 'Transdanubian Province' thing. As for Macedonia, we'll keep quiet. Y'know, that issue isn't going anywhere. Time isn't helping. Austria is this way and that. The Triple Alliance—somehow it just doesn't add up."[75]

"What about the youth? What are we going to do about the younger generation?" added Gochoolu. "They've also begun to stir up trouble."

"We'll pull the wool over their eyes. What else can you do with a bunch of young troublemakers? Once in a while, we'll tip our hat to them. It's come to that; there's nothing else to be done," said Bai Ganyo with a sigh.

"There's nothing else to be done, eh?" growled Danko the Thug, and his expression darkened. "If I had a club, just let me at 'em."

"Take it easy now, Danko . . ."

---

75. The Triple Alliance was a coalition of Germany, Italy, and Austria-Hungary dedicated to maintaining the status quo in the Balkans. First signed in 1882, the treaty that established the alliance was renewed four times between 1887 and 1902. On the Macedonian question, see 138n85.

"I'd smash 'em to p-p-pieces."

"Come on now, just forget about them. Sit down and relax. There's time."

"Could we hurry up and get down to business, Bai Ganyo? My clients are waiting for me," cut in Gunyo the Lawyer impatiently.

"Listen, Gunyo, don't start in again with your damned clients! You know what? Sit down tonight and write an editorial. Draw up such a loyalty statement to our sovereign that the prince himself will be amazed. Put in 'your obedient children,' 'our Sire and Father,' 'in the dust at Your august feet' . . . String them together like rosary beads. You know how to do it! Put in a word or two about the Bulgarian people, as always; you get what I mean? That's it. And then, smear the opposition. Say, 'Those traitors, those . . .'"

Gunyo corrected him. "'Traitors' is already old hat. Let's put in abominations.'"

"Oh, that's good! Put down 'abominations.' And don't forget to add that they're catastrophic for the Bulgarian nation. Damn, I love the word 'catastrophic.' When I say it like that, 'c-c-c-catastrophic,' it's like I'm c-c-catching someone by the throat. I really, really like it."[76]

"As for me, what I like best of all is raking someone over the coals," Danko the Thug cut in candidly. "It does me good."

"Bravo, Thug, that's the spirit!" shouted Bai Ganyo with delight, slapping Danko on the shoulder. "This job is a done deal, then. Gunyo, you'll write what I told you, the editorial, OK? And as for you, Gochoolu, and you, Dochoolu, you two will cook up some news reports and some dispatches."

"What sort of reports and dispatches?" the two of them asked in confusion.

"What do you mean, 'what sort'? All sorts! Haven't you seen the other papers? Put down something like 'Your Royal Highness, the people rejoice on bended knee and pray to the Almighty in unison,' and so on. Put down whatever pops into your head. Put in 'The Bulgarian nation has proved a thousand times that when its rights are threatened, everyone to a man will rise up and whatever, with tears in their eyes,' and so forth. After all, you don't really have to go into so much detail. Curse the opposition for all they're worth—they can't do a thing about it—and your day's work is done.

---

76. In the original Bulgarian the words are *fatalen* (fatal, catastrophic) and *fashtam* (grab, catch). The adjective *fatalen* was a favorite epithet of the Stambolovite press, which Aleko is mocking in this vignette (as elsewhere). It was applied to the politician Petko Karavelov and to Metropolitan Kliment (see 105n62), among others.

No point in philosophizing and all that drivel. Who'll know what you're talking about anyway? After all, the whole idea is to pull the wool over their eyes, and then we're off and running. That's the idea, isn't it?"

"Then it's settled. I'm going. My clients are waiting," muttered Gunyo the Lawyer as he picked up his hat.

"The hell they are. Well, never mind. Off you go. Good-bye. But listen, Gunyo, I want that editorial ready first thing tomorrow morning. So long!"

Gunyo headed to the door. Behind him Gochoolu and Dochoolu got up, and Bai Ganyo gave them the necessary instructions.

"Wait, gentlemen! We forgot the most important thing," Bai Ganyo called after them. "What shall we call our paper?"

"That's right. Tell us, Bai Ganyo. What were we thinking?" responded both Dochoolu and Gochoolu.

"This is a very serious matter," said Gunyo the Lawyer. "And do you know why it's so serious? It's because those other papers, damn them, have already taken all the good names. They haven't left anything for us. But we'll come up with something. I think it would be best to call our paper *Justice*, and then we'll add in parentheses 'fin du siècle.'"

"Huh?"

"That's a French expression. You don't know it."

"We don't want any French. Put in something in Latin, if you can. It's customary."

"How about *'tempora mutantur'* . . . ?"[77]

"Put it in if it's to the point. You, Gochoolu, what do you think?" Bai Ganyo turned to him.

"'Justice' is a beautiful word, but it seems to me that *Words of Wisdom* would be even better," answered Gochoolu.

"I don't agree," said Dochoolu. "That name sounds too preachy. I think it would be better to name it *Bulgarian Pride*."

"What about you, Thug? What's your view?"

"Who, me? What do I know? Why not go with the *Courage of the Nation* and then come what may. We'll put down Yellow-Boot Mehmed Aga as the editor in chief."[78]

---

77. *"Tempora mutantur et nos mutamur in illis"*: "The times are changing and we are changing with them."

78. The editor in chief was the one sent to prison if a newspaper got into trouble, and so it was common practice to use fictitious names. Here they have made up a name left over from Turkish times.

"This is all nonsense. Should I tell you what we'll do?" announced Bai Ganyo with authority. "We're going to name our paper either *Bulgaria for Us* or the *National Grandeur*. Choose between them."[79]

"The *National Grandeur*. It's agreed. *National Grandeur*! That's it!"

"All right, then! Good-bye now, Bai Ganyo."

"Good-bye."

Gochoolu, Dochoolu, and Gunyo the Lawyer left.

"Hey, Danko, stay here. You and I will write the columns."

"Good. Order some *mastika* and snacks, and then let's get to work. But tell 'em not to bring any of that pickled okra again. Get 'em to bring something fit for human consumption. We're publishing a newspaper here, and that's no joking matter!"

The *mastika* and snacks arrived. Ah, but now Bai Manolcho will ask, what sort of snacks? It doesn't matter. What matters is that Bai Ganyo and Danko the Thug got down to the task of shaping public opinion.

"You know, Danko, our neighbor is really putting on airs. He says he's so educated, he says he's so honest and other nonsense . . . Shall we take him down a notch or two?"

"A notch or two? We'll take him right down to the ground," says the slander specialist.

And so the writing commences . . . "We have learned that . . . ," Bai Ganyo writes, and across that white sheet of paper his pen leaves a trail of black calumny against his neighbor, allegations that he had never "learned" about, nor even dreamed of.

Bai Ganyo writes and writes, then crosses out, constantly dissatisfied with the poison in which he's dipping his arrows. "Thief" is too tender a word for him, so he crosses it out and writes "robber," but this word has become too routine, so Bai Ganyo adds "highway" before it and combines that with "murderous." The neighbor, his wife, his children, his ancestors— Bai Ganyo's pen turns them all into phenomenal monsters. He reads his work to Danko the Thug. Danko, with eyes glistening from the *mastika*, eggs on this master of the column with his enthusiasm.

"Go, go, go! Blast him, damn it all! Don't let up! Don't let anything stop you! Go get him," thunders Danko the Thug, as if he were commanding an artillery assault.

---

79. Aleko is mocking the "patriotic societies" and committees called Bulgaria for Itself founded in Bulgaria under Stambolov. The implication is that the Stambolovites are out to grab all they can for themselves.

"And that, gentlemen, sums up the story of how Bai Ganyo founded the paper," Gedros concluded.

We reopened the door to the inner salon once again. The orchestra was thundering through the wondrous march from Wagner's *Tannhäuser*.

Farewell, gentle reader! In these pages you will encounter some cynical turns of phrase and cynical occurrences. I couldn't avoid them. If you can portray Bai Ganyo without cynicism, be my guest!

Farewell to you, too, Bai Ganyo! As God is my witness, in writing of your exploits I was always driven by good intentions. Neither cruel reproach, nor contempt, nor flippant derision has ruled my pen. I, too, am a child of my time, and perhaps certain specific events have clouded my strict objectivity, but I have endeavored to reproduce the essence of this sad reality. Your brethren, I believe, are not molded from the same clay as you are, Bai Ganyo. But they remain in the background for now, in the shadows. Only now are they barely beginning to show signs of their existence. But you, you're very much in evidence. Your spirit hovers around and adversely affects every aspect of our society. It leaves its imprint on politics, on the parties, and on the press. I firmly believe that there will come a day when, after reading this little book, you will stop and reflect. You'll sigh and say, "We are Europeans, but still not quite."

Farewell! I wouldn't be surprised were we to meet again.

SOFIA, 17 MARCH 1895

13

Bai Ganyo at the Palace

*"What a shame! You should've been at the palace
for the breaking of the fast to get some material."*

"Hey, there, Bai Ganyo! Happy Easter! Were you at the palace for the break-ing of the fast?"

"Who, me? Are you kidding? If I didn't go, who would?" said Bai Ganyo, twisting the left end of his mustache and casting a sly glance in my direc-tion as if to say, "As long as there are suckers, is Bai Ganyo going to pass up a free lunch?"

"So, how was it? Did you have a good time?"

"Who cares about a good time? What a feast! I got as smashed as a, as a whatchamacallit. Y'know how it is, Holy Week. I fasted and fasted. I got bloated on those damned beans, and then sauerkraut juice on top of that. I became as hungry as a tapeworm. On Saturday I didn't put so much as a crumb in my mouth. And they went and put the breaking of the fast at two in the morning. While I was standing there in church, I felt as if three hundred leeches were sucking on my stomach. You spit and spit and there's no saliva left. You say to yourself you'll light up a cigarette—no good, you get a bitter taste in your mouth. At midnight they said, 'Christ is risen.' How are you going to wait till two in the morning? I told my family to go break the fast on their own, and I went to the Red Crab. The place, my dear friend, was full of people like me: top hats, epaulettes, medals. They were all wait-ing for the clock to strike two. I sit down near a long table, I look over. A bunch of young guys are breaking the fast. They had set that table up with appetizers, a suckling pig, and on top of that, good red wine from Varna. It really got your juices flowing. Just looking at the skin of that piglet I almost lost my mind. What can I say? I could have asked those guys, 'Hey, what are you eating there? Is that a suckling pig? Bravo! So, blah, blah, blah, a little of the skin . . .', and those folks would have given me some. But there you are.

I've been shy since I was a little boy. (Hey, pass your tobacco tin over here. You smoke good tobacco. Ivan's is lousy. It smells like cheap Russian stuff!) Those young guys were smacking their lips. I couldn't stand looking at them, so I looked the other way. I said to myself, 'I'll spit,' but how can you spit when there's nothing to spit? It was as if my guts were glued together. I thought of ordering a beer, but I decided to pass it up. After all, is that why I starved myself, so to speak, for these past two days? So I turned away so as not to see those guys, but as if on purpose, they kept chomping away and praising the suckling pig, damn them! You know, I felt like getting up and grabbing that damned pig right out of their mouths. If I could have, I would've bent over to press on my stomach. I don't remember ever being so hungry. But I couldn't bend over because my evening coat was too tight. It would've split down the middle. Devil take the damned thing. And the collar was starched so stiff that it cut into my neck like a saw blade. Everything grew dark before my eyes. I left the Crab and headed toward the palace. It's no good to go in early. I have a friend who's a guard, and he's a good friend; in fact, if you ask, he's even something of a relative, but there was no way to put a fix in. And even if you do go in early, they're not going to lead you straight to the table. I walked round and round by the gates till my legs were sore. Then all at once, cloppity-clop, a carriage! After a little while, cloppity-clop, another carriage. They entered the courtyard, thank God! I twisted my mustache, coughed a bit, and followed them. I go inside, look around, guards all over the place, the escort is already set up. A clean-shaven lad swooped down on me to take my overcoat. I murmured to him, 'Excuse me, sir, mind your own business,' and didn't let him take it. He got embarrassed and went to take someone else's coat. Why on earth would I let him take my coat, eh pal? The cuffs on my coat—or rather not the cuffs but the linings inside—were in shreds like a, like a thingamajig. Never mind. I went upstairs, but before I did I glanced at the lower rooms. The tables were groaning, that's for sure. People had collected all around. We waited there a bit, and out came the prince and the princess. This time, they were a proper Christian host and hostess.[80] They gave each of us an egg."

"And did you kiss their hands again?"[81]

---

80. Prince Ferdinand and his consort were neither Bulgarian nor Eastern Orthodox (the dominant Christian denomination in Bulgaria), so following Orthodox custom was an important public relations move. At the same time, Aleko is satirizing Bai Ganyo's lack of awareness of any other kind of Christianity. Ferdinand was born in Vienna and

"Yes, of course. Hey, for a feast like that I'd kiss a hundred hands. Never mind. So we got through that ordeal, and then how we rushed down those stairs, my friend. Believe it or not, I took the stairs three at a time and almost crashed into the mirror, but I didn't let anyone get in front of me. I got a hold of the caviar, and boy, how I dug my spoon in. If I got less than half a kilo, then shame on me. And that fish mayonnaise of theirs and those hors d'oeuvres, I don't know what they were called, but how my mouth opened wide. Oh man! I ate and ate. I really stuffed myself. I'm still amazed that my stomach didn't burst. And the drinking! When I left . . . How did I leave? Slit my throat, but I don't remember. Oooff! My head still aches from that damned champagne. But never mind that, I went and stuffed my pockets with pastries, and they were soft, damn it, and what a mushy mess they made all over my pockets . . . Oh well, so long."

"So long, Bai Ganyo."

SOFIA, 5 APRIL 1895
ALEKO KONSTANTINOV

---

was Prince of Saxe-Coburg-Gotha, and his wife was Princess of Bourbon-Parma; they were both Catholic. Ferdinand was proclaimed prince regent of Bulgaria in 1887, after the abdication of Prince Alexander in 1886, and he married in 1893.

81. Kissing the hand of one's elders and/or superiors was an old-fashioned custom that Ferdinand encouraged and that Aleko disapproved of as humiliating.

14

Bai Ganyo in the Delegation

Oh, come on now![82] Couldn't it have been done without him? I mean, wasn't it quite sufficient for the official delegates to do the job themselves? But no, Bai Ganyo had to stick his nose in. As if those guys, the officials, weren't in a position to show the world what it means to be a Bulgarian and what Bulgarian patriotism is all about. Weren't there enough characters like the personage with the "imposing Russian beard" or then again the one who "resembles a Frenchman and speaks French very glibly and smoothly" or finally the "well-known Bulgarian diplomat?"[83] In fact, if you ask me, just the last one alone was enough for the Russians. The person whom the Russian press calls a "Bulgarian diplomat" is in fact a Plovdiv soap maker. Now that's a progressive nation! If Bulgarian soap makers pass for diplomats in Russia, imagine what will happen if a real Bulgarian diplomat appears in Mother Russia, eh? No matter how modest you are, you can't help being proud. Indeed, justice requires you to admit that even the French resemble us a bit. Their Félix Faure went from being a leather maker to president of the republic. And the Romans, too, have a similar case. Do you remember Cincinnatus? But we'll surpass both of them. Just try, for example, standing blindfolded in

82. In 1895, after the death of Czar Alexander III, who was ruler during the Russo-Turkish war and regarded as the liberator of Bulgaria, Prince Ferdinand of Bulgaria decided it was time to restore diplomatic relations with Russia, which had been broken off nine years before owing to Russian interference in Bulgarian internal affairs. A delegation was sent with a golden wreath to lay on the grave of Alexander III. The delegation was received by Czar Nicholas II. Relations between Bulgaria and Russia were officially restored with the conversion of Ferdinand's infant son and heir apparent to the Eastern Orthodox Church on 2 February 1896.

83. In Aleko's original, these descriptions were taken from Russian newspapers and left in Russian. The bearded one is Dimitûr Mollov, the Francophone is probably Pantelei Minchevich, and the Bulgarian diplomat is Ivan S. Geshev, a merchant from Plovdiv.

the middle of the marketplace. I assure you that the first Bulgarian you grab and ask, "Do you want to become prince of Bulgaria?" will answer in the affirmative without a moment's hesitation; perhaps he will just add the condition that the gifts and bribes that he gives out should not come out of his salary but from the treasury.

But we're talking about Bai Ganyo here. And, as I said, couldn't it have happened without him? Why did he have to go and represent the Bulgarian people, too? Surely, you will say that he's not an official delegate. It makes no difference. As soon as the correspondents from important newspapers go to interview him, and his words, like oracular prophesies, are spread all over the world by the press, just try to prove afterward that the Bulgarian nation speaketh not through the mouth of Bai Ganyo.

But I'm an incurable optimist. I think that fate insinuated Bai Ganyo into this mission precisely so that the delegation would preserve its genuine Bulgarian national character. Because say what you will, "large Russian beard, Frenchie, diplomat" don't sound Bulgarian. And from the following interview everyone will see that Bai Ganyo held high the banner of Bulgarian patriotism with aplomb. (There is no need for us to mention the fact that the first gentleman dressed in a frock coat that entered Bai Ganyo's room and to whom Bai Ganyo managed to pour out his brotherly feelings was not a correspondent but a waiter from the hotel. A small misunderstanding, but what are you going to do? His breast was roiling with sincere feelings, his eyes were dim with emotional tears—a natural mistake.)

A Russian correspondent enters. I don't know whether Bai Ganyo had prepared a sliced onion or not, but I can definitely confirm that his eyes were full of tears.

"Hey there, hello, dear brother, hello! Nine years, dear brother, nine! Not one day, not two; nine years!" And Bai Ganyo began to cry.

Anyone would have thought, quite naturally, that a fraternal reunion after a long and sad separation had filled Bai Ganyo's breast to overflowing with tender sentiments, and the flood of these feelings was pouring out in the form of emotional tears; but imagine the amazement of the correspondent when he saw the face of his interlocutor clear all of a sudden and heard from his lips the following words, pronounced furtively, with a wink:

"So, do you know what kind of wreath we had made up? Hoo boy—the real thing! Not that nickel silver stuff, but pure gold.[84] Do you have any idea

84. Bulgarian émigrés in the Russian Empire laid silver wreaths on the czar's grave, but Bulgaria sent their delegation with a golden one. Nickel silver (in Bulgarian, *bakûr*

how much it costs? What do you think, dear brother? If the Russians brought me, for example, as it were, such a wreath, I'd kiss their feet. What do you say? It's no joke. Gold! And pure gold at that, not some kind of . . ."

"Well, some sort of Macedonian movement has begun in your country," said the correspondent, changing the subject. "Do you consider this movement to be timely?"[85]

"A movement? What movement?!" said Bai Ganyo in surprise, as if he were hearing of such a thing for the first time. "Don't you worry about it. There's no movement whatsoever. A sleazy business! Hooligans! As if now were the time for an uprising! And what is it those bums want, anyway? I can't understand it. Do you know what, Your Grace? I don't know if you know; there was a proclamation by the Sultan in 1870 about six bishops for Macedonia. They've appointed three, and they'll appoint three more, and then everyone will sit contentedly on their behinds. That's what they want!"[86]

---

srebro [copper silver]) is a copper-nickel-zinc alloy that shines silvery white when polished but contains no silver and is used for cheap filigree. Aleko is mocking the Bulgarian government's extravagance.

85. The Treaty of Berlin (see 57n29) set the stage for uprisings and rebellions inside the territories that remained part of Turkey. These uprisings were variously supported or thwarted by conflicting interests in neighboring states, which interests could also be internally divided. In Bulgaria, political interests were divided over the timeliness of attempting or supporting armed intervention in Macedonia. Aleko, like many Bulgarians, felt that it was Bulgaria's duty to make Macedonia a part of Bulgaria and regarded those who advocated caution ("Now-Is-Not-the-Timers"; see 140n90) as opportunists looking after private interests. In Macedonia, however, revolutionary sentiment was already divided between those favoring union with Bulgaria and those favoring autonomy or independence. On 29 June 1895 the Supreme Macedonian Committee, a pro-Bulgarian organization based in Sofia, sent its armed bands into Macedonia to engage Turkish troops.

86. In 1870, after decades of struggle, the Sublime Porte recognized a Bulgarian Orthodox Church, to be ruled by an Exarch (a rank between metropolitan and patriarch in the Eastern Orthodox Church hierarchy). This was a challenge to the hegemony that the Greek Orthodox Church had enjoyed in the Balkans for quite some time. Since nationality was determined by religious confession in late Ottoman Turkey (the so-called *millet* system), religious confession had potential linguistic, political, and territorial consequences as the Ottoman Empire declined and the Balkan nation-states gradually expanded. Since the church had quasi-political powers in strictly internal matters, including the ability to judge court cases in which only Orthodox Christians were involved as well as to collect fees and tithes, and since the affected bishoprics in Turkey—especially in Macedonia—had to declare for either the Exarchate or the Patriarchate, the

"But what about the Treaty of Berlin?"[87]

"Ah, forget about all that stuff. C'mon, let's talk about something else. Do you know Dragan Tsankov?"[88]

"Yes, I believe I know him quite well."

"Well"—and Bai Ganyo emphasized the question with an ambiguous wiggle of his fingers—"how does that guy seem to you?"

"I think he's a good patriot."

Bai Ganyo gave a forced laugh and shook his head. "Pa-tri-ot, you say? Oh boy, if you only knew what a piece of work he is. As if he thought for even one day about his fatherland! He's just looking to set himself and his son-in-law up nicely. He's been like that since he was little; I should know. As for patriots, we're the real patriots. Have a good look at me! You wouldn't have to pay me 200 rubles, just 150 rubles a month, and you'd see what your Bai Ganyo can do. What do you take me for, Your Grace! This isn't Abyssinia."

"Have you dined, Mr. Balkanski?"

"Why are you asking? You're not inviting me to dinner, are you? Well, I accept. After all, aren't we Slavs?"

The interview broke off.

SOFIA, 1 JULY 1895

---

stage was set for bloody struggles over loyalties and territories. Greek and Bulgarian bishops and their supporters were thus in violent conflict over who would control the Orthodox bishoprics of Macedonia.

87. Here the reference is to the reforms promised in the Treaty of Berlin, the non-fulfillment of which could justify Bulgarian intervention.

88. Tsankov was Bulgarian Prime Minister in 1880–81 and 1883–84. Aleko is mocking both the Russian press's fascination with all things Bulgarian as a consequence of the reconciliation and its uncritical reproduction of whatever the delegates (Bai Ganyo) happened to say.

15

Bai Ganyo in the Opposition? Don't You Believe It!

Mr. Editor:

A certain gentleman who knows I'm friends with the fellow who collects material about Bai Ganyo gave me the enclosed letter to deliver to that fellow. This letter is so original and so typical that it would not be remiss to publish it in your paper, the *Banner*, as an insert. How the letter fell into the hands of this gentleman is not known to me.

Sofia, 30 October 1895

A LUCKY GUY[89]

To the editor of the paper *Now Is Not the Time*:[90]

You young whelp, you, why did you slander me in the paper *Now Is Not the Time*, alleging that I was in the opposition, huh? How much sense have you got? None at all, kid. Would your Bai Ganyo be in the opposition? Or maybe you said to yourself, "Hang on. If there are fewer of us, then we'll each get a bigger share." You're not so dumb; I know you. But then again, to tell you the truth, you are dumb. Or rather, not dumb, but just a little

---

89. *Shtastlivets*, literally "lucky/happy one," was Aleko's nickname.

90. "Now Is Not the Time" was Aleko's name for the weekly magazine *Progress*, edited by Konstantin Velichkov and others. During the Stambolov regime, the journal was the organ of the United Opposition, and Velichkov worked with it even though he was in exile (see 149n102). After the fall of Stambolov, *Progress* became the organ of the Progressive-Liberal party and supported the government of Konstantin Stoilov, criticizing Dragan Tsankov and Petko Karavelov. Before the unification of Eastern Rumelia with the Principality of Bulgaria in 1885 (see 57n29), the editors campaigned on the slogan of unification for northern and southern Bulgaria. Once they were in power, however, in conformity with the Treaty of Berlin, they announced that "the time has not yet come." As a result they were dubbed "pseudounitarists" and "Now-Is-Not-the-Timers."

wet behind the ears. When it comes to these types of things, ask your big brother. Just yesterday, as it were, you dug up a tasty bone, but your big brother has already been gnawing on that same bone for nine sweet years, and he has no intention of ever letting it go. And anyway, you know, kid, to tell you the plain truth, there's enough for the both of us. Long live the Nationals![91] Back when I went to Sofia in the delegation, in order to beg that scoundrel not to resign,[92] even then, remember, in the taverns of Vrazhdebna,[93] even then I understood that there's no percentage in being in the opposition. "But why?" you will ask. Why? It's perfectly clear. You do the work, and other people get all the goodies. And what kind of people? The cream of the crop! They're all educated, talented. Our predecessors were a totally savage bunch. They stole right before your very eyes, by force, like rank amateurs. They even indulged in debauchery; they sullied the honor of women, of girls, of . . . Well, kid, isn't that so, huh? And finally, they landed in the trap with both feet. You see, our folks today aren't like that. There's no one up for debauchery. That is, how can I put this? It's not that there isn't anyone up for it, but who's going to follow them up one Plovdiv hill and down another[94] or make the circuit of the Turkish baths and ask what's up? They know a trick or two, how money changes hands, and that's the truth! And they've got things arranged so that whether it's embarrassing or not—I have to admit it, my friend—I'm awestruck. Nice work, sons of bitches! Now that's education for you! You can do business with people like that—I know what it's like. Those who preceded us had gone berserk. They were shooting and hanging and beating and maiming the populace right and left. And for what? For nothing. And today, do you see? It's only at election time that they clamp down and won't let you budge. Otherwise, you're free to do whatever you like! Shout, curse, sling as much mud as you want—no one says anything to you. And why should they bother with the opposition? Let 'em make a stink; who cares? *Our people* that are now at the top can just sit back twirling their mustaches and laugh at them! The power is in their hands. They don't care about anything. And now, when so many railroads

---

91. This is a reference to Stoilov's party. See 103n59.

92. The reference here is to Stambolov. See 94n52.

93. Vrazhdebna was popular with Aleko's circle, that is, the opposition. See 89n45.

94. In the original text, the Plovdiv hills are specified as Dzhendem Tepe and Nebet Tepe, the Turkish names of hills in the old-town section of Plovdiv, which is located on the site of Thracian Pulpuldeva, one of the most ancient cities in the Balkans. Today Plovdiv is the Chicago of Bulgaria (second city, industrial center, etc.).

are going to be built, so many investors' groups are going to be formed, so many ports are going to be constructed, you pick the moment to slander me with allegedly being in the opposition.[95] Don't do it, my friend. Is that the kind of a pal you are? Are you envious of me or something? Do you think you got less of a deal than I did? Go on, add it up; how many different places are you lining your pockets from? As for me—what? I'm just looking after my little business, that's all. Besides, don't forget that one hand washes the other. If you help me get into some juicier enterprise, do you think I won't pay you back? I know how these things are done. But no, now on top of everything else, you devil, you've gone and twisted things in such a way that if someone reads your article, he'll even think that I'm against His Majesty. Who, me? Is that what you think of my loyalty? Didn't we agree that *now is not the time?* Now if we weren't in power, if we were sniveling on the sidelines, then of course you could get all hot and bothered and curse them one and all, His Majesty included. But when we've got hold of this bone with both hands, when *now is precisely the time* to guarantee a secure old age, do you think I'd up and say something untoward about His Majesty? Your Bai Ganyo is no fool. He knows when the time is right to shout, "Long live His Highness!" One "Long live . . ." would get me a corporation, just like that! Sure, *when the time comes*—we know how to shout all sorts of other things, too. That's the way the world is. If nothing else, at least we've plumbed the depths of this philosophy, dammit.

Anyway, listen, lad, didn't *our people* go a bit overboard with that protest rally in Lom?[96] I hear that people were wounded, even killed. Listen, we have to be careful, you know. They cut off the hands of the old prime minister; we have to watch out lest times get tough.[97]

---

95. During the rule of the National Party (1894–99), the network of railroads increased from 479 to 1002 kilometers. In 1895 a record number of corporations was formed—seventeen—with a capital of 11,286,000 levs.

96. On 29 October 1895 a rally was organized in Lom, a town on the Danube in northwestern Bulgaria, to protest the rigged elections of 22 January. The city was surrounded by police, who met villagers coming in for the rally with clubs and beat them viciously, driving them away. Nonetheless, the organizers began the rally peacefully with the signing of a letter of protest addressed to parliament. At that moment, the mounted police descended on them, sabers drawn and whips flailing. The police wounded almost all the demonstrators and shot one man dead.

97. On 3 July 1895 ex–prime minister Stefan Stambolov was attacked with sabers and knives in the center of Sofia, in full view of the police. His doctors amputated his hands in an attempt to stop the bleeding, but he died of his wounds.

Well, enough of that for now. Long live his Royal Highness!

See how I shout out, "Long live . . . !" And you've gone and said that I'm supposedly against him. You're jealous of me, damn you. If we begin a shouting match, you don't know who will win it. And as for showing His Majesty respect, if it comes to that, I won't give ground. You'll kiss his hand, I'll kiss both hands; you will kiss his hem; I, his feet. You'll kiss him on another place, and I on yet another. Do you think you can beat me, you whelp?

GANYO BALKANSKI

16

The Temperance Society

A SHORT SHORT STORY

Taki the Beer-maker was still sleeping, even though the sun's rays had long since pierced the clouded, grimy windows of his stuffy room; the rays gradually illuminated his legs, then crept up toward his potbelly, shone on his lower lip, which was dried and cracked from an internal fire; then they moved toward his open mouth and penetrated down his throat, from which emanated waves of snoring, deafening to the ear.[98] Just then, the postman knocked three times at the door; but don't imagine that Taki's ear comprehends such gentle signals. Had it been a workday, well, then, maybe, but this was a holiday; and on the eve of a holiday, you know, a person lets himself go a bit more. You clink glasses with this guy, you clink glasses with that guy, and eventually you get completely clinked out! That's just what had happened to Bai Taki. In his desire to promote his beer, he got himself pickled. My point is that you won't be surprised that the postman repeated his knocking on the door. But when no one appeared, he delivered to that totally innocent door such a hard, merciless pounding that even if Bai Taki's stomach had met up with an entire vat of beer, he would've woken up; and wake up he did. He opened his eyes, blinked in the sunlight, and, in a voice worthy of the throat whence it emanated, asked, "Who's there?" "The mail," answered the postman. He entered the room, crossed over to the bed, handed over a letter, and hastened to escape the stifling atmosphere of the

---

98. This is the only story in *Bai Ganyo* that does not have his name in the title. Some popular editions have added "Bai Ganyo Founds" to the beginning of the title, but these additional words are neither in the original nor in scholarly editions. See the preface for original publication details.

unventilated bedroom. Bai Taki coughed for a little while, as was his habit, rubbed his eyes, and opened the letter. An invitation!

> My Dear Sir, Your presence is requested tomorrow, Sunday, at five o'clock in the afternoon at the cellar of the Suhindol winery, where the question of founding a Temperance Society will be addressed.
>
> YOUR HUMBLE SERVANT,
> TANAS DOCHOOLU,
> TAVERN KEEPER, FOR THE INITIATORS.

Good God! This invitation had come at a most auspicious time. Bai Taki's parched throat and chapped lips were at that very moment such strong agitators in favor of temperance that he enthusiastically took to this noble idea, and by the time it struck five in the afternoon, he had declared himself to be the most ardent defender of temperance. Throughout the day, Bai Taki drank only water. (Actually, truth be told, he drank two little glasses of wine, but that's what he said.) As soon as five o'clock struck, Bai Taki crossed the threshold of the spacious cellar of the Suhindol Winery.

"Is Bai Tanas here?" he asked the boy who was standing behind the counter.

"Right this way. They're here in the back room," the boy answered politely and stepped forward to open the door for him.

The owner, Tanas Dochoolu, greeted his colleague amiably and invited him to take a seat. Sitting stolidly and silently along the walls were several citizens who had been inspired and drawn here by the noble idea of this proposed society. Bai Taki greeted everyone, and once again silence reigned, broken only by unobtrusive coughing. It was clear that those present were waiting for someone without whom they dared not call the meeting to order. It wasn't long before the outer doors opened. Dochoolu rushed to see whether the anticipated guest had indeed arrived but immediately returned with a dissatisfied expression. Danko the Thug burst quite unexpectedly into the room. "We hit the jackpot!" Bai Tanas whispered to Bai Taki. It was obvious that this was not the expected personage. Danko opened his mouth to say something—Danko's idea of conversation would be to curse someone out—but no one showed the least desire to listen to him, and he fell silent. Several more minutes passed and (thank God!) the boy dashed headlong into the room and cried out as if frightened, "He's coming! He's coming!"

They all rose to their feet. The outer door opened, and on the threshold there appeared in all his glory none other than our mutual friend Bai Ganyo Balkanski.

"O-o! Long live!" the long-awaited guest exclaimed enthusiastically and without specifying who or what should live; but even without any explanation everyone understood that this referred to the future society.

"Long live!" answered the assembled gathering, and they began to take turns shaking Bai Ganyo's hand. Danko the Thug, always a little less polite, allowed himself (just imagine!) to give Bai Ganyo a familiar slap on the back of the neck, but Mister Balkanski's eyes flashed at him so fiercely that Danko tucked his tail between his legs and cowered in a corner. "Don't pay him any mind, Bai Ganyo," whispered the owner. "After all, you know him. Danko will always be Danko—a lush."

The meeting began. Eh, gentlemen, if only you had had the good fortune to stumble upon this assembly! When Bai Ganyo opened up that mouth of his, you couldn't tell whether it was a person talking or a nightingale singing. That Bai Ganyo sure knows how to persuade you! Not just about this society—he could talk you into believing that your father was Musala and that Vitosha was your mother.[99] Never mind! Everyone was convinced that precisely now was the time to found a temperance society;[100] only Danko the Thug (wonder of wonders!) was a veritable doubting Thomas. No matter what they proposed—nope, he just sat there in his corner and smirked behind his mustache and uttered an occasional word of skepticism. "It's already time to, time to whatchamacallit," orated Dochoolu, "for us to establish a, a thingamajig, y'know, a society." And Danko let loose with a single "Whatever." Bai Taki strung his words like pearls. "Drunkenness, honorable gentlemen, has a negative effect on our work, on our health, on our offspring." "Bullshit!" whispered Danko and smirked behind his mustache. But time and tide wait for no man. We're not going to give up on this

---

99. That is, he could make you believe anything. Vitosha is the mountain just south of Sofia (see 91n50). Musala (2,925 meters) is the highest peak in the Balkan peninsula (8 meters taller than Olympus). It is located in the Rila Mountains in what is today southwestern Bulgaria (a region also known as Pirin Macedonia). In Aleko's time, it was in a part of Turkey to which Bulgaria had territorial aspirations. Bulgarian rebel bandits took refuge in the mountains, and thus reference to the mountains as one's parents was a trope for rebel banditry in Bulgarian folk poetry.

100. See 138n85 and 140n90 about "Now is not the time" and the group called Now-Is-Not-the-Timers.

lofty ideal now because of someone like Danko. They left Danko chewing on his mustache and began the business of establishing the society. They decided to christen the society "Abstinence" and to ask the teacher to write them a set of bylaws. The teacher, like it or not, had to write the bylaws, because if you must know, he was the first to come up with the idea of this society. For the present, the initiators limited themselves to voting in a slate of officers, as has been the practice from time immemorial. They elected Bai Ganyo, of course, as chairman; Tanas Dochoolu, being the host, as vice chairman; and Bai Taki as treasurer. All done! And have you ever heard of an election where the winners didn't treat everyone to a drink? Impossible! That's how it's been, that's how it is, and that's how it always will be. The vice chairman, as the owner, was the first to acquit himself. He summoned the boy and whispered to him, "Two liters of the old stuff, quickly!" Wine was brought in. Now *there* was a wine if ever there was one, that Suhindol wine, like crystal, the devil take it!

"Let's have a toast, for good luck!"

"Long live the chairman, hurrah!"

"Thank you. Long live His Royal Highness and the honorable government."

"Hurrah!"

"Down with drunkenness!"

Then Bai Ganyo returned the favor. And then Bai Taki returned the favor. And someone seconded it, and then thirded it, and so on until night fell.

It was already dark when I was walking with a friend along Chista Rabota Street.[101] As we passed the cellar of the Suhindol Winery, an unusual sound emanating from within caught our attention and aroused our curiosity. We entered the wine cellar, and through the window of the back room, this is the picture that greeted us: Most of those gathered there were snoring, sprawled all over their chairs. Bai Taki, arms folded over his paunch, wheezed heavily with his head hanging down and his eyes half-opened. A tall, thin gentleman in a shabby frock coat and dark glasses was turning in all directions and shouting into space, "I'm against machines; you can say whatever you like, but I'm against machines." Dochoolu was sitting at the table. The boy was holding a candle for him, and he was entering the final tally in his ledger with a quivering hand. Bai Ganyo was pounding on the table with all his might, and with a savage look on his face was screaming, "Me? I'll show them, I'll teach them just who Bai Ganyo is." And Danko the Thug,

---

101. The street name is colloquial Bulgarian for "the real thing."

enthralled by this energetic tone, sat as if transfixed across from Bai Ganyo, asking him with his eyes, "Just tell me then, Bai Ganyo, go on and tell me, brother, who is it I should grab by the throat? Who should I kick out the door?"

The boy left, taking the candle with him.

"Hey, kid! What group is this?" my friend asked.

"The society against drunkenness," answered the boy.

———

If they gave out prizes for being overwhelmed by the most carefree laughter, my friend and I would have taken first place for that moment.

SOFIA, 12 MAY 1895

17

Letter from Bai Ganyo to Konstantin Velichkov

Bai Velichkov![102]

Good for you, Bai Velichkov! That's the way to go! Why should we deceive the younger generation? Let's put our cards right on the table. Ideals? Nonsense! Our very own personal satisfaction, right here on this earth, that's the ideal we should pursue. I'm glad that you've finally figured it out. Why should we work up a sweat for this contemptible nation? When we were young, it was no big deal, but now that we're over forty, it's time to think of ourselves. We're through roughing it! And especially you, poor guy, you really wore yourself out in those Constantinople alleys and Italian lanes, and wasn't that a deed of derring-do! When you saw that Stambolov had blown his top, you snuck out of Bulgaria, you ditched those slaves; let them rot in slavery. They're used to it. You're not used to pulling your weight, and like any fine gentleman, you tried to cut and run. And how you suffered on Khalki! Sometimes, you didn't even have enough money for medicine. Bobchev and Madzharov fell silent.[103] Enough with the heroics, already!

---

102. Konstantin Velichkov Petkov (1855–1907) was a writer and social activist. He was arrested during the April Uprising (1876) and spent four months in Turkish jails. In 1886 he went into voluntary exile as a protest against the Stambolov regime, but his exile, which lasted eight years, was interpreted by some as flight, hence Aleko's sarcastic remarks. In 1889 Petkov went from Italy to Constantinople, where he worked for the Exarchate (see 138n86) for three years. In 1893 he went to Khalki, an island in the Dodecanese west of Rhodes, where he lived among the fishermen, worked hard, and painted pictures. In his letters to friends he complained of poverty and illness.

103. Stefan Bobchev (1853–1940) was a prominent activist in the National Party. He held various public offices and was professor of the history of Bulgarian law at Sofia University. Mihail Madzharov (1854–1954) was a leader of the Unitarist Party and also held numerous important public offices. Bobchev and Madzharov were the editors of the journal *Bûlgarska sbirka* (Bulgarian Collection), with which Aleko was involved.

And you know what? Chuck your damned poetry, too. That stuff is OK when the wind is blowing through your empty wallet. But now, thank God, we've fixed things up! Now all kinds of lowlifes, nasty little socialists and idealists, are going to start bashing you, but don't you bat an eye. Just you turn a deaf ear and take it easy—take it easy and laugh in their faces. Of course! And why are they bashing you? I mean, really, is it for some treachery of yours, for some deception, out of disillusionment? Nope! It's envy! Of course! There's no doubt about it; they're envious! And why is that? Simply because they've been beaten black and blue and coughed their lungs out, and then you (what a devil you are, damn you!), you go and land yourself the cushiest job.[104] So, do you see now? Do you agree? Wasn't I the one who told you that in this world the best thing to do is to take it easy? This social struggle, ideals, and I don't know what all other foolishness—it's all hot air! And now, look, when you hold out your moneybag at the end of the month, they shovel fifteen hundred big fat levs into it. It's a beautiful thing, goddamn it! Hang in there now! If you dig yourself up a tasty bone, hold on to it! Don't you give a thought to whose hide those levs are coming out of. You squeeze that blood out of that turnip, goddamn it! Squeeze away! It'll keep dripping.

But maybe you're wondering why I'm writing to you. I'm writing to praise you for your speech the other day in the National Assembly.[105] Good for you, Kocho! Well, to tell you the truth, I wept for joy. I almost came right up to you and kissed you in front of all those deputies. But they would have started to kick me—I mean, raise objections. Do you remember the speech I'm talking about? Of course you do! Everybody is talking about it. And you're right, Kocho! No way twenty cops and a gang of fifty drunkards could have gone and busted up thousands of voters. Big deal! The cops would have shot at most a hundred voters. Is that such a big deal? All in all, they would have put about two hundred households into mourning. And let's say that the next Sunday, soldiers come, and they start shooting and kill at most, at most three hundred people. How many orphans? Five hundred! Big fat deal!

---

104. Velichkov was elected to parliament and almost immediately thereafter became Minister of Public Buildings and Information in Stoilov's cabinet. See 103n59 on Stoilov.

105. In his speech before Parliament on 24 October 1894, Velichkov responded to attacks from the opposition, who complained about the violence at the Svishtov elections (described in "Bai Ganyo Does Elections"). He mocked the citizens of Svishtov, saying that five thousand voters had allowed themselves to be intimidated by a mere twenty mounted police. Instead of fleeing, he said, they should have engaged the police in battle.

But those dumbbells went and calmed the mob so not a hair on anyone's head would be hurt! How could you not be outraged? Because of those namby-pamby dumbbells, you waited eight whole years on Khalki. You go and write them so many poems about stars and sighs, and they make you wait eight years. Eight years! Shame on the Bulgarian nation! If at least a hundred thousand voters from all of Bulgaria had gone down under a hail of bullets, you could have taken your present cushy place much sooner. But what a good-for-nothing nation! Gutless wonders! What the hell good is rule of law and freedom if at least a thousand voters aren't wiped out? Hang in there, good ol' Kocho. That's the way to go! Give speeches like that more often so you can inspire more trust in the palace. Do whatever makes you happy! So what if they say the younger generation's gonna complain, that people will get upset. Don't you bat an eye! The people! The people are sheep when you wave a stick at 'em. But then who am I to tell you about such things?

I was especially happy that you were the one who rushed to give that speech; no one could get ahead of you. After all, if you haven't inspired them with trust by now, then there's no doing it! All the fat cats are singing your praises! Attaboy, they're saying. Kocho has become one of us; he finally got some sense into his head. You just keep your wits about you, stick to your guns, and don't be afraid! But you watch out, Kocho. Salt a little money away. After all, you never know—here today, gone tomorrow.

Kocho, after you've read this letter, tear it up so that it doesn't fall into the hands of that guy who wrote about my travels in Europe, or he'll expose me again somewhere. I heard him that day. He was saying to someone, For shame! I really didn't expect those words from our Velichkov." I listened to him, and I wondered what's inside his head. Apparently, nothing. But come on, Kocho, why are you still publishing that damned *Progress?* Tear it up! Really, its name is so childish. It's no longer fitting for a solid citizen like yourself. And if you've got such an itch to write, then write, but it would be most appropriate to call the newspaper *Now Is Not the Time,* and our partisans will be called Now-Is-Not-the-Timers.[106]

I've brought a few *muskali* in my *disagi.* Couldn't you get a little law passed requiring that they spray public buildings with rose oil?[107]

Sofia, 28 October 1894

YOUR *GANYO BALKANSKI*

---

106. See 138n85 and 140n90 concerning Now-Is-Not-the-Timers.

107. This is a reference to the fact that Velichkov was Minister of Public Buildings and Information.

18

From the Correspondence of
Bai Ganyo Balkanski

I

My Dear Mr. Balkanski,

Perhaps you have already forgotten me, but I shall remind you of certain events, and I believe that you will remember who I am.[108] Do you recall that when you were traveling around Europe, you stopped off in Prague, and all the Bulgarian students treated you so coldly, even Jirechek? I was the only one who invited you home, and you stayed several days with me. Do you recall how you surprised me with the landlady's daughter? And do you remember, when you were left alone, how they entertained you and you sang "Terrible Is the Night" for them?[109] I am the very same Bodkov. I have finished my higher education and returned to my homeland. Since I do not number among my acquaintances any other influential person save yourself, I am turning to you with a request, and I beg you to ask someone from the editorship of some government newspaper to print the enclosed dispatch, a copy of which I am enclosing for you as well, in case it gets lost in the editorial offices. I believe that this letter is sufficient for the government to form an understanding of my ideas, and I am even in a position to write much more than this, should the need arise. I have completed my degree in philosophy. Mr. Balkanski, in addition to this, I have another request for you. My father is an entrepreneur, and the government is now rejecting as defective fifty thousand levs' worth of shoes, so I beg you to intervene so that they

---

108. This feuilleton was found among Aleko's papers after his death. It is known that he also wrote a feuilleton titled "The Moral Principles of Bai Ganyo," which Aleko read publicly, greatly upsetting members of the National Party. Unfortunately, the manuscript has not been found.

109. See 71n35.

accept them from him, just as they have accepted those of the very same material made by a Jew. Is this patriotic?

Do not think that I am writing my letter in order to butter up the government. Absolutely not. The fact that the shoes were rejected as defective has nothing at all to do with this letter, and finally, you should know that I am not a person who would trade on his convictions.

BE ASSURED OF MY EXTREME RESPECT TOWARD YOU,

YOUR BODKOV

P.S. The editorial office may change my text if they see fit. I am not a pretentious person.

THE SAME.

P.P.S. The shoes were rejected three days ago.

THE SAME.

Here is the text referred to in the above letter:

Copy

Letter to the Editor

Mr. Editor,

My blood freezes in my veins, my brain congeals in my skull, my heart stops beating, and I, with trepidation in my soul, address myself to the respected Government and beg it to answer whether or not there will be an end to its tolerance of the destructive lack of restraint on the part of the opposition press. The people want to know (boldly I can affirm this) when they will break the sacrilegious fingers of the opposition, which dare to touch—O horrors!—the Chaste and Sacred Person of our common Father, the guarantor of our happiness and well-being. Instead of an unquestioning reverential prostration before the glorious embodiment of our independence, instead of a submissive readiness for the gratification of the royal lusts and desires, there appear Bulgarians among us (misbegotten monsters of the Bulgarian people) who dare to ascribe human weaknesses to the unapproachable Personage! This is more than a betrayal of national interests. This is a depravity unheard of in history! There are even such scoundrels of the pen who have rebelled and tried to halt and to desecrate the most virtuous act of our communities, the bestowing of municipal forests, islands, and gardens on their Beloved Prince. The majesty of the throne is likewise the majesty of the people, and instead of being proud that our municipalities demonstrate their love for the Crown and the Dynasty for all to see, instead of rejoicing that our fatherland, until recently uncivilized, is covered with luxurious palaces and villas, one can find Bulgarians—just imagine, Bulgarians!—who, even after all this, are not satisfied! Such malcontents sow degeneracy in our society, and the Bulgarian people must gaze upon them with revulsion. They are the reason for the moral decline of our society and for the distrust that is insinuating itself between the government and society and that is having such an evil influence on the national economy.[110] This mistrust damages the private interests of the most respected and scrupulous merchants, as is the case with our well-respected citizen who only recently has had fifty thousand levs' worth of shoes of the finest material rejected owing to a misunderstanding. And so, the government must take steps immediately to stop the mouths of the opposition once and for all. This is the most fervent desire of the Bulgarian people.

ANONYMOUS

Mr. Editor,

I promise you henceforth to write you as many such letters as you want against the opposition. I will only beg you to allow my name to remain unknown to the public. I have a degree in philosophy.

WITH DEEP RESPECT,
BODKOV

II

Mr. Bodkov,

It has come back to me who Your Honor is. How could I not recollect? I remember not just you but your fiancée and her mother as well. She wasn't bad at all. And then, didn't I teach them to prepare some dish or another, and we played the piano? I remember quite well. You have become a master in your trade; when I look at you, I see that this philosophy stuff isn't just for suckers to study. But as for the shoes you're writing about, you are somewhat mistaken. That problem can't be dealt with through a letter to the editor.

---

110. By 1896 the Bulgarian government had spent more than twenty-five million levs on palaces and properties for Prince Ferdinand, who was also in the habit of confiscating private property for his personal use. That year, Representative Nikola H. Gabrovski complained in a speech before Parliament that while palaces were being built for the prince, the people were living in shacks.

You see, don't you, that they accepted the shoes of the Jew that you talk about. They accepted them because he knows whose palm to grease; you should open up your purse, too. I read your letter from beginning to end and figured out what your problem is. Not everyone can be a businessman. It's not like philosophy, and as for accepting your shoes, sorry, your father's shoes, you yourself ought to realize who that depends on. And what you say about the dynasty, never mind, keep it up, it's the fashion. After all, talk is cheap.

WITH KIND REGARDS,
YOUR GANYO BALKANSKI

III

Most respected Mr. Ganyo!

I appeal to you. You are the people's representative, and I ask henceforth that such things not continue, specifically, that an entire regiment goes through a forest barking like dogs so the gentlemen officers can hunt hares, because we've not been sent to learn to bark but rather to preserve our fatherland, and even though you're completely exhausted, dead tired, tears flowing from your eyes, starving, they still force you to bark, and it better be good or else you get a beating, because you didn't know how a hunting dog barks and they killed only five (5) hares. At least they didn't wound a soldier, because then you get another beating for not being careful. Besides which, they made me an officer's orderly and I wash his kid's underpants and the carriage too. This is a shameful thing and I beg you to issue a law and since there's nothing more to tell you, I'll stop. Tear up this letter.

HUMBLY YOURS,
TRÛPKO TRÛPKOV,
PRIVATE[111]

IV

Mr. Trûpko,

You wouldn't happen to be the son of Trûpko the *komitadzhi*?[112] I know your father. What you say about them forcing you to bark at rabbits in a

---

111. In Bulgarian, *trûpka* means "shivers," "shudders," "thrills," or "pins and needles." The opposition press published many reports of such abuses of power by army officers. In another report, a commander sent an entire company to gather raspberries for his family and then punished them for not cleaning the thorns off the stems.

112. A *komitadzhi* is a member of an insurgent group (*komita*).

forest, even I heard about it, but patience is a virtue, as they say. You can't fight city hall. After all, under the Turks we suffered for a whole lifetime. Whatever we have to suffer under the Bulgarians for two short years is no big deal. As for the underpants, that's not a good thing for a man to do. That's woman's work, but what can you do? Wash the underpants and hold your nose; politics demands it. After all, you know how it is; just grin and bear it, and don't forget to say hello to your father for me. Patience, there's no other way; these things work out with patience and not by rocking the boat. As you well know, the saber doesn't cut off a bowed head.[113]

YOUR WELL-WISHER,

GANYO BALKANSKI

V

Kind Uncle Ganyo,

I want to send our Rada to study abroad this year, but so that I don't have any expenses, I beg you to go up to the big shots and get me sent abroad on some business trip, to study some questions or for some sort of lobbying; perhaps, for example, to study the question of whether it would be possible to promote our homespun cloth to the Belgian army, or to investigate the ethnography of the Kutsovlahs in Switzerland, or something like that.[114] If they want to, they can think up ninety-nine business trips. A per diem of even three napoleons would be satisfactory. Answer me as soon as possible.

YOUR FAITHFUL LIKE-MINDED KINSMAN,

VASIL

P.S. You won't be left empty-handed from this business trip either. If they ask about my education, tell them that although I don't have a diploma, I have still read a lot, and it's just as if I had a college education.

THE SAME.

---

113. This proverb is well known in Turkish and all the Balkan languages. It is the quintessential expression of how to avoid trouble from brutal authorities.

114. Kutsovlah is a name for Aromanians, a group that speaks a Romance language and lives in the southern Balkans. Their language separated from Romanian about a thousand years ago. Also known as Vlahs, many Aromanians were migratory shepherds, but those who lived in towns were often wealthy merchants. The name Kutsovlah means "lame Vlah" and is considered pejorative.

I couldn't find an answer to this letter in Bai Ganyo's ledger, but in the envelope I found a draft of the following telegram:

Urgent   To Zheravna Village

Vasil Mangov[115]

You're much too late, Vasil. Someone more educated than you has already been sent on that business trip.

BALKANSKI

VI

Most Respected Uncle Ganyo,

Man proposes, but God disposes. All the plans we concocted for my future have been reduced to dust and ashes. My career is completely ruined. I have been expelled from school and sentenced to three years of hard labor, and the reason for all this is that damned Bulgarian spelling system; they've been promoting a new fashion: we're supposed to write foreign words and names as they would be pronounced; for example, we aren't supposed to write *ministr*, but to write *ministûr*; not to write *ansambl*, but to write *ansambûl*, not to write *Bokl*, but we should write *Bokûl*—because this is supposed to be more characteristic of the Bulgarian language, as if the character of our language resembles that of the Afghan language.[116] We protested to our learned tutors, and they declared us mutineers. On the very day of the birth of Jesus Christ, the savior of mankind, they escorted us under a convoy of mounted police, us unwilling tourists on foot, along the snowy highways of mother Bulgaria, and we're trudging, trudging from one stop to the next, sleeping in police stations. We were met by policemen and seen off by gendarmes, and where they're taking us even we ourselves don't know. They say that for the triumph of the Bulgarian spelling system they intend to educate us for three years in prison gangs. Who knows? Maybe such a miracle could happen, too. I have now been brought here to your city, and I write this letter from my cell. If you would be so kind, come visit me and bring a doctor, because I don't know if it's from the journey or from the cold, but lately I've begun to spit blood.

YOUR NEPHEW,

STOYKO

115. The name Mangov suggests *mangup* (rascal) or *mango* (Gypsy, pejorative).

116. Aleko did not approve of the orthographic reforms promulgated by the philological commission of the Ministry of Public Education.

P.S. I have heard, uncle, that the Turks had a custom for major holidays, such as Christmas and Easter, to let Christian prisoners out on bail to visit their relatives and to spend the holidays with them. Is this true, uncle?

THE SAME.

Dear Nephew Stoyko,

As you have sown, my boy, so have you reaped. Whose fault is that? I wonder that they didn't give you a good hiding on top of it all. It's only natural. Are we playing tiddlywinks or running a kingdom? What do you mean by this abuse of freedom? How dare you prattle on to me about the Turks as if they were more merciful? They're not merciful, but they are suckers. If they were smart, they wouldn't have given up the kingdom to someone else. If you ask me, I'm even glad that they've finally handled you folks properly. You just rot now in the police stations and barracks so that you get some sense into your head and remember what happens when you stick your neck out. I couldn't understand from your letter just what the reason was; you write about some kind of *Bokûl-Shmokûl* stuff, but I don't believe you, even though I don't know anything about grammar. Who knows what mischief you've been up to? I don't have time to make the rounds of police stations, disgracing myself in front of big shots, just to meet with rebels. How many times have I tried to teach you that the saber doesn't cut off the bowed head? But no, you wouldn't listen to me. You're paying for it now with your head. As you have sown, my boy, so have you reaped.

YOUR WELL-WISHER,
GANYO BALKANSKI

Glossary

bachka: a card game

bashibazouk: Turkish irregular troops, paramilitaries noted for their ferocity

boza: lightly fermented, sweet, grain-based drink, about as strong as near-beer

Chifut (plural Chifuti): Jew (derogatory), miser

Chingene: Gypsy (derogatory)

disagi: a kind of saddlebag made from a rectangular piece of colorful, heavy-woven cloth whose ends are folded and sewn at each side to create two sacks that can be slung over the back of a pack animal or the shoulder of a person

chorba: soup (from Turkish)

efendi: Turkish title of respect, now archaic

kalpak: a high, circular, brimless, woolen cap with a peak in the center, typically worn by peasants in Bulgaria and neighboring regions

kelepir: free lunch, unearned profit, windfall, freebie

kilim: a flat-weave Turkish rug, often with geometrical patterns, that can serve as a sort of rural sleeping bag

komitadzhi: member of a *komita*, a Slavic, Christian insurgent band that fought the Turks (and sometimes also Greeks and Albanians) in the nineteenth and early twentieth centuries

kvass: lightly fermented grain-based drink, about as strong as near-beer

kyoravo: something for nothing

mastika: anise-flavored, unaged grape brandy

muskal (plural muskali): a measure of rose oil equal to either one and a half or three drams; the glass phial containing such a measure of rose oil

muzhik: peasant (Russian)

nazdar: hello (Czech)

oka: a measure of weight equal to about 2.5 pounds (1225 grams)

rakia: brandy

Shumi Maritsa ("The River Maritsa is Murmuring"): the Bulgarian national anthem from 1886 to the end of World War II

traktir: inn, tavern (Russian)